A TIME TO LOVE

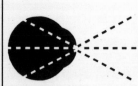

This Large Print Book carries the
Seal of Approval of N.A.V.H.

A TIME TO LOVE

BARBARA DELINSKY

THORNDIKE PRESS
A part of Gale, Cengage Learning

GALE
CENGAGE Learning·

Detroit • New York • San Francisco • New Haven, Conn • Waterville, Maine • London

GALE
CENGAGE Learning®

Copyright © 1981 by Barbara Delinsky.
The book was originally published under the name Billie Douglas in 1982 by Silhouette Books, a Simon & Schuster Division of Gulf & Western Corporation.
Thorndike Press, a part of Gale, Cengage Learning.

Thorndike Press® Large Print Famous Authors
The text of this Large Print edition is unabridged.
Other aspects of the book may vary from the original edition.
Set in 16 pt. Plantin.

LIBRARY OF CONGRESS CATALOGING-IN-PUBLICATION DATA

Delinsky, Barbara.
    A time to love / Barbara Delinsky. — Large print ed.
        p. cm. — (Thorndike Press large print famous authors)
    "The book was originally published under the name Billie Douglas in 1982 by Silhouette Books, a Simon & Schuster Division of Gulf & Western Corporation"—T.p. verso.
    ISBN-13: 978-1-4104-5084-5 (hardcover)
    ISBN-10: 1-4104-5084-8 (hardcover)
    1. Large type books. I. Title.
PS3554.E4427T5 2012
813'.54—dc23   2012032483

Published in 2012 by arrangement with Avon, an imprint of HarperCollins Publishers.

Printed in Mexico
2 3 4 5 6 7 16 15 14 13

To Nancy and Joel,
the most patient of friends

A NOTE FROM THE AUTHOR

A Time to Love is one of my earliest books. It was written in 1981 for publication as a romance and centers around a theme often seen in that genre, the lack of forthrightness between man and woman and the misinterpretation of feelings that results.

As with so many of my books, I chose to write *A Time to Love* about something I knew, in this case photography. At the time of its writing, my children were very young, and I was the designated picture taker. I taught myself about F-stops and shutter speeds, about developer, stop bath, and fixer. To support the habit, I began to do photo work for newspapers and even taught an adult education course for several years. Though I believe I was a better teacher than doer, that interest in photography left me with some pictures of my boys and their dad that Arielle Pasteur and Christopher Howe would surely appreciate.

I am told that St. Maarten, the setting for *A Time to Love,* has changed much since I was there. Those of you who have visited in recent years will have to forgive the discrepancies between how I depicted it in 1981 and how it is today.

Finally, please note that *A Time to Love* was originally written under the Billie Douglass pseudonym. That name is gone, as is the original cover of the book. All else remains the same.

Barbara Delinsky
September 1996

ONE

Arielle Pasteur stood, enchanted, a lone figure on the beach. Beneath her bare toes the play of the fine white sand was soft and alluring. The warmth of the afternoon sun caressed her with its golden glow, and she opened her arms to welcome it. The pale aqua roll of the surf mesmerized her with its rhythmic motion, gathering and breaking, then retreating to the darker depths of the ocean once more, taking with it, bit by bit, her fatigue and tension and replacing them with an incredible sense of peace.

Closing her eyes and tilting her head back, she reveled more deeply in the sensual masterpiece. The balmy tropical breeze fanned through her raven-black hair, drawing it back from her face with the gentleness of a whisper, tenderly baring her features to the healing flow of the trade winds. Each breath she took of the moist sea air brought growing relaxation through her slender limbs and shapely form.

Her pre-dawn waking on this day, the hassle of a sunrise takeoff, the long hours in flight from Boston, through Philadelphia, then on to this small Caribbean isle of St. Maarten — all were happily cast to the tropic winds, relegated to the far reaches of memory as she greedily drank in the elixir of pleasure flowing freely all about her. In this moment of delight nothing mattered but that this exquisitely beautiful and secluded stretch of beach was hers, and hers alone, for the next four weeks. Nothing mattered but that the charming villa, high on the craggy hillside behind her, would be her haven for the days and nights of solitude and serenity she craved. Intuitively, she knew she had found the perfect spot to organize her thoughts and her photographs, to compile her work of the past five years into the book for which she'd been commissioned. Here she would relax and enjoy each day as it came, responsible to no one but herself, committed to no schedule but that which she chose to create. At her private whim she would sprinkle her hours with sun and surf, work and play. It would be a month of self-centered indulgence, and she had earned every last minute of it.

After a final deep breath of the fragrant

air of paradise, she opened her eyes. Slowly, she walked the stretch of beach, a gleaming ribbon bounded on one side by the lava-gray of volcanic formations shaping the rugged cliff, and on the other by the clear aqua ruffle of the Caribbean waters. With each step her bare feet dipped into the softness of the sand. It was warm and pliant, capturing her, bidding her linger in its hold before moving on. She readily complied, for there was no reason to rush. Time was now her ally. With a contented sigh, she feasted on the beauty of her surroundings.

The sight was breathtaking! Azure skies speckled with the occasional fluffy cloud, misted gray-green peaks of neighboring isles far in the distance, the shimmering dance of sunlight on the emerald-blue of the waters — it was magnificent, and it was hers!

A smile tickled her lips as she sank down on the sand, stretching her long, graceful legs before her toward the sea, propping herself up on straightened arms, now bare of the heavy winter attire she'd sported just this morning. Again she closed her eyes and cocked her face toward the sun, absorbing its warmth, willing its rays inward, then sighing with delight.

This was everything she wanted in a vacation, she mused with a tingle of excitement, directing a silent message of thanks to her brother, Michael, back in frosty New York City, who had first suggested this trip, then had found the villa through his own travel agent and had taken it on her behalf for the month. Expensive as it was, she could well afford it, having become a respected and successful child photographer in the five years since she had graduated and gone out on her own. She lived a modest existence from choice, rather than need. This was an extravagance she had waited for; on first impression, it would be well worth it.

Shifting in the sand, she reached behind the even fall of hair at her collar line to daringly release the tie of her navy halter top, freeing her shoulders of covering as she pulled the knit bands across the upper swell of her breasts, wound them around her back and secured them there. She rolled the cuffs of her white walking shorts as high as possible, even as she realized that, in the end, only a bathing suit would do. But the laziness of the moment, the glory of this afternoon, her first in the sun, were not to be disturbed. The glance she cast back toward the sturdy wooden steps, nestled in against the rock and leading up to her seaside retreat, turned indulgently back toward the sea.

The sand molded itself to the slimness of her shape as she lay back, stretched flat against its warmth. Her breathing was deep and even, her every muscle at rest. Only then, as the waves lapped the beach yards from her toes and the palm fronds murmured softly atop the cliff high above, did her mind retrace the events of the day. It had started with the ringing of the bedside alarm, goading her into action, prompting her to shower and dress before the night sky had begun to yield to the breath of day on its eastern edge. Her friend Sean had been at her door, as promised, at five o'clock, managing by some miracle to fix them both a cup of coffee while Arielle saw to her last-minute packing. With the endearingly unpretentious sculptor behind the wheel of his battered Volvo, they had headed for Logan International Airport, an hour's drive from Rockport, on the Massachusetts North Shore. How someone so skilled with a hammer and chisel could be so inept with a stick shift Arielle would never know. But she indulged him his jerks, lurches, and swerves, refraining from comment in the mercifully negligible new-dawn traffic, eternally grateful to him, her closest friend, for having sacrificed his own precious hours of sleep to help her. Even now, she pictured him in his small studio, carving masterpieces out of wood with a flair and sensitivity most artists strive for yet never achieve.

Friend, artist, inspiration — Sean had been all of these things to Arielle during the past five years. He had been entrenched in the Rockport colony for several years prior to her arrival, and had taken her under his wing, helping her to find her way in what was now, in every sense, her home. The vulnerable, shy, unsure young woman, fresh from college, had grown into a more confident and capable one before his eyes. He had encouraged her, then had stood back to watch her spread her wings and take flight; her success had been his as well. But there was more; Sean, seven years her senior, was her confidant, and her protection when the occasional male became overly persistent. For Arielle had no wish to become involved with any man, and Sean understood and respected her wish. What the world needed was more men like *him,* she decided with a sigh, stretching her arms out from her sides to furrow the sand with her angel wings as she more fully welcomed the rays of the sun.

She smiled in idle recollection of the morning's flight. It had been an interesting few hours, even amusing at times. Once the semblance of breakfast had come and gone she had indulged herself in her favorite form of distraction — people watching. Her trained photographer's eye studied the faces about her, supplementing images with bits of conversation that filtered over the mercifully steady hum of the engine. There had been the new parents occupying the two seats immediately to her left, their soft chatter focused on the young child they had left behind, the merits and demerits of the particular baby-sitter they had chosen, the contents of the freezer and cupboards and, finally and with odd reluctance, the prospect of a week without responsibility. To Arielle, theirs was a remote world. She could not deny that she adored children. How else could she devote herself exclusively to the photography of them? No, it was the male of the species who evoked her anger, rather than his offspring, yet the two were eternally interrelated. Without a man, she would have no child — and there would be no man. Once burned, she had vowed to maintain her independence. If her innate maternal instinct sought expression, it would find it in her work. Any further yearnings for a man or a child of her own were doggedly cast aside, squelched by the memory of one night of trauma, heartbreak, and disillusion long, long ago.

15

As always, such emotional meanderings sent a shudder through her; as always, she quickly found an alternate focus for her attention. Diagonally across the aisle had been two "ladies-of-the-world," as she had dubbed them, each several years older than Arielle, each dutifully wearing her wedding band, each openly bent on enjoying her week of freedom to the hilt. There were "the old-timers," a couple who proudly informed each stewardess of their impending forty-second wedding anniversary, and "the high rollers," two loud and obviously well-acquainted couples whose main goal was to hit it big at the gaming tables in the casinos for which St. Maarten was renowned. There was "the perfect family," consisting of three unusually well-behaved young boys — were they terrified of the airplane, too, she had wondered? — and their parents. There was "the dynamic duo," two bachelors of dubious intent to whom she threw her most disinterested look each time they walked along the aisle in search of their prey. And, finally, there was "the brooder."

Strangely, of them all, he was the one who held her thoughts even now, as the warm sea breeze touched her cheeks, her nose, her eyelids and lashes, as the sun's vibrant beam cast its glow on her winter-pale skin.

16

"The brooder" — closed and mysterious, seemingly out of place, a dark cloud in the brightest of azure skies, a gray stone in the whitest of soft sands, a shrill cry amid the gentle rustle of the coconut palms above. Clad in a dark gray turtleneck sweater and even darker charcoal gray slacks, he sat quietly; when he stood, his towering presence dominated the cabin. He was an enigma, allowing no clue to his identity to penetrate his taut mask of composure. Was he headed for St. Maarten on business? Was his chore so awesome that it demanded the glower he had worn ever since boarding in Philadelphia? What were the secrets hidden behind those one-way mirrored sunglasses, beneath that casually disarrayed thatch of dark brown hair, in the angular set of that squared-off jaw?

Drawn to the puzzle he posed, Arielle found herself uncomfortably aware of him, a vague but nagging sense of familiarity lurking in the recesses of her mind. She felt his sober presence in the seat directly across the aisle every time she leaned forward — to offer her coffee cup to the stewardess, to extract a paperback novel from the carry-on bag at her feet, to retrieve a pen so she could complete the landing form before touchdown in St. Maarten. Yet, try as she might,

Arielle could not quite pinpoint where, if ever, she had seen him before.

Even he slipped to the periphery of her thoughts, however, when the first of the island jewels studding the emerald waters of the Caribbean emerged from beneath the giant gray wing of the airplane. From then on, it had been smooth sailing all the way, in every sense of the word. St. Maarten, from the air, was an intriguing amalgam of ponds and lagoons, hills and valleys, jutting peninsulas and ribboned roadways. The landing had been easy, her rental car had been waiting, and the small, but fully-equipped and modern house had even been stocked with canned goods and fresh produce by way of welcome.

And now the sun, warming her, painting her skin with a delicate orange blush, threatening to hold her forever in its heavenly spell — what could be more divine?

A sudden shadow fell across her, instantly robbing her of the warmth in which she had reveled seconds before. Her eyes flew open to determine what dark cloud hovered in otherwise clear skies, then widened in alarm. It was the towering figure of a man which loomed above, tall, ramrod straight, and infinitely threatening. He wore nothing but a ragged pair of cut-off denims, which

18

concealed little of the muscled strength of the legs rooted in the sand mere inches from her. Long fingers splayed over hips, and he exuded a readiness, an acuity, in his mockingly casual pose. His torso was sculpted to manly perfection, a narrow waist yielding to an ever-broadening stretch of chest crowned by classically molded shoulders. Though lacking the tan that would label him an islander, his skin was a shade darker than her own, its hue accentuated by the coarse mat of dark brown hair which covered his chest before tapering gradually to a fine line which disappeared beneath the snap of his denims. He was, in her judgment as a photographer as well as a woman, a magnificent physical specimen whose power surged in each taut cord, in every well-developed muscle of his lean body. Scantily clad as he was, there was a primitive aura about him, a savagery which was oddly out of place in this gentle and serene setting.

With a barely audible gasp, Arielle bolted to a sitting position, one hand flying up to reassure herself that her halter top provided adequate covering for her own softer curves. But when she raised her eyes to the intruder's face she gasped with a mixture of fear, surprise, and recognition. The set of his square jaw was more taut than before, his lips were thinned in a semblance of control, his shaggy brown hair fell at the whim of the breeze, and those mirrored sunglasses revealed nothing but her own startled expression. It was "the brooder," the man she had recalled but moments before. Dark and mysterious still, he dominated this open stretch of beach much as he had the infinitely smaller airplane this morning. But there was a difference. Then he had been self-contained and impassive; now there was an unleashed quality about him. And by every modest estimate, he was very, very angry.

"What in the devil are you doing here?" His fury exploded deafeningly, its roar bearing a venom she could not fathom.

Shock reverberated through her before Arielle could find the strength to respond. To have been wrenched from utter relaxation to . . . to this, was more than she had counted on. Forcing herself to display a calmness she did not feel, she answered him simply. "This is my beach."

"My foot it is!" Each word was drawn slowly out, underscored with an undeniable sneer. "This is a private beach," he roared on. "You have no right whatsoever to be here. Now, get out!"

Incredulity held her frozen, her gaze

locked to his iron-hard features. Never had she encountered anyone as instantly offensive as this man, who obviously had his facts mixed up. When he made no move to evict her bodily from the spot she grasped at the first germs of resistance.

"You must be mistaken," she argued quietly, the blue of her eyes deepening with resolve. "I'm living in that villa" — she cocked her dark head toward the structure at the top of the cliff — "and understood that this beach went along with it. The stairway from the house leads directly here."

His shaded gaze held hers a minute longer, then angled up toward the hilltop. Not at all impressed, he renewed his tirade. "*I* was told that the house was unoccupied. You're lying through your teeth —"

"I beg your pardon," she interrupted loudly, growing less intimidated and more incensed by the minute, "but it *was* unoccupied . . . until this afternoon. Now *I'm* living there, and, for your information, *you're* trespassing." She rose lithely to her feet in hopes of diminishing the advantage he held so long as he towered so far above her. It was a futile measure; even standing at her full 5'6" height, he surpassed her by an easy head. And, as if height alone were not enough to enforce her impotence, the breadth and sturdiness of his leanly muscled shoulders echoed it. Arielle couldn't remember having been in such a situation before — and she wasn't quite sure how to handle it.

As though sensing her dilemma, he let the issue of the occupancy of the house pass. "What are you doing here?" His voice was lower, yet still deep and piercing in intensity. She could no more have fled a buffalo stampede than evaded his interrogation.

Tilting her chin up in a confident gesture, feigned at best, she saw no point in delaying. "I'm here on vacation — and to work."

"To work? Hah!" he exclaimed, his even, white teeth showing in a bitter laugh, then went on as if talking to himself. "At least this one is honest about it. Somewhat evasive, perhaps, but honest. Most of them claim they're lost!" He paused for a breath, his chest expanding to claim her involuntary attention before she caught herself and dragged her gaze to his face once more. "And would you go so far as to identify the nature of your, er, work?"

As his voice softened a fraction, his features followed suit. In that instant Arielle felt the same tug of familiarity which had nagged at her on the plane. She had seen him somewhere . . . but where? If, indeed, she recognized him, he could hardly be the dangerous savage she might have imagined; in her fairly limited circle of acquaintances, and beyond, to *their* circle of acquaintances, there were no maniacs that she knew of. Buoyed by this feeble thought, she spoke freely, half hoping to evoke a similar chord of recognition in him.

"I'm a photographer." He snapped, if possible, to even greater attention, prompting her to elaborate. "A child photographer. I was hoping to organize a collection of my photographs while I'm here. I purposely rented this place for its seclusion and never imagined," her voice rose in open accusation, "that I'd be interrupted this way." With a will of its own, her spirit broke through.

For the first time, his lips curved faintly upward in what could not quite be called a smile. "It certainly looked as though you were getting a lot of work done just now." His smooth challenge mocked her. Though hidden by his sunglasses, his eyes were unmistakably thorough in their survey of her body, his dark head dipping imperceptibly in the endeavor. Goaded by his insolence, she jumped to her own defense.

"For heaven's sake, I just arrived! Part of what I came for was the sun — and I was thoroughly enjoying it until you came along.

23

I have no intention of working *every* minute. And, if it's not impertinent of me to ask," she jeered sarcastically, "what are *you* doing on my beach?"

"*My* villa is the one over there." He indicated the high face of a cliff to the immediate north. There, largely concealed by a hedge of broad-leaved greenery, was a second house, similar in stuccoed structure to her own, though much larger. "I *own* it and that one, too," he shot a glance at hers, "not to mention this lovely stretch of beach. So, it would seem that *you* are the trespasser. Now, shall I call the police, or will you pack up and leave quietly?"

His smugness infuriated her. On impulse, she launched a counteroffensive. "Now, wait just a minute, Mr. — Mr. —"

"Howe," he supplied, with a note of expectancy she promptly ignored, leaning a fist on her own slim hip and glowering her impatience.

"Just a minute, Mr. Howe. My brother rented this house through an agent, Thomas Kendrick, in New York. If there's been a mix-up, you should take it up with him. I have already paid the full month's rent, and, if you really *do* own this place, you should be ashamed of the sum you're getting! But the fact remains that I paid it willingly and

24

I have a canceled check to prove it." Of course, the canceled check was back in Rockport, she realized with a grimace, praying that he would not demand to see it. Howe . . . Howe . . . why was that name so familiar?

"I'll refund your money." The steel was back in his deep voice, cold and hard. "I want you out by this evening."

"What?" she shrieked. Momentarily nonplussed by this unexpected turn of events, she stared, open-mouthed and incredulous, at him. Then, anger slowly surfaced to dominate her whirling emotions. "Are you kidding? I'll have you know that I've waited a long time for this vacation. I haven't been away in years! And I didn't travel all this way only to be evicted from a place I rented in good faith!"

A slow smile spread across his lips, twisting them in what could only be termed blatant mockery. "A hard-working girl . . ."

"As it happens, yes! I owe myself this vacation and I have every intention of taking it right here, in that," she pointed to the hilltop, "house. And if you don't like my presence, *you* can leave." Slightly breathless, she paused. *Let him digest that,* she concluded determinedly, only to be appalled moments later by the abrupt evaporation of any semblance of humor from his features.

"That would be preposterous," his voice lowered dangerously, "particularly since you and I both know that *I'm* the main reason you've come."

This was a new twist, and even more ludicrous than the first. Once again, Arielle found herself dumbfounded, staring at him in disbelief. When she finally spoke, her voice was puzzled and high pitched. "What are you talking about?"

His patience seemed to wane. "Oh, come off it, what did you say your name was? Honey, Kitty, Dolly?" The disdain with which he tossed off the possibilities puzzled her further.

"I didn't, but it's Arielle. Arielle Pasteur." There was no need for secrecy. If he did, indeed, own the houses and the beach, he would simply have to put through a call to his rental agent in New York to ascertain her identity and the validity of her claim.

Undaunted, he picked up where he had left off, his anger smoldering perilously close to the surface. "Arielle Pasteur — a fitting name for a would-be glamour girl. Now, let's be honest with one another," he growled impatiently. "You came down here in hopes of being . . . discovered is the term I think they like to use. And you want me to photograph that lovely vision of innocence and purity. How am I doing?" His show of good humor held not an ounce of the real thing. He hadn't moved an inch, but held the stance of the master, taunting her with both his words and his arrogant manner.

Arielle's finely-shaped brows drew together, furrowing her forehead beneath her bangs. "Photograph?" It was all she could do to restrain the skepticism which threatened to erupt from deep within at the thought of that other photograph, hidden but vivid, in a far pocket of her wallet. "Photograph?" The word echoed in her consciousness. "Whatever are you talking about? Photograph?" Howe . . . photograph . . . *oh, no!* The tremor in her voice could not be hidden in her urgency. "What did you say your first name was?"

His smile was cold and shallow as he threw her own words back to her in mocking echo. "I didn't, but it's Christopher. Christopher Howe."

Christopher Howe. Christopher Howe. *The* Christopher Howe? In an instant of stark recognition, she knew it for fact. The tall, menacing figure before her was none other than Christopher Howe, the world-famous fashion photographer, before whose lenses many a young, fresh face had posed her way to the very top of the high-fashion ladder. He had appeared on many a cover, himself, though as a newsworthy playboy rather than a model. As a fashion photographer, there was no better. Arielle had admired his work on many occasions, including that on which she and Michael had viewed one of his shows, a superb collection on temporary exhibit at the Museum of Modern Art in New York City. It was, ironically, on that visit that Michael had first proposed this vacation. Had her interest and involvement in photography played any role in Michael's choice of this particular cottage for her? That was a detail she would clarify later. For now, she found herself engaged in open warfare with this brilliant photographer, this most masculine of men, and she had to sort this situation out before tackling any other. For a brief moment, she stood in awe of him.

"Christopher Howe . . ." she whispered. "I should have realized. There was something very familiar about you, but I couldn't quite place it. Your work is magnificent —"

"And so is yours," he interrupted curtly, shifting to cross his arms over his chest with an air of superiority. "You're quite an actress. But then, most of them are. You're just a little more convincing than some." His sneer sent a chill through her. "Tell me," he growled darkly, "how did you manage to find me? This house is a well-kept secret." Then, suddenly, before she could even begin to protest, his rage exploded anew. "It was Felicity, wasn't it? That scheming witch is bent on revenge! She and that pathetic modeling agency of hers will be the death of me yet!" With a muttered oath of disgust, he turned and stalked toward the sea, shaking his head in exasperation, standing for several moments with his back to her before he stormed back to resume his assault. With mind-shattering bluntness, he vented his anger.

"And you're as bad as she is, to go along with her little plan. Did you really think I'd fall for the trick? You're not the first pretty face she's sent to me, you know. Nor will you be the first precious body I've bedded along the line of duty." He ignored her gasp as he raged on. "Did you really think that, simply by propping yourself up on my beach, you could win my attention? Do you really expect me to spend my own vacation photographing you? Did you really think you could worm your way into my life, with your air of wide-eyed sincerity, and then use me for your own devious ends? Well, *you were wrong!"*

Appalled by his contempt, bewildered by his surliness, Arielle stuck by her claim of innocence with a fierceness which surprised even her. "No, *you* are very wrong. You may well have hordes of ambitious young women scrambling for your attention, but I assure you I'm not one. Even if I *were* looking for a man," her flaming blue-eyed gaze raked over his body, then flew back up with a fury, *"which I am not,* I would never be so stupid as to dabble with the likes of someone as arrogant and offensive as you. All I want is to be left alone. If you treasure your own privacy so highly, please respect mine." Suddenly drained and breathless, she saw no point in continuing the conversation. If for no other reason than pride, he would not yield — she knew the type. "Now, if you'll excuse me, I have other things to do." Pivoting on her heel, no small feat in the shifting sand, she attempted to escape his overpowering presence. But steel fingers seized her arm in a bruising grip, halting her instantly.

"You bet you do," he seethed, teeth clenched in anger, apparently undaunted by her pithy denunication. "You'll take your precious little body back up there and pack, then head somewhere else. I don't care if you stay on the island — just stay away from me!"

Angrily, he moved closer. She tried to back away, but his hand tightened painfully. Even though his eyes were hidden, he threatened her in a way she had never been threatened before.

"Look, Mr. Howe," she blurted out defensively, holding her palms out and open to him, "I honestly want nothing from you —" But he cut her off sharply, shaking her for an instant before thrusting her away.

"Spare me! You're as sly as the last one. All women want something — money, favors, a shooting session, a night in bed. If it isn't one thing, it's another. And they resort to any trick in the book to get it! Well, Miss Arielle Pasteur, this is one you've blown. Why don't you just move to a hotel and spend some time in the casino? Who knows, maybe you'll get lucky and recover the money you've wasted on this little venture. Or maybe you'll find a man willing to make your stay worthwhile."

His crudeness held Arielle speechless, yet his implication was enough to trigger her own form of violence. Without thinking beyond stilling the tongue responsible for such an outrage, she raised a hand and swiftly slapped his face. Never before had she hit a man. Never before had she been brought to the point of such raw fury. Never before had she even thought herself capable of this kind of response. This man had evoked a hidden side of her nature — and that disturbed her as much as anything else.

Her hand flew to her mouth as she realized what she had done. Yet her own pride precluded an apology. Christopher Howe had deserved it! All the professional skill and success in the world could not excuse his scathing disrespect. Apprehension surged through her, nonetheless, as she awaited his retaliation. To her dismay, he seemed almost unaffected by the blow, still every bit the simmering demon he had been before.

"Did that feel good, Arielle?" he taunted as he let go of her. "Do you feel better now?" A new quality had entered his tone, one she could not yet identify.

"You asked for that!"

"For hitting on the truth?"

Trembling all over, she struggled to recapture her composure. "For making vile accusations and even more vulgar suggestions," she cried defensively, further disconcerted by the low rasp of his voice. "You're the one who's blown it this time. You're way off base. I want nothing, *nothing* from you!"

Her cry was abruptly stilled by his long stare. Though his expression was unfathomable, the air was suddenly charged with a new form of energy, one that had not been there before. Fighting the urge to flee, she held her ground in a show of conviction.

"Nothing, Arielle?" he drawled, shattering her composure with two words, as he had been unable to do with twenty. For his drawl reeked of seduction, sending a shaft of fear through her body. She stepped back involuntarily. Surely as reputable a man as this talented image-maker would do her no harm. Then his own other image, that of the noted playboy flashed before her eyes, and she held her breath. When he took one determined step toward her, then another, her pulse accelerated to panic-driven speed.

"Please," she cried in desperation, her eye skirting his oncoming form to calculate the possibility of escape, "just leave me alone. That's all I ask!"

Again he challenged her, his voice lower, thicker. "Is that all? Are you sure, Arielle? You're a very attractive woman. I can't believe that you would turn away what I would freely offer. . . ."

Unwittingly taken steps had backed her to the ocean. Even now, the warm waves lapped gently at her heels. But, growing more frantic by the second, Arielle was oblivious to it. Mustering her last bits of courage, she attempted to deal him a verbal blow in hopes that it would have greater impact than the earlier physical one. "I most certainly would! You're self-centered, egotistical, a chauvinist from the word go. I wouldn't even allow you to *photograph* me, much less crawl into my *bed!*" Her lips thinned in disgust, then her mouth opened in astonishment moments later when he burst into loud and unexpected laughter.

"You have a novel approach," he choked out at last. "Very refreshing, and exactly the type of challenge no red-blooded man could ignore." Instantly, he sobered. "I sure as hell won't."

She had gone too far; her own defense had backfired. This time, when he moved to within inches of her, she tried contrition. "Look, I'm sorry for this misunderstanding, truly I am. I'm sure there has to be some solution here that would be agreeable to us both." Shifting sideways, she prepared to circle him. "Why don't I try to call . . ." She took another step to the side, but he stopped her, clamping a hand on each of her shoulders.

"Not so fast," he taunted softly, wickedly.

Momentary paralysis seized her limbs as she wondered just what he would do next. The leisurely lowering of his head snapped her out of her frozen state. Horrified, as his lips approached hers, she struggled away, pushing at the warm wall of his chest with every bit of strength she could muster, resisting the pull of his hands. Her high-pitched "Let me go!" was choked out in desperation as she kicked at his shin with her foot.

When her fingernails raked the solid column of his neck, he cursed beneath his breath, then hauled her writhing form against the steadiness of his. "So you want to play rough, do you?" he drawled mockingly, securing her arms behind her back with one deft motion. "Fine with me."

Even as she twisted futilely, his lips captured hers, stealing her breath in momentary shock. She wrenched her face to the side and gasped for air. So he intended to carry out his threat, to seek his own satisfaction! Terrified, she groped for some means of evasion. But when her knee came up he was prepared, hooking his leg behind her stationary calf an instant before her blow hit its mark, knocking her off balance, then tumbling beside her onto the sand.

Fear surged through her trembling body

with the realization that her fight had only served to augment his determination and his ardor. Yet the past had trained her; she would not lie still beneath his attack. From deep within, she found the strength to maintain her resistance. Wildly, she squirmed and thrashed, until his hand anchored hers above her head and the weight of his body, now partially atop her, stole what little breath she had.

"No . . . no, please," she moaned, turning her head from side to side. But he caught her chin with fingers of iron and held her still as his mouth covered hers once again, smothering her protest with the totality of his possession. Strangely, there was no pain. His lips mastered hers, consuming and devouring without punishment. Sensation hammered in on her — the foray of his tongue across her lips, against her teeth and beyond, the strength of his leg, thrown across hers, pinning her down. She felt herself the prize of a timeless pirate, bent on taming her, body and spirit. Her smothered cries of protest went unheeded, as did the quivering of her limbs. In panic, her thoughts flashed back to another time, to pain and degradation, to humiliation and betrayal. Helpless tears formed, then flowed, as finally he released her lips and raised his face to look long and hard at her.

She no longer noticed that his breathing matched hers in unsteadiness, so blinded was she by her own emotional upheaval. Her eyes, fluid and pleading, looked up at him, conveying the terror she felt to her core.

In an unexpected movement, he raised a hand to his glasses, removed them slowly, then tossed them down on the sand. For the first time, she saw his eyes — coal-black but glittering, their murky depths as much of an enigma as his mirrored lenses had been. But when he lowered his mouth this time, there was a difference. This kiss held an incongruous softness, an unexpected gentleness as it first feather-touched her lips, then firmed into a caressing lure against her own locked lips. It was as though he offered her comfort, steadied her, gave her his strength. Confused, she held his gaze when he lifted his head once more, only marginally aware when he released her hands and threaded his fingers through the hair on either side of her face. His thumbs rested lightly against her cheekbones, coaxing her imperceptibly. Even his body, long and firm against her, gentled mysteriously.

Overwhelmed by the emotional battle which was raging within her, she felt herself floating in a limbo of numbness, too weak to resist him, too frightened to yield to his demand. The force of her dilemma brought a soft cry from her moist lips, a sigh, a protest, an exclamation of helplessness. It was what he wanted, as his lips repossessed hers, now open and vulnerable to his advance. But he continued to coax, tasting her sweetness with the gentlest persuasion, sending shudders through her with the touch of his tongue, soft and tentative against the curve of her lips, the tips of her teeth, the inner recesses of her mouth.

A strange lethargy enfolded her, bringing a range of feelings she could not comprehend. He was a stranger — yet not a stranger. He was her assailant — yet this was no attack. He was her lover — yet she had no lover.

It was the last thought which wrenched her back to reality. Horrified now at the extent of his conquest, she jerked her head away and twisted anew beneath him. Moments later, she found herself free, crouched on her knees, her back to her tormentor, her face to the sea. Panting, she dropped her chin to her chest, aware of the quivering of her muscles, alert to the man behind her.

His voice came to her, deep and husky. "If I didn't know better, I might believe you."

His shadow on the sand lengthened as he stood. The coldness of the words that poured out belied the warmth of his caress moments before. "It seems to me that you have something to think about. The next time you see me, you may want to head in the opposite direction." Anger and disdain were in his voice, but both were held safely in check once more.

As he retreated to his own house, moving beyond the curve of the rocks to the stairway she had been unable to see, she sat in mute bewilderment. It was only when a small shell, exquisitely colored but pathetically empty, was washed up by the waves that she mustered the strength to move. Reaching forward, she rescued the shell from the retreating surf and clutched it to her. An empty shell — the implication was devastating. Was she an empty shell, devoid of life, of feeling, of love? For the first time in five years, she wondered what it might have been like to have known the fullness, the wholeness that a man might have brought to her life. But a man who loved her, and only her — had such a man ever existed? Did one exist now?

Driven by doubt, she stood and headed for her house, *his* house.

Two

The solitary shell, with its delicately swirled blend of ecru, coral, and cocoa, lay atop the white-lacquered sheen of the nightstand by her bed, capturing her attention as she sprawled across the nubby cotton coverlet. It represented all that had happened earlier that afternoon, all that she wanted to push from her mind. The irony of the situation was striking. Arielle had left the rush and structure of a life she did, nonetheless, love, to taste another, more peaceful, more exotic existence on a distant Caribbean isle. In her wildest dreams she had not anticipated having to cope with an antagonistic neighbor in the form of the exceedingly virile Christopher Howe.

A frown tugged at her gentle features as she concentrated deeply, trying to remember everything she had ever read about the man. To her dismay, there was little to retrieve beyond the broadly generalized image which had come to her earlier. He was in his late thirties, she recalled, and worked out of New York, where his studios were located. How much time he spent there, however, was open to question. His assignments took him to the far corners of the earth, from teeming cities to the remotest of spots. His photographs regularly graced the covers and inner pages of the top American fashion magazines, as well as comparable publications out of Paris, Milan, and London. His vision was bright and new, creative and trend-setting. Subtlety was his trademark, which was remarkable, considering the undercurrent of flamboyance which his work conveyed.

He had "made" any number of beautiful models, and only photographed the cream of the crop. How ridiculous, she mused, that his eye should mistake her for a potential subject! Or, she asked herself, had he seen something she had never seen?

Impulsively she moved from the bed to stand before the dresser, above which hung a large, white-framed mirror. Though the young woman who stared back at her was pretty enough, in Arielle's judgment, she had none of the attributes of a model — neither the fine bone structure which the prime agencies sought, the willowy height

41

which was customarily required, nor the inner core of seductiveness which would make a photograph appealing.

Rather, here was an innocent face, framed by a bob of glossy hair, blunt-cut to just above shoulder-length, and sporting a thick row of bangs curving lower at the temples. Her complexion was fine and creamy-white, dotted now with a faint sun flush. A small nose stressed the symmetry of her features; a rounded chin and jawline gentled them. Her lips were finely curved though thin, made even more so by the grimace which graced them in self-examination. If anything, however, it was her eyes which held a world of promise. They were blue, blue as the azure skies beneath which she had reveled earlier. Shifting in hue with her moods, they were compelling, adding a depth to her face, a hint of mystery, that suggested a woman on the verge of discovery.

As the figure in the mirror did a slow pirouette, an unobserved bystander would have labeled it a lovely one. Slim and graceful, she possessed all the right curves, underplayed but latently feminine. Had she been draped in a slim-fitting *pareu* such as she would later see on display throughout the island, she would have been divine. Clad in nothing but the skimpiest of bikinis, she would have been provocative. But she wore a sober navy halter top, properly tied, and sedate white walking shorts, whose pleats disguised the true richness of her shape.

Regardless of how much time she spent before the mirror, Arielle would always think of herself as heavy. It was a self-image with which she had grown up, one which was impossible to erase despite the slenderness which the past five years had brought. Chubby as a teenager, overweight through her college years, she would always recall that other Arielle when she saw this new one. In her mind, she would always be gently rounded, introspective, socially self-conscious. Though her years in Rockport had brought a certain maturity, a professional self-confidence, a kind of detached poise, that other self-image was etched too deeply to ever be completely erased.

How absurd that Christopher Howe should misinterpret her intent! Perhaps the sun had gone to his head, or the long flight had taken its toll on him. Perhaps his anger had blinded him.

The large white wicker chair by the window welcomed her as she sank down into it and let the ocean breeze refresh her. What was it she felt toward him? She admitted to an undeniable fear, both of his size and his threatening, overtly sexual intent. But there was also something else — a curiosity, a sense of mystery. If only she could be sure she would not see him again. But a month was a long time to live in such proximity to a man without running into him. What was she going to do?

As she hugged her knees to her chest and rested her dark head back against the brightly flowered cushion of the chair, she examined her options. She could leave the island. Certainly not! This cottage? No way! If there was one thing she had vowed after that fateful night in Peter Stoddard's dormitory room, it was that no man would ever manipulate her again! She *would* stay here. The debate was on how to handle this already uncomfortable situation, not on how to avoid it, because it could not be avoided.

Here in the villa, she was safe. A smile of satisfaction dimpled her cheeks as she rose and wandered into the main room of the house. As it had on first impression, it pleased her now. The decor was light and modern, an airy arrangement of whites and vividly tropical colors. The living room was focused around a long wicker sofa and its matching end tables; in addition, it had a casual array of armchairs, similar to that in her bedroom, open-backed shelf units, and a low, closed piece, white and gleaming, housing a stereo and a bar. Windows dominated the walls, allowing for no more than a sampling of the local art, which hung in a brightly-colored display. The true beauty lay beyond the windows in the lush greenery and landscaped growth whose glory invaded the simplicity of the room, and in the vibrant shards of sunlight, now orange in its late-afternoon intensity, which spilled across the furnishings and the polished tile floor. To the right was a kitchen, small but crisp and immaculate, as was everything else. To the left was the bedroom from which she had just come, its deep-pile carpeting a renewed lure. The bathroom was connected to the bedroom and was luxurious in its simplicity, its tub sunken and shiny, its bright pink and green towels rich and oversized. Arielle resumed her seat by the bedroom window with a bolstered resolve to remain in this delightful haven for the full month for which she had contracted.

Yes, here in this house, she was safe. The beach was another matter. Yet hadn't she taken the exorbitant lease with that beach in mind as well? Every piece of written material she'd skimmed prior to her departure from Rockport had stressed the magnificence of St. Maarten's beaches. There were, she acknowledged, many others to choose from on the island — but this was *hers.* Her gaze was drawn to the window and beyond to the stretch of ocean which dominated the vista. From where she sat, the small, sandy beach was hidden well below the cliffs which fell just beyond her house. Would she feel comfortable, after the debacle this afternoon, in going there? Would she have the constant fear of attack each and every time she luxuriated in the fine white sand or romped in the gentle warmth of the waters there? He had issued a warning; did she dare ignore it?

A sudden brainstorm brought her to the edge of her chair. Michael — she'd call Michael! He would get on the phone to the travel agent and he would straighten out this whole mess from his comfortable New York office. He would surely know how to handle Christopher Howe! Heading back toward the living room after a stop in the kitchen, where she fixed herself a tall, ice-filled glass of tea, she settled into a corner of the sofa and pulled the telephone from the end table into her lap. Pausing for a few minutes, she indulged in a journey back in time to the childhood of which Michael had been such a vital part.

A late-in-life baby, she had been born

when her parents, then in their forties, had long since given up hope of providing their only child, Michael, with a sibling. Her arrival had sparked a joy in the family which was shared by all three. Pampering this new member was their given right, and they exercised it with no holds barred. As a youngster, she had been coddled and adored. Even now she grinned at the thought of the large portrait, still sitting in the living room of her parents' house in Longmeadow, Massachusetts. Roly-poly and chipmunk-cheeked, she had resembled an elf, with her ruddy cheeks and dark-thatched hair.

The teenage years had brought a few modifications of that cherubic charm, the natural flush of childhood giving way to a crystal-clear pallor, the hair growing longer, tamer, less mischievous, the baby-fat yielding to an adolescent plumpness. Her family had championed her through it all, but Michael had been her savior.

Twelve years her senior, he had been her idol. Michael was always right. Michael was always in control. Michael did everything to perfection. And, best of all, Michael treasured his sister. There was a mutual bond of love between them. When Arielle had a problem, it was her brother to whom she went. Fortunately, he had spent his college years at Amherst, not far from the family home. Even during his years in law school in Boston, they had kept in close touch. When he had settled in New York, it had been a blow, but by then she was old enough to carry on a correspondence with him, to phone him, even to make the trip on the train to visit him. When he married two years later, his wife became the sister she had never had. Many a vacation, during those socially painful high-school years, had been spent with the two of them and then with their baby girl, when she finally arrived.

You will be a beautiful woman one day they had all told her, over and over again. But the promise of a future in full bloom was small solace for the girl who felt dowdy and unattractive. Saturday nights were spent either alone, when she refused to accompany her parents to a movie or a show, or with them, when they stayed home. Even now she doubted that they understood the pain she had felt sitting between them in a lovely restaurant while dating couples amused each other at adjoining tables. New Years' Eves had been the worst, and she grimaced in hindsight. Though she had a circle of close female friends, they always had plans and dates, while she had none. Perhaps that explained her unadulterated joy when Peter Stoddard had first expressed interest in her.

But enough! This was to be a time of pleasure, not a terror trip into the past. Lifting the receiver, she placed the call to New York. She was grateful that she could call direct, rather than through Holland, which had been the case until recently; in fact, her lovely villa was located on the Dutch half of the island.

"Michael! Hi!" she exclaimed. He would have just gotten home from the office.

"Arielle? Arielle! How are you? Is everything all right? I didn't expect to hear from you, not so soon, at least!"

"I'm fine, Mike! Really fine!"

"The flight . . . ?"

"Great! Smooth all the way."

"And the weather?"

She gave her response without hesitation. "Magnificent! It's warm, sunny — the island is just beautiful! How are things there? Are Jane and the kids all right?" Michael and Jane were now the proud parents of three girls, all gangly adolescents themselves, all absolutely beloved.

"Everyone's fine here, hon. Is the place OK for you?"

"Ah . . . that's why I'm calling." Her voice lowered, and she cleared her throat. "There's been a slight mix-up; I need your help." As succinctly as possible, she explained the situation.

"He *what?*" His disbelief came through clearly.

A light laugh, bearing a blend of sarcasm and apprehension, preceded her words. "He told me to stay out of his way. He was really a brute about the whole thing." Then, she recalled an earlier thought. "Did you know that he owned these houses, Mike? Did you know that he would be here?"

There was a distracted note in his voice as he replied. "I had no idea, hon. Tom and I have been friends for years. I'm sure he knew that you were a photographer, but I had no idea that he would try anything like this." There was a pause as he struggled to grasp the information. "Christopher Howe is *there?* What a fantastic break for you!"

"*Break?* Michael, the man is insane! He's convinced that I'm after him. He's as paranoid as they come! I want no part of him!" Her elaboration of the situation had deliberately left out the part about the kiss; so much for brother-sister confidences, she mused with a touch of guilt. But then, she had never told him about Peter Stoddard, either. Her brother's retort startled her.

"What a terrific opportunity, though, Arielle!" His excitement was unaffected by her protest.

"Michael," her firm voice held a warning note, "he has nothing to offer me."

"He's a photographer, hon, a very successful one. Maybe you could pick up pointers here or there."

"He's a *fashion* photographer, not a child photographer! His work is a world away from mine, Mike!" Much as she adored her brother, he was wrong on this one. "It's like . . . like you taking tips from a trial lawyer even though you never set foot inside a courtroom. Your field is corporate law. Would you waste your time taking hints from a trial lawyer?"

Michael mulled over her argument. "If he had something to offer, yes. But I do see your point. So, what can I do?"

Now she was getting somewhere. Relieved, she nestled deeper into the cushions. "You can start by calling your friend Tom and asking him what the story is. Then you can call me back and fill me in. Until then, I'm not sure I dare set foot outside this house for fear of running into that monster!"

"OK, OK. Relax, hon. I'll call Tom. But," he quickly interjected, "don't expect a call back from me tonight. Tom is a pretty lively bachelor and rarely sees the inside of his apartment until the wee hours of the morning, when your dear and stodgy brother and his family are fast asleep."

"Oh, Michael," she chided gently, "you're not one bit stodgy. If you were a bachelor, you'd have every girl on the block after you!"

"Well, little miss prim and proper," her brother retaliated easily, "if you relaxed a little bit you could have every available guy on your string! Why don't you start down there and have a little fun?"

Suddenly the conversation hit too close to home. "I will have fun," she began, fighting to keep her bitterness at bay, "but I don't need a panting male to provide it. Now, will you call Tom for me, or do I have to put the call through myself?"

Michael laughed loudly. "Of course I'll do it. You might spend half your vacation trying to reach him. I'll get back to you when I have any news. Good enough?"

"Good enough!" Her tension evaporated with the smile that brightened her features. As Arielle replaced the receiver, she felt a surge of optimism. Everything would work out. In a day or two she would look back at this misunderstanding and laugh. Or so she hoped!

For a brief instant, more sober thoughts intruded on her happiness. No, she had never told Michael, nor her parents, about Peter Stoddard and that terrible night. Her subsequent depression must have been obvious to them, knowing her as well as they did, though the fact that she had been living at college at the time had helped. Still, there was the self-consciousness she felt for months after that when her parents, or anyone else, looked at her — and the awful sense of guilt at having betrayed the values with which she had been raised. Had it been a just punishment for her stab at womanhood? A determined shake of her downcast head denied that possibility. Nothing, *nothing,* could justify what Peter Stoddard and his friends had done. To have heartlessly lured an innocent, inexperienced young woman, who so obviously craved affection, into an intimate relationship *on a dare* — nothing could have been more cruel! Yet, the facts were unarguable. She had gone willingly with Peter that night, had submitted to him by choice, had later discovered the ruse — then had been utterly crushed.

In the weeks and months that followed, she had struggled with a bruised self-image and nonexistent self-confidence. She had fought her way to peace of mind day by day, step by step. When she had finally attained it with her success as an individual, as a photographer, in Rockport, she cherished it. She had been happy in the past few years. No man, *no man,* would spoil that happiness!

Determination provided the momentum as she changed into a high-collared sundress and a pair of low sandals, grabbed her purse, and headed for the small Chevette she had rented. Even as she slipped behind the wheel and rolled each window down in turn, she had to laugh at coming all the way to a foreign island to drive a slice of Americana. Not terribly different from her own Pinto, it started easily, lapped up the early evening breeze, and cooled quickly. One glance at the map provided by the rental office and she was off, bent on finding Philipsburg, the Dutch capital of the island.

The road was only marginally paved at first, and her tires raised a large dust cloud behind her. She drove slowly, enjoying the scenery she had rushed by earlier. Then, her sole intent had been to ferret out the hidden drive that led to the villa; now, she was more sure of her way, more open to the sights around her. The rural, at times almost barren, quality of the landscape fascinated her. Aside from the more cultivated and manicured patches on which her cottage and the various hotel, resort, and condominium complexes were located, the central stretch of the island was dry and hilly. The vegetation was drabber and lower to the ground, rugged in a beautiful way, offering broad vistas to the appreciative eye. Along the route she would come to know well over the next few weeks, the string of tourist havens fell before her — Mullet Bay, with its low apartment groupings and its luxuriant golf course, the Maho Reef, and the Caravanserie, on a small peninsula, teasing the ocean.

The sun, lowering quickly now toward the sea, streaked the waters with its reds and golds and swept the skies with its pinks and purples and oranges. The map spelled out the way, a simple one, given the sparsity of roads, and one that took her gradually higher to hug the hillside which overlooked the bay. There, at its highest point, she stopped, enchanted. Pulling up at a roadside turnoff, she gazed out over the Caribbean, drank in the sunset, marveled at the scattering of boats, now headed for shore. It was a breathtaking sight; instantly, she regretted not having brought her camera.

Returning to the roadway once more, she followed its curves downward toward the center of civilization. Natives, dark-skinned and proudly erect, filled the streets on their way home. Again she made mental notes for future photographic endeavors. Gradually the number of roads increased. Within a few minutes, she found herself on Front Street, the first of the two main thoroughfares which bisected Philipsburg. It was, to her surprise, a narrow street, lined on the right by parked cars which allowed no more than a single lane for through traffic. It was a far cry from the wide, modern streets of home and she was delighted. Parking in the first available spot, she eagerly began her exploration. To meet the oncoming dusk, the lights of the stores and restaurants went on one by one, creating a charm, an intimacy, which she found infinitely appealing. The sidewalk was as narrow and uneven as the road had been, suggesting a provinciality which was belied by the elegance of many of the shops and the sophistication of many of the restaurants. A free port, St. Maarten offered its visitors the finest wares from many European establishments. There were shops filled with perfumes, cameras, jewelry. There were those stocked with incidentals — books, toys, and notions.

There were those whose window mannequins wore the latest fashions. And there were those which specialized in a more local variety of goods.

It was toward the latter that she gravitated, fascinated by the splash of colors, intrigued by the simplicity of style, captivated by the Caribbean flavor. And though there were many tourists, like herself, who roamed the evening street, there were also the local residents, clustered in small groups by the roadside, chatting in pairs on the sidewalks, leaning against a car or a store window, watching the stream of visitors as they passed, to draw her artist's eye.

Darkness loomed ahead as Front Street tapered to its end. Instinctively, she turned and retraced her path, suddenly struck by the realization that she'd eaten nothing since lunch on the plane and that she was, indeed, very hungry. The dilemma of where to eat was a delightful one; the choice included one interesting possibility after another. In the end she entered a small seafood restaurant housed in a charming, distinctly West Indian building. It was aptly called La Bouillabaisse, and she ordered the specialty, savoring the exquisite blend of fresh fish, milk, butter, and seasonings as her eyes drank in the bayside view. In most of the local spots, as opposed to the more elaborate hotels, air-conditioning was non-existent and pleasantly unnecessary. Whereas the mid-day heat hovered in the eighties, the evenings cooled to a more balmy seventy. The ocean breeze was restive and gentle, circulating about the small room and its array of gay round tables, with the aid of quaint, Casablanca-type ceiling fans which had recently become the vogue at home, Arielle noted. The diners had an unobstructed view of the port beyond, the boats now lit and dancing softly in the lapping waters. The island cast its spell over her as she sat, entranced, sipping the small cup of espresso which was her sole dessert. If this was a sampling of what she could expect over the next few weeks there was a lot to look forward to. She smiled in satisfaction. Taking a deep breath of the shore-fragrant air, she dragged her gaze reluctantly from the diamond-studded dark of the night and moved to settle the bill which her waiter had quietly presented. As her eyes shifted across the room, her breath caught.

There, in a far corner of the room, leaning comfortably back in his chair, was Christopher Howe. *Looking directly at her.* Now there were no sunglasses to camouflage his gaze. Now there was no rumpled thatch of hair to disguise his roguery. And, mercifully, there were no less than eight tables separating his commanding presence from her. His eyes locked onto hers for a moment before she determinedly broke the visual link. She studied the bill, then signed a traveler's check and handed it to the waiter, who disappeared instantly to get her change.

She refused to raise her downcast eyes and risk another encounter. The nearly-drained coffee cup became the object of her intense scrutiny as she sought to re-create the island spell in which she had reveled moments before. But her mind was elsewhere, analyzing with acuity the man who had irrevocably broken that spell. That he was also alone had been clear, as was the fact that he, too, had finished eating and was now simply relaxing, content to reissue his arrogant challenge in silence. There was a different air about him now; he looked more civilized but no less potent. But the depth of his gaze shook her, speeding her pulsebeat with maddening persistence. For though she no longer met his eye, her entire body felt his presence as clearly as if he were intimately close.

Infuriated by the effect he had on her, she recalled the vow she had made earlier that day, that she would not be intimidated by any man, much less Christopher Howe. When the waiter reappeared with her change and the offer of more coffee, her stubborn streak reared its head. *He will not chase me away,* she thought. Her nod was one of adamant determination. If he had thrown down the gauntlet, she would not ignore it. If she cowered before him, the last five years of confidence-building would have been in vain. This was a test, she mused, and she refused to fail.

Her eye followed the thin brown stream of coffee, dark and richly aromatic, as it slowly filled her cup. Then, alone once more, she doggedly swallowed her hesitancy. Defiance was bright in the gaze she lifted to meet the eyes that still studied her. With deliberate slowness, she raised the cup to her lips and sipped. Then, with an equally rebellious air, she shifted her gaze abruptly from his, hoping that she had made her disinterest clear.

When at last she gathered her things together and stood to leave, she steadfastly avoided glancing toward the corner in which the dark figure had been. When she reached her car, she had no idea of his whereabouts, whether he had left the restaurant or not. But the open street reassured her, relaxing her once more as she began the return drive to the cottage.

With the countryside bathed now in darkness, there was little to see. Wayward thoughts filled her mind as she drove carefully over the still-unfamiliar roads. How pleasant the evening had been until that man had forced himself into her awareness! What was it about him, she asked herself, that so unsettled her? Why had she let him affect her, both this afternoon and tonight? On the one hand, he *was,* much as she might like to deny it, an eminent personality, a celebrity in his own right. It would be natural to stand in awe of him, particularly as she could appreciate the brilliance of his work. On the other hand, he was, stripped of camera, portfolio, and entourage — much as he had been this afternoon on the beach — no different from any other man.

Slowing to negotiate a particularly sharp curve, she pondered this last thought. Was he the same as other men? In some ways, yes. He was arrogant, selfish, and dictatorial. And the lewd gleam was as fast to enter his eye as that of any other man. But, she acknowledged with grudging reluctance, he was also forcefully tall, magnificently built, and ruggedly handsome in a way that instantly set him apart from the others.

Now, as her mind re-created that scene on the beach, she admired his body from afar. Safe in her car, and immune from the fear he had inspired then, she examined that body, line by line, and found nothing wanting. In the eye of the artist, his was a form which captured the spirit of virility to perfection. Dressed as he had been this evening, clean-shaven and with his hair neatly combed, he exuded an aura of masculinity that was undeniable.

With a grunt of dissatisfaction at the direction of her thoughts, she gripped the wheel tighter. What difference did it make, her inner voice argued, that he was tall, dark, and handsome? Hadn't she always been told — particularly in those awkward and unattractive years — that it was what was inside that counted?

The sight of the moon, full and half-hidden behind a chain of small, dark clouds, brought an analogy to her mind. He was indeed a dark cloud, hovering over her head in this Caribbean paradise. When he stood, he cast his pall of gloom over her. When he passed by, the weight of darkness lifted.

The concentration she needed to relocate the drive that led to the villa was enough to push him from her mind. As she sighted the drive and turned in, she felt strangely relieved of a burden. Her haven was here, welcoming her, offering her its sanctuary. Moments later, having parked the car, opened the house, and turned on a soft light in the living room, she found herself outside once more, standing on the small patio which led to the wooden stairway and overlooked the sea. How peaceful it was. She sighed. There was no cloud in sight, either real or imagined. The thought that a mere twenty-four hours earlier she had been huddled beneath a heavy quilt to ward off the January chill brought a smug grin to her lips. The warmth of the air was heaven, the sound of the tide a nocturnal rhapsody, the seascape itself a masterpiece before even the rankest of amateur's lenses. Time lost all meaning as she stood, savoring the bounty served up by the Caribbean.

By ten the next morning, she was on the beach. It was a beautiful day, and she felt rested and eager to enjoy her vacation — and unafraid of Christopher Howe. A burst of excitement had awoken her much earlier, at an hour which would have seemed too early for normal functioning at home. Wasn't it always the case, she had mused, that late-morning sleep only mattered when one had to get up early? Here, where she could sleep as late as she pleased, there was no desire to do so.

She quickly spread the long, lime-hued beach towel out on the warming sand, allocating one corner each to a pair of sunglasses, a book, and a bottle of suntan lotion. With the purr of a kitten, Arielle stretched out atop the thick-piled terry. She wore her bathing suit, a stylish though conservative navy blue maillot which sported the thinnest of spaghetti straps, left in place today as a precaution. For the only thing that had dampened her spirits on this morning was her constant awareness of the man in the other house, the rogue who shared her beach, Christopher Howe, who might, at any time, choose to bother her again.

Until her brother returned her call, she was in a strange limbo. She had mulled the issue over and over that morning, unsure as to how many liberties she dared take without risking retaliation. As she lay here absorbing the warm rays of the sun, she marveled at her own determination, which had brought her down to the beach this morning. She could as easily have basked in the sun atop her patio, but that wouldn't have been the same. Something had driven her to express her defiance once more —

but what that something was clearly mysti-fied her.

Actually, she had been quite cautious, scanning the beach before she climbed down to it, every so often casting a watchful eye in the direction of *his* house, *his* end of the beach. But the temptation of the sun, the sand, and the water had been too great to resist. Before the sun grew too high and hot, she intended to indulge herself. Which she did. Thoroughly. When the heat began to build on her skin, she skipped into the waves, swimming in the shallows, emerging refreshed to scan the craggy cliff once more before sinking down onto the towel and reapplying a rich layer of lotion to her pale skin. Annoyed that she should spend *any* time in contemplation of Christopher Howe on this glorious morning, she put her mind at ease with the reminder that Michael would be calling at some point today. If she wasn't in, he would call back. But the mat-ter would be settled by this evening, of that she was sure.

An hour in the sun was all that she would allow herself. The last thing she wanted was a painful sunburn to spoil her vacation. Much safer, she had decided, to limit her exposure, particularly at first, and gradually build a deep tan. After all, she had to have something to show for her month in the Caribbean! A smooth, bronze tan and the format for her book — two very noble objectives. Having finished with the first for the day, she turned her thoughts to the second.

She stood, shook out the large towel, and folded it. She would begin her work while she awaited that phone call, rather than yielding to laziness and staying on the beach a little longer. There had been no sign of Christopher Howe so far; why tempt fate? Yielding to a last shard of curiosity, she cast a final look toward the far hilltop. A sharp gasp accompanied the realization that she had spoken too soon. For there, outlined starkly against the sky, surrounded by greenery yet standing alone, was a dark figure that could be none other than her nemesis. Her heart suddenly pounding, she stared up at him, convinced that she held his gaze as well. It seemed to pierce her, to suck out her complacence, to lift her and twist her, then set her down with a thud. Pulse racing accordingly, she stood, hypnotized. It was only the flight of a yellow-breasted sparrow, soaring in from overhead to land on the beach, which broke the spell. She glanced down at the bird, then back up at the ominous figure. His boldness was undeniable; even when discovered at his spying, he made no move to withdraw, but, rather, held his stance firmly.

Arielle bent to slowly retrieve her glasses and lotion, tucked the book under her arm along with the towel, and, stiffening her back, headed for the stairway which, in the crook of the rocks as it was, would remove her from his range of vision. Her thoughts roared in tumult as she climbed steadily higher, stunned and shaken, and furious at herself for both. What was it about him that disturbed her so?

The merciful jangle of the telephone interrupted her musings as she neared the top. Quickening her pace, then running the last few steps to the cottage, she flung the screen door open and raced for the phone. The sound died in mid-ring as she reached toward it; a dial tone was all that met her ear when she lifted it. Cursing softly, she thrust the receiver back onto its cradle. *It must have been Michael,* she snapped at herself, then transferred the blame to that dark figure on the hill, for whose benefit she had slowed her retreat. If he had not been there, she would have been back at the cottage minutes earlier, easily in time to get the phone call. But Michael would call back, she reassured herself. He knew how much she wanted this mess cleared up!

Determined to stay close until she received that return call, she spread the first of her photographs on the floor in the living room, propping the large brown portfolio which contained the others against the sofa. There were, all told, seventy-five photographs which she had selected for inclusion in her book. All were pictures of children, some alone, some with adults. Some were close-ups, others included the whole figure, perhaps with a taste of the surroundings. All had been taken during the last five years, then carefully printed in her own darkroom. Each had its own story to tell and, in turn, a story to tell about the art of child photography. It was precisely for this last reason that each had been selected.

Her eye moved from one print to the next, seeking a thread to tie them together, hunting for a theme around which to organize the lot. Nothing came. Carefully scooping up the photographs, she returned them to the portfolio and withdrew the next group, spreading them out and studying them, with similar results. Determined not to be discouraged, she stood and walked about the cottage, assuring herself that the formula would suddenly appear, if not today, then tomorrow, next week, or even the week after that. The final sets of prints met matching fates. It was when she was about to return the last shot to its spot in the pile that the phone rang. She grabbed the receiver before it rang a second time.

"Hello?" It suddenly occurred to her that it might *not* be Michael. What then?

Mercifully, it was. "Arielle? It's Mike. I tried you earlier. Is everything all right?" The connection was not as clear as it had been the night before. Michael's concern was laced with heavy static.

"I'm fine!" She spoke loudly into the phone to overcome the static. "I was at the beach and got back to the house just as you hung up. Did you have any luck with Thomas Kendrick?" Since the rental agent was a friend of her brother's, she kept all trace of a sneer out of her voice.

"I reached Tom this morning," Michael quickly informed her. "He says to tell you that everything has been straightened out. You *do* have the cottage for the month."

That was fine and dandy, she mused sarcastically, but what about her caustic neighbor? "Does Christopher Howe know that?"

"Tom was going to put a call through to him just after I spoke with him. He should have received it by now. Was he any trouble

69

last night — or when you went to the beach this morning?"

"Trouble?" she echoed his word skeptically. How did one explain the many faces of "trouble"? "No, he behaved himself properly enough." After all, if glowering was his thing, he had every right to indulge in it. But there was more to learn from Michael. "What caused the confusion in the first place?" she asked.

Even amid the static, Michael's sheepishness was evident. "Ah, Tom thought he knew what he was doing."

"What he was doing?" she cried in disbelief at the implication that the mix-up had been no mix-up at all. "What do you mean? Did your friend do this to me on purpose?"

"Come on, Arielle," her brother was quick to chide. "He's really not a monster, you know."

"You're not down here facing him, Michael. Now tell me exactly what your 'friend' did."

Michael paused, letting the static fill the silence, wondering just how much he dare say. In the end, his affection and respect for his sister brought out the whole truth. "He believed that you would be very good for Christopher."

Arielle bridled in anger. " 'Good for

Christopher'!" she shrieked in disgust. "What about me? What about my vacation — well paid for, I might add? 'Good for Christopher'? And how would your friend Tom know that much about me?" This new thought gave her a jolt; she was subtly accusing her brother of conspiracy in this plot.

"He's a good friend of mine, hon. I told you that. You can't begrudge me telling my pals about my family. But take it easy. Your vacation will go along just fine, now that this is cleared up. Once Tom has informed Chris of your right to be there, the fellow should leave you alone. Tom was very apologetic about the whole thing. He honestly did believe that you would be a good change for Christopher. The two of them are very close; Tom sounded pretty exasperated at his friend."

Everything suddenly sounded very sane, very rational. How could Arielle, in good conscience, argue further, particularly when she had been assured that she would be bothered no more? Yet now she was curious. "He thought that I would be a good change for the man, huh? What did he mean by that, Mike?"

"I'm glad you asked," her brother laughed slyly, "since I went to quite some trouble dragging as much information about Howe from Tom as possible. Despite the image, his private life is very private. Tom was reluctant to tell me much about him."

"So what did you learn?" she interjected impatiently, even as she chided herself for her interest.

"He's never been married, though he's thirty-eight years old. He's had a number of steady relationships over the years, but none has amounted to anything. The last few years have been particularly difficult ones for him. Though his work has thrived, he's become even more of a loner — hence his desire to spend the winter in seclusion down there *and* his anger when he found you on the beach. The man has become very closed, according to Tom. You know, Arielle," he paused expectantly, took a breath, then threw in the kicker, "you *could* be very good for him."

Arielle was both dismayed and infuriated. A chill passed through her at the thought of this game that the two men — Tom, whom she had never met, and her very own, supposedly more sensitive brother — appeared to be playing. She recalled another game, so long ago, and had to stifle a momentary wave of nausea. Bent on calmness, she decided to hear her brother out. If she was to be a pawn, it helped to know something about the knight. "I don't see where he needs anyone. What seems to be his problem, as Tom sees it?" Any unsteadiness in her voice blended into the static.

"He's been surrounded by the women of his trade, most of whom are shallow and ambitious. Tom felt you would be different."

"And how would he know?" she asked defiantly, wondering just how much Michael had told the other man about her.

Her brother appeared undaunted by her accusatory note. "He knows me, sis, and had to imagine that you were even partly as . . . upstanding, should we say?" Again there were echoes from the past; again she fought the trembling which shook her. "At any rate you have a unique look about you. I always told you —"

"How did Tom know what I *look* like," she screamed hastily.

Finally sensing the extent of her dismay, Michael sought to comfort her. "He's been at my office plenty of times, Arielle. Your picture sits right up there on the credenza next to Judy's and the girls'."

For a frantic moment she struggled to recall exactly which photograph was there. A sigh of relief accompanied her recollection. It was the one that had been taken for her brochure, the one she used for advertising. Mercifully, it was a recent picture, one that had been taken by another photographer, a good friend and an able technician. It was, if she dared to admit it herself, very flattering, though a far cry from the kind of woman that Christopher Howe was accustomed to photographing.

Sarcasm tinged her words. "Well, at least *he* knows how different I am from the usual Christopher Howe woman —" She fell silent and caught her breath as she realized what she had said. She was *not* a Christopher Howe woman! Never would be one! The man had little worth admiring save his talent and his good looks. He was hardheaded, selfish, and crude, also arrogant, aggressive, and chauvinistic. No, Arielle Pasteur would have nothing to do with the man — if she could possibly, possibly help it!

THREE

Possibility was one thing, inevitability another. On an island as small as St. Maarten, it would have been a minor miracle not to have run into the man at some point, even without the added factor of the proximity of their homes and the stretch of beach they shared. After speaking with Michael on the phone, Arielle decided that there was only one course to take. She could not spend her vacation looking over her shoulder. Nor would she alter her plans or hamper her enjoyment because of Christopher Howe's presence. Rather, she would proceed with life as though there had been no ugly encounter on the beach, as though there had been no visual communication in that small restaurant. Life would progress as though there were no such animal as Christopher Howe in the wings, much less next door.

Though her first full day on St. Maarten

passed harmlessly enough, with some exploring in the car, a return to the beach later in the afternoon for a swim, dinner at an informal Indonesian restaurant, and an evening of reading by the soft light above the living room sofa, she was ever aware of the possibility of a confrontation. Despite all her vows to the contrary, she did search the passersby on the streets of Philipsburg, the faces in the market where she shopped for food, the diners at the surrounding tables in the back-alley restaurant where she ate. Though Christopher Howe was nowhere in sight, he was everywhere in her mind irritating her by his absence almost as much as his tall, lean presence had irritated her in person.

The inevitable occurred on the afternoon of the following day. Having spent the morning sunning, then going over her prints, she hopped into her car and headed for Philipsburg in search of postcards, a comfortable place to write them, and a post office. Fully relaxed, she let the traffic flow around her, content to find a parking space once she got to town and take a leisurely walk. The capital's streets were as fascinating in their daytime activity as they had been at night. Natives, other than those manning the occasional shop, were a rarity.

Rather, the downtown population consisted primarily of tourists like herself. In addition to English, her ear caught fragments of both French and German as she moved quietly among the pleasantly sedate groups in the various shops. Finally she returned to the street, postcards in hand, to contemplate a remedy for her dry throat. Across the street and several doors down was a small café, now cleared of the best part of the lunch crowd and seemingly just the place to satisfy her needs. Moments later, she was seated at a shady table on the open-air patio, pen in hand, awaiting the arrival of a large soda.

She took out the colorful cards she had gotten for her parents, Michael and his family, her favorite and, to be more precise, only, great-aunt, a spritely old lady in her late eighties whose spirit was as indomitable as her physical energy was astonishing, and, of course, Sean, perhaps the closest friend she had.

"Dear Sean," she wrote, the neatness of her handwriting, even after five other such notes, as faultless and precise as the quality of her photography, "I think of you, back there in the snow, as I lounge on the beach and bask in the sun in the balmy 80-degree air. It's gorgeous here. The villa is everything I had hoped, plus a little bit more." She would explain the tongue-in-cheek remark when she returned to Rockport. "I only wish you were here to share the latter with me." Indeed, with Sean as her protector, she would never give Christopher Howe a second thought. "I assume you made it back to the house in one piece the other morning. How are my plants doing? And the mail — anything interesting?" Sean had generously offered to care for her houseplants in her absence, to take in the daily mail, and watch over the house; she had readily taken him up on the offer. "You know where to reach me if inspiration hits and you feel like sharing it. In the meantime, my thoughts will be with you. Love, Arielle."

"Love letters?" The deepest of voices broke into her concentration, bringing her head up sharply and stiffening her spine. As on the other night, he looked civilized enough wearing well-tailored white ducks and a blue, open-necked safari-style shirt. The soft rubber of his sneakers had hidden the sound of his approach from her. Now she struggled to contain her surprise and the instant tension brought by his appearance, clearing her throat, searching for properly indifferent words.

A shrug seemed the most appropriate opener. "Whatever you say." Let him make whatever interpretation he wanted, if he was so impertinent as to read over her shoulder. Dragging her eyes from the maddening impassivity of the mirrored sunglasses so far above her, she returned her attention to the postcard, ignoring his unbidden presence as she reread the note, then placed the card, face up, on the top of the pile. The faint quivering within her was harder to ignore.

"Who is Sean?"

Her turmoil this time was not so much from his sudden materialization as from the very personal nature of his intrusion. But turmoil quickly turned to indignation when he remained by her side, towering above her, intent on an answer. She had only one answer to give him, however. Despite the half-full glass of soda, she pushed her chair back as though to leave. A hand, its pressure forceful yet not painful, stilled her.

"You haven't finished your drink," he observed calmly, motioning to the waiter for another, then audaciously folding his long form into the chair opposite hers. Dumbfounded, Arielle simply stared, unaware of the gamut of emotions which flickered in and around the blue of her hard-set eyes.

She was annoyed that her delightfully relaxing afternoon should be disturbed.

Even more, she was bewildered that the disturbance had come in the form of the very man who had warned her to stay away from *him*. She was perplexed as to how to handle this enigmatic man. And she was frightened, very frightened, of herself as much as of him. In the end, she did nothing but lift the straw to her lips and sip her drink as she willed her eyes to the scenery beyond the patio. If Christopher Howe had something to say, an apology perhaps, she mused, swallowing hard, let him say it!

Apparently he did. But first he very slowly and deliberately reached up and took off the sunglasses, his own emotional smoke-screen. It was her undoing. Had the shutters remained in place, Arielle might have succeeded in responding to him with indifference. With them gone, however, she didn't have a chance. For the darkness of his eyes glittered at her, their power drawing her gaze magnetically, subtly augmenting her fears.

As her head slowly turned, she saw his face as though for the first time. There was a new softness which subtly altered his rugged features, an openness that had been there neither on the plane nor on the beach. His mouth was set in a firm line; his eyes were sharp and intense. Yet there was no anger, no chill, no disdain. The strength that remained was compelling, casting its magic over her until the arrival of the waiter broke the spell. Embarrassed, she tore her gaze away and concentrated on her own soda. It was far easier, she mused in dismay, to recall his arrogance and the vulgarity of his previous behavior when her attention was focused on something other than his face.

"Are you enjoying your stay on St. Maarten?" he asked, breaking a silence which had seemed eternal but which had, in fact, lasted only a few minutes. His voice was smooth and low, the harbinger of something even deeper.

Good manners prevented Arielle from simply ignoring his query, since it had seemingly been offered in a spirit of truce. "Very much." Even to her own ears, her words sounded stilted. Determinedly, she looked toward the full-sailed sloop that had just come into view.

His eyes followed hers for a moment, then returned to their study of her. "Your tan is building up nicely," he complimented her, confirming what her own mirror had told her before she'd left the cottage. Yet his motive puzzled her. Compliments, flattery, these were things she could do without. An out-and-out apology was in order. The evaporation of his anger indicated that he must have spoken with Tom Kendrick; why didn't he say as much? Or wasn't he man enough to offer an apology, to admit that he had been wrong, totally wrong?

Perhaps the grim set of her lips betrayed her thoughts; she really didn't know. At first she wasn't sure whether she had only imagined the words, so closely did they resemble her thoughts. Her ears perked up nonetheless.

"I spoke with Tom Kendrick yesterday. It seems we may both have been victims of his slightly warped sense of humor." He paused, sipped his drink, then waited until she looked back at him, as he had uncannily known she would. "I'm sorry for having lashed out at you the way I did. I jumped to the wrong conclusion."

At the reminder of that afternoon's ordeal, Arielle's eyes flared with anger. "You certainly did!" But her outburst was short-lived. Something in his expression conveyed his sincerity, calming her instantly. Chagrined at having dropped the controlled face she preferred to wear, she looked down. "Are you always that bullheaded?"

She knew he was grinning even before she looked up to see the broad crescent of white against the tan which he was, himself, building. "Usually. And I'm usually right. In this case, though, I wasn't. Do you accept my apology?"

He seemed to be making a point of dwelling on it, this apology that had meant so much to her moments before. Now the thought of accepting it and meeting this man on a more open, less antagonistic footing frightened her. But she had no choice. Her eyes locked with his for a moment of intensity. Although it had been underscored with an arrogant note, he had nonetheless apologized. Would she accept?

"Yes." It was nearly a whisper, surprising in its timidity, even to her. *This won't do,* she told herself, dragging her eyes from his in a spurt of self-reproach.

As though relieved of the burden of apologizing and content to leave that unpleasant task behind him, he went on more lightly. "Is the cottage all right? Do you have everything you need?"

"It's fine!" Helplessly, and in spite of the awkwardness she felt, her enthusiasm surfaced. "I love it! Have you owned it long?" His features relaxed even further at her expression of interest. It was an inevitable cycle; once rewarded by his smile, she felt herself begin to warm to the discussion — despite all attempts at maintaining a calm, cool indifference.

"I had the villa built five years ago. I wanted a place to" — he hesitated before filling in the word, seemingly reluctant to reveal more than she might learn from other sources — "escape to. The smaller cottage — yours — was originally designed as a guest house, an adjunct to the main house. I don't use it for that purpose, though. Hence, the rental."

Genuine interest spurred Arielle on. "Do you come here often?"

Again he hesitated before responding, and she sensed that he still distrusted her motives. Yet she held her own silence, awaiting his answer. It was a small victory when it came. "I try to get here two or three times a year. The winter months are the best, when everything is cold at home."

"But you travel a lot, don't you?" she countered spontaneously. At his frown, she clarified her source of information. "I *am* marginally involved in the field, Mr. Howe."

"Chris."

She took a deep breath, gaining the courage to say his name. "Chris. I read the magazines. You must be shooting on location for a good part of the year."

"Too much of it."

His curt reply and its underlying revelation momentarily startled her. Here was one of the most renowned fashion photographers in the world today, a man in whose shoes hundreds of aspiring photographers would give their all to stand, and he hinted that all was not as wonderful as it might, on the surface, appear. She frowned as she studied him, her dark brows drawn together in puzzlement. But before she could probe further, the line of his jaw tensed. It had been a slip which he had evidently not intended to make. Perhaps bitterness was not part of the public image, she mused with a touch of her own cynicism. It was all she could do to avoid an outright burst of laughter. What harm could a bitter note do to *her* opinion of him after she'd seen the boorishness of which he was capable?

The low hum of his voice captured her attention once more. "Tom tells me you plan on staying the month?"

It was purely a gimmick to redirect the conversation away from himself. She had made her intentions clear during their confrontation on the beach that first day. For the time being, she indulged him; his civility had successfully counterbalanced her chill.

"Yes. It didn't seem worth the effort of flying all the way down here for a shorter time. Once having gone through the trouble of clearing up everything at home — you know, rerouting the mail and the parcel post, letting clients know that I'd be away — it made more sense to really splurge. I suppose this is one of the luxuries of being in business for myself." She paused, catching her breath as she lowered her gaze. "Of course, I have to confess that there are disadvantages. I worry a little about my business. I mean, I wonder about all those potential clients who might be calling . . ."

"They'll call back." His seemingly unshakable confidence, mysterious as it was, comforted her immeasurably. "But I do know what you mean, even though my situation is somewhat different. It's tough to feel out of touch. And, for those of us who like to control things . . ." His words trailed off suggestively, drawing her gaze up once more. It was as though he understood, as though he identified with her fear, as though he felt it himself. His deduction was correct. She *was* a person who wanted to be in constant control of herself and her fate. Was he the same, as his words implied? If so, she mused, the two of them were bound to clash again and again!

Yet what she felt now, as she looked into his eyes, dark and black, deep and compelling, was far from a clash. Rather, she felt hypnotized, drawn forward, enveloped. It was very much what she had felt on the beach that second time, when she had looked up to find him watching her from the cliff's edge. There was something almost physical about his gaze. Sitting no more than the width of this small table from him, her sense of him was positively electric. Gasping at the shock of it, she tore her eyes from his. Even with the cloak of civility properly in place, there was a dangerous side to this man. Struggling to reestablish her self-control, she tried to steel herself against his magnetism. It was easier said than done.

"Tell me about your work, Arielle. You're a child photographer?"

"Yes." Her tone steadied as she discussed her work, letting it relax her, involve her, as it always did. "I have a small studio in Rockport. That's on the North Shore of Massachusetts."

"I've been there," he said with irritating nonchalance.

Arielle sighed, staring at the man, realizing how difficult it would be to remain calm before him. Either he mesmerized her, terrified her, or infuriated her. Was there no middle ground?

He had to prompt her to continue. "Do you do children exclusively?"

"Yes. I enjoy working with them."

"As opposed to working with grown-ups?" One eyebrow arched, he posed the challenge, putting her on the defensive again, tightening the knot which twisted in her stomach.

"Yes."

"Children are less threatening?"

She tipped her chin up in defiance. "In many cases, yes."

"Is it only men who frighten you?"

His eyes, frighteningly direct, took in the tautness of her face. As he stared at her, however, a flicker of puzzlement passed through them, disappearing as soon as she spoke.

"Only those who threaten me — as you did."

"*Did?* Is that why your fist is balled up right now?"

Dismayed, Arielle looked to her hand on the tabletop. He was right. Instantly, she flexed her fingers. "I didn't invite you to sit down with me. I was enjoying myself until you appeared."

"My point exactly," he answered promptly. "I apologize if I make you tense. You have nothing to be frightened of, you know."

His words, spoken low and deeply, brought her head up to face him. If only he knew how truly intimidating he was, she mused sadly. But then, she could never tell him *that*! A forced smile was her best defense. "That's two apologies in one day. Is it a record?" she asked softly.

The dark head was thrown back in a strangely comfortable laugh. "I think it is. Perhaps *I* should be frightened of *you!*" The eyes that returned to hold hers were warm and gleaming, searing her with heat. Where the knot of tension had been she now had a quivering mass of nerves, which perplexed her thoroughly.

"I really should be going. I've got to mail these postcards," she began, wanting only to escape. As she dug into her purse for change to cover her soda, she stood.

"Wait."

His quiet order froze all movement save that of her eyes, which were riveted to his with sudden fear. He met her terrified gaze with an unfathomable amusement.

"Look," he ordered softly, pointing to the wall behind her. Puzzled, she turned, gasped, and then smiled, all in rapid succession. There on the stone wall behind her chair was a small lizard, not more than a hand's length in all. "They're usually better camouflaged than that. But you'll find them all over the island. Watch it."

As she stared at the small creature, her peripheral vision took in Chris's approach around the table to a spot a hair's breadth behind her. She held her breath, chagrined at the loud hammering of her heartbeat.

"There." His voice was close by her ear, directing her attention to the sudden puffing of the lizard's throat into a delicate yellow bubble. Mesmerized, she watched — they both watched — until the bubble deflated and the lizard, as though satisfied with the quality of his show, scampered across the wall and out of sight.

Arielle drew in a long, deep breath. "That was terrific. I'll have to keep an eye out for them; they'd be great to photograph!"

His mouth was still uncomfortably close to her ear. "Very nonthreatening, just like children, huh?"

The sharp glance she threw his way as she stepped quickly — too quickly — away spoke of her annoyance. Yet as she left the restaurant and emerged into the brightly sunlit street, his dark presence moved right along with her. It was a thorny situation. On the one hand, he intimidated her, made her nervous; on the other, she feared being too blunt and asking him to leave her alone.

In the deepest recess of her consciousness, there was something that precluded the latter course of action, but she was reluctant to identify it just yet.

"Who is Sean?"

His question jolted her, breaking the rhythm of her steps, which she had struggled to keep steady and brisk. Chris matched her pace easily, no doubt shortening his usual stride to match hers.

"A sculptor," she replied evasively, keeping her eyes straight ahead.

"Oh. He lives in Rockport, too?"

"Yes. His studio is next door to mine."

"How cozy."

For the first time since they'd left the restaurant, she looked at him. Was he curious? Angry? Mocking? To her dismay, the glasses were once again in place and she could decipher nothing about his mood.

Grasping the first thing she could think of to shift the discussion from Sean, she let go with a taunt of her own. "Is that your personal disguise? Do many people here recognize you?"

Not in the least offended, he answered her smoothly. "No. Most people outside the field wouldn't think to make the connection. You were the exception. Glasses and all."

"Not quite; I wasn't sure until I heard the name," she corrected impulsively. "So you really do prize your privacy?"

"Yes." The firmness of his assertion left no room for doubt. Its quiet force held a renewed warning for Arielle as well. In light of it, she reacted with alarm when he took her arm and steered her away from the street down a narrow walkway. Eyes wide, she began to pull away.

"The post office."

A flush of embarrassment rouged her cheeks as her gaze flew to the building before them, then back to the smug face above her. Mustering what little dignity she had left, she squared her shoulders, shrugged her arm free of his hand and proceeded into the building. When she reemerged a few minutes later, Chris was waiting, arms crossed over his chest in a sign of lordly confidence, legs stretched before him as he leaned against a low, wooden fence. He straightened when he saw her.

"All set?"

She nodded. As she headed for her car, he fell into step beside her.

"Where did you park?"

She cocked her head further to indicate a spot down the street. "Way down there. You really don't need to bother this way," she added, uncomfortable and unsure of herself.

As though sensing the latter, he quickly reassured her. "I left my own car on one of the side streets in that direction anyway. It's no bother." He paused, subtly guiding her around and between a group of tourists coming from the opposite direction. "It's really a shame to have brought two cars downtown when we're both going back to the same place."

Mercifully, he let conversation fall prey to the peacefulness of the afternoon at that point. His steps matched hers all the way to her car. When she retrieved her keys from the depths of her pocketbook, he took them smoothly from her hand, before she could issue the slightest protest, unlocked the car door, rolled down the window, and held the keys out, dangling them just above her waiting hand before dropping them into her palm.

What followed was a moment of odd expectancy. Should she thank him? For what? His presence? It had only brought tension to her otherwise relaxed afternoon. Her cool drink? She had paid for it herself. His guidance to the post office? She hadn't asked for his help, and would certainly have found the building on her own, perhaps even sooner, without the distraction. His gallantry here at her car?

With a smile, she finally yielded, relaxing, since she knew that escape was only seconds away. "Thank you for your help. I doubt I could have managed without it." Despite the sarcasm, Chris returned her smile.

"I think I deserved that one." Then he hesitated, as though debating whether to mention a deeper issue. "Is all forgiven?"

His gaze held hers. What could she say? Never one to hold grudges, she would not in this case. "For the other afternoon, yes." It was as honest a statement as she could make. The fact remained that the man disturbed her deeply. The fact also remained that she needed freedom from his presence to begin to cope with it. With a faltering glance toward the car, then back at him, she slid behind the wheel, silently allowing him to shut the door tightly, then started the motor. It took every ounce of self-control to keep from looking back at him, to concentrate on pulling out into the line of traffic, to rest her elbow atop the rolled-down window with a nonchalance which mocked her inner turmoil. It was only after she'd gotten out of the downtown traffic and turned onto the road home that she breathed deeply in relaxation.

The twenty-minute drive back to the cottage was barely enough to allow for a sorting out of her thoughts. Today she had seen a softer side of Christopher Howe. It was, she admitted to herself with reluctance, quite impressive. What with the magnetism of his person and the air of self-confidence which was an intrinsic part of him, this civility had been, in its way, pleasing. Now, in hindsight, she thought of all of the questions she would have liked to ask him — about his work, his plans for this stay on St. Maarten, his celebrity status.

With a grunt of disapproval, she stopped herself. That was exactly what every little star-spotter would have done. Hadn't the man himself repeatedly stressed his desire for privacy? No, her curiosity was certainly understandable, but it was better that she had not succumbed to its demands. As it was, she had been more concerned with other things at the time — such as the strength of the reaction he inspired in her. Why was it, she asked herself, that she had faced so many men in the last five years without the nervousness, the tension, the raw fear that this man's presence engendered? What was it about him that was so different?

It was this that she could not pinpoint.

And it was this, above all, that frightened her. Could she assume, now, that he'd leave her alone? Or should she still be looking over her shoulder, fearing his imminent arrival? But why fear? The question gnawed and nagged as she neared the cottage and turned into the drive. *Why fear?*

As she stilled the engine, she knew. He was virile and good-looking. He was the embodiment of sensuality. He was infinitely attractive, yes, even to her. *That* was why she was frightened. Whether enraged or impassioned, Christopher Howe was a threat to her peace of mind. She had as much to fear from his arrogance as from his charm. Perhaps it would be best if she continued to avoid him, despite their supposed burial of the hatchet. Yes, that was what she must do, she told herself. But would Chris abide by that?

She had neither requested nor welcomed his company this afternoon, yet he had imposed himself on her until he chose to let her go. What did he have in mind? This new question surged to the fore as she left the car and wandered to the patio to sit atop the low, stone wall which overlooked the sea. What was it he had wanted from her this afternoon? Merely a chance to apologize? Perhaps, but not likely. There had been a softness in his expression; it had been very obvious when he had removed his sunglasses. What did it connote? Was he legitimately sorry for his outburst? Perhaps he was worried that she might talk about his rude behavior to people who might, one day, hurt him. Doubtful. Christopher Howe didn't seem the type to give one hoot about the media. He seemed strangely removed, above it all. Why, then, had he sought out her company?

For a moment she pondered the challenge she had unwittingly issued that day on the beach. At the time, he had vowed he would not run from it. Was that his present motivation? Would he seek to prove, during her stay in his cottage, that he could manipulate her at his whim? Did he see her as a potential member of his scattered entourage?

Anger surged through her, and she brought her open palm down hard against the rock on which she sat. That would not happen! Not as long as she remained her own person. Not as long as she recalled the pain she'd suffered on the way to establishing Arielle Pasteur as an independent being, an artist commanding respect, a woman of principle.

Armed with a firm resolve, she walked idly toward the wooden stairs. It was too bad that things had to be this way. There had been a pleasantness about him this afternoon, despite the other, more disturbing elements of his company. He had the potential, she mused, to be a charming companion. But dangerous, very dangerous.

What was it he had said, she asked herself, about being out on location too much of the time? She thought back to his statement. In reflection, it was not the words but the tone which had made its impression on her. There had been a bitterness which she hadn't understood. Nor did she now. Was he dissatisfied with his work? With his life?

Her eyes skimmed the waves below as she descended several steps and sat, her back propped against the wood support. Something on the beach caught her gaze — a towel, she decided. Instinctively, she searched the aqua swells, quickly finding that which she sought. A head, dark and bobbing, moved among the waves. He must have gone to the beach the instant he'd returned home, just after her. As she watched, tucked into her snug perch, he stood in the chest-deep water and waded slowly, pensively, to shore. Gleaming wet in the sunlight, his body was breathtaking. From this distance, all detail was lost, leaving her full attention to focus on his shape, his stance, his gait. An animal, she had thought him once. Now she repeated the comparison. His stride along the sand toward his towel was lithe and graceful, yet proud and manly. He was a jaguar, sleek, muscled, and strong. The sight of him set off a tingling within her, one she had no more power to understand than she had power to drag her eyes from the figure. He stooped to catch at his towel, then stood and dried his face, his shoulders, his chest. The ripple of muscles was only imagined from where she sat, yet it was a potent stimulant. Catching her breath, she gripped the wood support with both hands behind her.

Then, as though touched by her gaze, he looked up and saw her. His eyes never left hers as he stared, stock-still for a moment, then continued to towel his body dry. Arielle felt the quickening of her pulse, the continuation of that tingling within her, so strange yet so automatic. For a heart-stopping moment she thought he might climb the steps to where she sat. Then he turned and walked back across the sand, pausing once, just before the turn that would take him out of sight, to look back up at her. He made a promise in that brief moment. She knew it as though it had been engraved in stone and delivered to her door. There would be another meeting. Oh, yes. There certainly would.

She hadn't expected it to come as soon as it did. After a night of unusual restlessness she headed for the beach earlier than usual, hopeful of sunning out the tension from her taut muscles. She had already spread her towel on the sand and was easing herself down onto it when he approached.

"Arielle, good morning!" His smile was bright. Obviously he'd had no trouble sleeping. But then, she acknowledged grudgingly, there was nothing particularly different in his life, was there? It was only she who had discovered a new well of feelings within herself, none of which she clearly understood.

As the familiar tension besieged her, she offered a casual, if stilted, "Hi," in response, shading her eyes with her hands as she watched him sink down onto the sand close beside her. For one panicked instant she didn't know what to do. On the one hand, she wanted to flee; on the other, she had to remain. One-half of her would have bounded toward the ocean for a swim; the other felt safer lying flat on her towel. The thin fabric of her suit covered everything, yet nothing. Frantic at her sense of exposure, she would have wrapped the towel around her, sari-style, had it not been for the heat of the sun and the absurdity of that move. Where had her composure gone? she cried mutely as she willed herself to remain still on the towel.

"How did you sleep?" he asked easily.

"Not bad," she lied blatantly.

"You're down early today. I'm usually back and finishing breakfast before you hit the sand."

Lying flat on her back, eyes closed, arms at her sides, she tried to imagine that it was anyone but Christopher Howe beside her, "You've been spying."

"No more than you have."

Her head snapped up and her dark lashes whipped open. "I was sitting there yesterday before I even saw you." Her voice held all the defensiveness she felt. "If you think I really sat there waiting —"

"Take it easy, sweetheart."

"Don't call me that!" she cried angrily, the blue of her eyes flashing her annoyance. Chris had no way of knowing that a large part of her frustration was directed at herself.

"Arielle," he began slowly, his voice deep and in stark contrast to her higher pitch. "I didn't mean any harm. Just relax. I'm not going to hurt you."

The thickness in her throat cut off any possible response. Appalled at her reaction, she closed her eyes and lay back again, throwing an arm across her forehead. But she looked at him again almost immediately when he spoke.

"Why did you tense up just now?" His dark gaze was focused on her face. "I can't believe you're that . . . testy . . . all the time. Do I do it to you?"

Sarcasm edged her laugh and the words that followed. "Don't pride yourself."

"I don't. That haunted look you get, the cornered look in your eyes . . . I would never be proud of putting that in any face. If I've done something to offend you, I'd like to know."

One lithe movement brought her up to tuck her legs beneath her, her face toward the sea. Chris was slightly behind her. "It's nothing. Perhaps I'm not a . . . a morning person." Though she had grasped it spontaneously, it seemed as good an excuse as any.

"I see." Did he? Did he see through her veil of composure, fragile at best? "Would you do me a favor then?" he asked gently, the very softness of his tone coaxing her head around. Silently, her eyes questioned him. "Would you lend me some of your tanning lotion?"

Suddenly relieved, she smiled, leaned forward, grabbed the plastic bottle and handed it to him. Then she lay back once more. If she thought she had overcome a major hurdle, she was mistaken. With her eyes closed, her sense of hearing was that much more acute. And she heard everything. The sounds painted a picture as vivid, if not more so, than her eye might have done. There was the whistle of the bottle as he squeezed the lotion out, the sound of skin on skin with that creaminess between. In her mind she saw his chest and arms as he covered them with lotion, the muscles flowing beneath the palm of his man-sized hand. His legs were next, long and firm, coarsely haired and textured beneath the run of his careless hand. Now, if *she* were to spread that lotion on . . .

"I think I'll take a dip," she blurted out, her voice thicker than usual. Desperate strides took her to the water's edge, then in. As the cool waves enveloped her she felt only minor relief from the heat within. A smooth crawl took her out a short distance. Turning, she headed in again, noting that Chris was now stretched fully on the sand. Marginally refreshed, she joined him.

But relaxation was not to come easily.

Again her auditory sensitivity to him over-whelmed her. Now there was the steadiness of his breathing, maddening in light of her own, less steady panting, mercifully attributable to her swim. The surf provided the accompaniment, its gentle rolling making a mockery of her keyed-up nerves. She heard a movement on the sand beside her, but dared not move herself. When the deep voice came from close beside her ear, she jumped.

"Arielle?"

He was on his stomach, his face very, very close. Humor danced in his eyes, belying the innocence of his tone.

"Would you do my back?"

Stunned into speechlessness, she could only stare with silent pleading at the darkly handsome face. To put lotion on his back would mean touching him. Touching that skin. Touching those muscles. Feeling their strength, their firmness. As though hypnotized into docility, she sat up, took a deep breath, and reached for the bottle he held out to her.

It was everything she had imagined that it would be. Her hand glided over the planes of his back, gently spreading the thin white lotion over the lightly bronzed terrain, circling the swell of muscles, retreating to the flatter expanses of spine and lower back. She knelt over him, his private masseuse. As if in salute to her talent, his eyes were closed, a warm and satisfied expression gracing his face, seen now only in profile.

At some unknown point the whiteness of the cream disappeared into his skin, yet her hands continued their massage, driven on by a will of their own. There was strength beneath her fingertips, and firmness, yes. But there was more. There was a man, breathing and vibrant, his skin sending beams of energy through her fingers and into her body. When she finally sat back on her heels and relinquished her hold on his warm flesh, she reflexively put her hands to her own arms so that they might absorb any excess of lotion though there was, in fact, none. It was in this pose of vulnerability, with her eyes widened in awareness, that Chris found her when he turned over.

Long moments of silence passed between them. Arielle struggled to accept what she had felt, what she still felt. Chris studied her closely, wondering at the hint of pain in her expression. When he sat up to face her she was helpless to move, hypnotized by his gentle manner, paralyzed by her own nascent arousal. Ever so slowly, he raised a hand to her face, his long fingers tucking her dark tresses behind her ears before returning to caress her cheek. When his thumb traced the curve of her lips they opened to him, responding instinctively to his command.

His low-whispered "Arielle" was all she heard before his lips lowered to touch hers, lightly, gently, carefully, as though testing her willingness to stay. Little did he know that she had no choice. A new and different force had taken over, one within her, one which she had never known existed. The brutal assault of the past was suddenly forgotten. There was only now, and the delightfully heady sensation the touch of his lips on hers created. It began deep within her, the tingling of which she had become aware earlier, and it bubbled upward and out in the faint beginnings of response. Timidly at first, her lips moved against his, craving the firmness he still withheld. His hands threaded into her hair, drawing her face back gently for his inspection. The question was asked and answered, all without benefit of words. When he resumed the kiss, she was waiting.

Tremors of excitement surged through her as his mouth devoured hers. Gentle yet thorough, he tasted everything she offered. And she did the same, following his lead in a ritual she had never experienced before. Her hands crept up to his neck, encircling its strong column to touch the thick growth of hair at the back of his head. His arms formed an iron band around her slimness, crushing her to him, her thin and damp maillot hiding nothing of the breasts whose fullness strained against the fabric.

"Oh, Arielle," he moaned softly, his breath fanning the back of her neck where his lips had found a temporary haven. "You disturb a man's peace of mind." The huskiness of his voice was further evidence of his own aroused state. As for Arielle, she couldn't speak. Her eyes closed tightly, she was intent on capturing the sensation, on committing it to memory and savoring it for eternity. There was a beauty in what she had felt, one which she wanted to hold on to forever. Her arms clung to his broad shoulders as he turned her and lowered her to the sand. Once again he held back from her for a moment.

The warmth of his gaze heated her body, tracing a molten path over her curves before returning to her eyes. When he kissed her again his hands traced that same path, curving around her shoulders, her waist, her hips, then moving inward. When the tips of his fingers circled her breasts she sighed against his lips, drugged by the powerful opiate of passion. When they found the pebbled peak and teased it even higher, she recoiled.

"No, Chris . . ." she murmured against his lips. "Don't do that. . . ." It was simply too much, too fast, too strong, too electric. It frightened her. Her hand pushed against his chest, but he grasped it firmly, lifting it to his lips and kissing it softly.

"I won't hurt you, Arielle. Stay with me a little longer." It was as though she was suddenly mindless, turned into putty by the sincerity of his request. She didn't fight when he released her hand and lowered his own to her breast once again, caressing it gently as he held her gaze in binding possession. His eyes continued to gentle her as his fingers had their way with her body, coaxing her to heights of excitement that had her arching and moaning. But when his lips lowered to her neck, her chest, and then touched the bareness of her breast, as he eased the fine maillot fabric down, she rebelled. Primal fear erupted, drawing a panicked cry from deep in her throat.

"Nooooo!" Her scream, and its underlying emotion, stilled Chris's every movement. Her eyes were moist and terror-shadowed as she opened them to meet his.

Openly quizzical, he stared down at her, stunned by the force of her withdrawal. "What is it?" he asked softly, a frown furrowing his forehead beneath its thatch of dark brown hair.

"I can't," she whispered, shaking her head weakly from side to side. "I . . . just . . . can't." Her whimper was barely audible.

For long moments he retained his state of suspended animation. Then, with a low curse, he released her completely, rolled away and to his feet in one lithe move, and ran toward the waves. By the time he returned to the beach, Arielle was gone.

FOUR

Arielle found a shady corner of the living room and burrowed herself in an armchair. Hugging her knees to her chest for comfort, she tried to fathom the events on the beach. The beach . . . It was ironic. Once before they had collided with each other there. He had kissed her, and his cruelty had torn into her. But today his kiss had been far from cruel; it had been warm and gentle, soft and divine.

If only it were a simple matter of hating it then, loving it now. But nothing was that simple. His kiss today had brought an unbelievable ecstasy on which she'd soared so high she'd been terrified. Was the past destined always to haunt her in this way? Yet even as she had been frightened by the liberties his masterful hands had taken, she had been curious. The pleasure she had known today was wholly new to her; how much further could it go?

At twenty-seven, she was far from naive. Despite the fact that she had only been with a man once, and then to the utter exclusion of both pleasure and satisfaction, she knew what to expect physically, biologically. But knowing was technical; feeling was entirely different. No amount of technical data could have prepared her for what she had felt today — the mindless frenzy, the disembodied rapture. And they had not even . . .

With a sharp intake of breath, she redirected her thoughts. It was the challenge. He had taken her up on the challenge. It had been his victory when she had responded so fully to his caress. Yet why had he let her go so easily? It seemed out of character — unless she was truly misjudging him. But how could she know the truth? How could she discern his character without compromising her own?

It was a dilemma she failed to resolve. When the sound of a loud rap at the door startled her, she glanced reflexively at her watch. Eleven-thirty — who could be here to see her?

It had to be Chris. A furtive glance out the front window confirmed her fear. Her eyes darted around the room, then toward the bedroom, contemplating a place, any place, to hide before she caught herself short. She was, after all, an adult. Hiding would solve nothing.

Before she had a chance to change her mind, she pulled the door open. In a moment of panic her eyes flew to the darkly disturbed ones before her. He wore a pair of faded jeans, equally broken-in moccasins, and a faded blue T-shirt whose message that "photographers snap to it" seemed poignant and apt.

"May I come in?" His voice was deep and cool. At her nod, he stepped into the room, moving to the far side before turning to face her. "I'd like to talk to you, Arielle." She had closed the door and now stood leaning back against its broad expanse. When she said nothing, he eyed her intently, then prodded more softly, "Are you all right?"

She nodded, then suddenly realized that she wore nothing but the knee-length terry cloth robe she'd put on to replace her damp bathing suit earlier.

"I'm, ah, not really dressed for this," she murmured self-consciously, feeling positively naked despite the thickness of the wrap-style robe. She tugged nervously at the ties by her waist, pulling them painfully tight.

In another situation Chris might have found any number of suggestive rejoinders.

Now, however, he was in no mood for teasing. "That will do just fine," he instructed, taking in the white robe at a glance, then refocusing on her strangely pale face. He looked away from her for a minute to gesture toward the sofa.

"Wouldn't you like to sit down?" he asked calmly. When she made no response, he went on. "I'd like to talk to you. Please sit down."

It was an order this time, offered softly but firmly. Moving away from the door with a pretense of confidence, she padded toward the corner chair from which she had been drawn by his knock. Surrounded by walls to her left and right, she felt more secure. If Chris sensed her ploy, he ignored it. Hands on his hips, he faced her from across the room, purposely keeping his distance. Arielle's gaze met his apprehensively.

"You're obviously terrified by something. What is it?" he began.

Swallowing hard, she nestled deeper into the chair. This was not the type of discussion she'd ever expected to have with Chris, particularly after that first afternoon on the beach. How could she answer him?

His voice held that same quiet command when he spoke again. "I'd like you to tell me what's bothering you." But she maintained her silence stoically. "Arielle?" he warned, lowering his head as his black eyes bore into her with an intensity so great that she had to look away.

Her whisper came from the heart. "It has nothing to do with you."

"Damn it!" he exploded, startling her with his outburst. "How can you tell me that? You look like a frightened rabbit, sitting there huddled in the corner. You won't even look at me."

Accepting his challenge, she raised her eyes to his. She laced her fingers together before her in a mocking pose of nonchalance. "I'm looking at you," she said quietly, then watched him regain control of his temper.

"Why do I frighten you?"

"Why does it matter?"

"It matters to me, Arielle. Take my word for it."

Some strange motivation drove her on. "But why? When I first showed up on *your* beach, you were furious. You wanted me to leave at once. You weren't terribly concerned then, I might add, for my frame of mind —"

"I've already apologized for that," he growled.

"Ah, that's right. But that doesn't explain

your interest now."

An unexpected grin gentled the taut line of his lips. "And you're changing the subject. Very clever, but I asked first. What frightens you so much?"

Without quite realizing it, she *had* tried to evade his question. She certainly couldn't give him the most honest of answers — not now, not ever, the humiliation would be too great, so she simply hung her head and said nothing, playing absently with her terry belt.

"Tell me, Arielle!"

Slowly, she shook her head. "I'm sorry," she whispered, still looking down.

She heard him pace across to the door. When the sound stopped, she steeled herself for the onslaught. It came instantly.

"Then I have to assume that I was right from the start," he stormed gruffly. "You can't be honest with me because it would tip your hand, is that it? Your motives for coming down here weren't as noble as all that after all, were they?" Arielle cringed in her chair, refusing to believe what she was hearing. But he wasn't done. "You're quite an actress. You'll get me to photograph you yet! But what's the matter? Is your conscience beginning to bother you? Or are you simply terrified at the thought of what I *will* do to you when I've learned the truth.

You're all the same —"

"No!" she shrieked, pressing her palms to her ears as she jumped from the chair. Enraged, she struck back. "You're insane! You have no idea what you're talking about. For a supposedly brilliant artist, you have the insight of a toad when it comes to people. For all I care, you can —" Her words died in her throat at the sight of the broad grin which lit his face.

"I can . . . what?" he asked expectantly.

On the instant she forgot what it was she was going to tell him to do. "What's so funny?" Frowning, she stepped back from him; in her fury, she had lunged closer than she would otherwise have thought wise. Now her blue eyes were clouded, puzzled. She shoved her hands into the deep side pockets of her robe as she awaited his answer.

"You are, Arielle. I certainly managed to get a rise with that one, didn't I? No," he quickly interjected, raising an open palm to calm her imminent rebellion, "don't get all huffy again." He sobered. As though momentarily lost in his own thoughts, he turned and strode toward the window. It gave Arielle a chance to recoup her lost composure, which she did. It also gave her a moment to contemplate her thoughts.

Sheer curiosity forced her back to their earlier topic.

"Why does it matter to you, Chris?" she asked softly, aware of his temporary vulnerability, which his stance, head hung low, conveyed. As though suddenly aware of it himself, he straightened and turned.

"Let's just say I've decided I might like some company every so often while I'm here."

He's decided? she fumed. *He* might like some company? This was sounding more like a let's-please-Chris party by the minute. But before she could protest, he had approached her again. "That came out all wrong. I'm sorry — ach, there I go again." His smile melted the anger that his words had inspired. "Look, let's go get something to eat. You probably haven't had a thing all day. Am I right?"

He was, and she nodded as much.

"Good. There's a fine place over in Grande Case. Have you driven in that direction yet?"

Her silken, jet-black hair shimmered as she shook her head. All ventures, as yet, had taken her in the direction of Philipsburg, to the southeast of the cottage. She'd never been to the north.

"Great! Why don't you go put something on —"

"I really shouldn't," she interrupted, acutely aware of the potential for trouble should she spend time with him. "I — I have so much work to do —"

"And were you really getting it done?" His arched brow dared her to deny her idleness; his gaze flew to the chair in which she'd spent the better part of the past two hours, then returned to impale her.

She gave it a final stab. "I don't want to." Bluntness, it seemed, was worse.

"Arielle," he sighed, a hand combing through the downfall of hair on his forehead in exasperation, "what if I promise not to touch you?" The pulse point at his temple throbbed, its revealing beat hidden as the hair fell over it once more. "You've rejected me once today, and no guy particularly cares for rejection. I'd be glad to make the promise if that would put your skittish little mind at ease. Would it?" Dumbfounded at this latest turn, she studied the firm set of his features. "I mean it," he went on solicitously. "I won't lay a hand on you. You see, I really do want the company." It was the poignancy of the last, a near plea, which decided the issue.

"I'll go change," she informed him, turning to pad back to the bedroom. "What should I wear?"

His low chuckle filled the room. "Whatever you want, as long as it's not provocative. I don't think I could take that!"

Without another word, she retreated to her room. A smile softened her features as she sorted through her sparse selection of clothes. The pink shirt and faded jeans were already in her hands when she paused, recalling his last words. Slowly their implication seeped through her, bringing with it a strange and new sort of satisfaction. For the first time in her life it was as though she actually *did* have the power to attract a man. And the fact that the man was as experienced as Christopher Howe was mind-boggling. It was a new thought, one that would take some getting used to. Yet she paid not one second thought to the extra care she took in dressing, to the fact that she rolled and rerolled the sleeves of her blouse three times before they were right, to the fact that, while she usually wore makeup only on the fanciest of occasions, she now put a careful dab of blusher on her cheeks, a dash of mascara on her already dark lashes, the thinnest line of pencil on her lower lid, and a skillfully drawn line of pink gloss on her lips. All in all, she concluded as she eyed herself a final time in the mirror, she looked a whole lot better than she had moments before.

Chris apparently agreed, staring at her at length when she emerged from her room. "Look, there's one other thing," he began, not taking his eyes off her. "If I'm going to have to keep my hands off you, you've got to promise to relax and stay relaxed . . . the way you are now." A flush rose to join the blusher on her cheeks, but he went on. "I don't want you knotting up on me in the car or in the restaurant. If I do something you don't like, just speak up. Agreed?" At that moment, as she looked down at the pocketbook clutched before her and smiled guiltily, she had no idea of just how feminine, how vulnerable, how desirable she was. His question, his demand, had captured every bit of her attention.

"Agreed."

"Good. Now, let's get a move on. I told them we'd be there by twelve-thirty. I think we'll be a little late."

"You 'told them'?" she echoed in disbelief as she passed through the front door ahead of him, then turned to stare.

Chris grinned endearingly. "I called from my house and made reservations. Not that they're really needed. But there's a special table overlooking the ocean that I wanted to have. You'll love this place."

"You knew I'd be coming?"

Humor danced in his eyes as he reached for her elbow to guide her to the passenger side of the car, then withdrew his hand quickly, vouching for the sincerity of his promise. "I figured I could con you one way or the other. This will be very pleasant — trying, but pleasant."

Ignoring his barb, she slid into the seat of the small car, a rental, just as hers was. When Chris took his place behind the wheel she angled sideways to face him. "I would have thought you'd have a car shipped over from the States."

Refusing to be baited, he simply grinned indulgently. "The anonymity of these little clunkers is much nicer. It works; that's all that matters."

She felt the same way, but she was surprised to find that he did. What with his image as an international playboy she would have expected something sleek, a Jaguar, perhaps. As they turned onto the main road, she wondered what other surprises were in store for her. She had already had plenty during just this one day, not the least of them her ability to relax in this car with Christopher Howe. She never would have believed it, but he had put her at ease. His words had been offered in apparent good faith, and she had accepted them that way. If he were a truly devious man, she was doomed. Yet something deep within her knew that was not the case. Crafty perhaps, manipulating perhaps, but not devious.

As the car chugged up and over the rugged hillside, headed toward Grande Case, a stone marker caught Chris's attention. "That's the official boundary between the Dutch and the French sides," he explained, pointing farther ahead to the sign that confirmed it. "This is the smallest piece of land in the world where two separate national entities exist in harmony. Did you know that?" There was something of the little boy in his enthusiasm as he darted a glance in her direction.

"Uh-huh." She smiled back. She had read up on the island before she'd come, yet his eagerness excited her, putting her even more at ease.

"Legend has it that when it came time to decide what would be Dutch and what would be French, a Dutchman and a Frenchman stood back to back in one spot, then commenced to walk around the island to mark off territory." As he spoke, he easily negotiated a curve to bring the car to a high point in the road, a spectacular island vista now spread before them as they began the slow descent. "The Frenchman walked farther, buoyed by his countrymen's wine. The Dutchman, they claim, was slowed down by his own Dutch gin." He gave her a sideways glance and caught the smile on her face. "You knew?"

Arielle could not restrain the gale of laughter which his expression of exaggerated disappointment set off. "I read the story," she consoled him gently, "but it had much more spirit the way you told it."

Satisfied once more, Chris continued. "The Dutch side actually proved to be the most valuable."

"I *didn't* know that," she interjected impulsively, subtly urging him on.

He rose to the occasion, growing serious with the truth of his words. "The French have their beautiful beaches and a whole assortment of restaurants which have since sprung up on their side, but the Dutch have the salt."

"Salt?"

"We'll see it another day; it's on the Philipsburg side of the island. The salt pond used to be the island's largest industry before the switch to tourism. Huge gates were opened to let the sea water into the pond, then the gates were closed and the sun did the rest. When the water had all evaporated, the salt could be picked up in cakes for exportation."

"That's very interesting," she mused, her gaze flowing over the landscape as they descended toward Marigot on the way to Grande Case. "And the two sides live in total harmony?"

"Total."

Her murmured "Interesting" was lost as they delved into the realms of their own thoughts. Yet the silence was companionable; when they reached their destination, Arielle was still relaxed.

Lunch was everything Chris had promised it would be. The small surfside restaurant was distinctly French in atmosphere, delightfully Creole in cooking. Chris ordered fish, Arielle chicken, then they shared each dish as it came. The wine was cool and refreshing, if mellowing, prompting discussions of childhoods and family backgrounds. Arielle's story, laundered of all references to her appearance and the pain it had caused, was the happier one as she spoke of her parents, her brother, the closeness of the family unit, the beauty of the family home in Long-meadow.

Chris's background was quite different.

The youngest of five children, he was a New Yorker by birth, the last of the litter, as he put it. His father was a poor, often unemployed musician, a violinist whose dreams of fame had fallen prey to crippling arthritis. From an early age each child had been forced to work, providing precious money for food and clothes, money which his father could no longer earn.

"Are your parents still living?" she asked softly.

"My mother lives with one of my sisters. My father died before I was ever able to do anything to really help." The tension in his squared-off jaw told of his frustration. "Not that there's much that can be done, even today, for that illness. But even a taste of this warmth," his eyes rose to indicate the clear blue sky over the water, "might have given him some measure of comfort."

Arielle sat in silence for a while before she ventured on. There was so much she wanted to know to be better able to understand this man before her. "Do you see your brothers and sisters often?"

He shrugged, frowning. "Not as much as I'd like. My work makes impossible demands on my time. During vacations — like this — I need to get away."

"Are there many grandchildren?" She

wasn't quite sure what had prompted her question. Though her brother had provided three for her parents, she had already abandoned the thought of providing any herself. Yet, she wondered . . .

His wide grin flashed her way. "There are, to date, if I've got the count correct, twelve — seven boys and five girls."

"Well photographed, I'm sure." She matched his smile.

He held her gaze sharply. "Actually, not. My field is fashion. What we need is a child photographer."

Arielle didn't know what to make of the suggestion. Momentarily taken aback, she quickly skirted the issue. "I'm sure you must take your fill of family snapshots. What does your family make of your career?"

Nursing the last of his wine, he leaned back in his seat. "Not very much. I'm still the same brat they knew and loved."

She nodded pertly. "I believe it." When his eyes turned to hers she sensed a depth, an intimacy she had not known before. It was a very pleasant sense of communion. With a surprising lack of inhibition, she commented on it. "This has been lovely, Chris. Thank you."

His dark gaze held hers a moment longer. "Come on, sweetheart; let's go," he suggested gently, standing to pull her chair out. Given the serenity of the atmosphere between them and the gentle tone of his voice, she raised no objection to the endearment which she had once rebelled so vociferously against. There was nothing offensive about it now; rather, it was a sort of caress, soothing, much as his hand might have been had it held hers just then, or curved around the slimness of her waist, or rested lightly on her shoulders. But she had made him promise to do none of those things, and he was behaving himself impeccably.

The drive back was slower and even more leisurely, if possible, than the ride out had been. From time to time Chris pulled over to the side of the road so they could watch the island life pass by. Most charming, in Arielle's judgment, were the roadside parades. Cows, goats, roosters — all ambled freely along the pavement's dilapidated edge. Natives moved in lines of two or three or four, narrowing to single file with the appearance of a car on the horizon. The roads were edged with more of the greenery, richer in some of the low-lying spots, that shaded the opposite side of the island. Buildings, few and far between, were low and well worn, crumbling in some instances, overgrown with vegetation in others. With the sun high and bright above it all, though, there was no sense of depression. Rather, there was a sense of freedom, of modest luxury, of simplicity and of rural splendor.

"Are you thinking what I am?" Chris's deep voice broke into her consciousness. Startled, she looked around, then followed his gaze to a side street from which a small group of children were being herded. A smile flirted with the corners of her lips.

"Uh-huh. I wish I'd brought mine, too. I haven't taken it out of its case since I got here. Very lazy."

He stopped the car to let the children cross the road, then resumed driving. "There's something you ought to see."

A little while later the car wound through the small center of Marigot, the French capital of the island. "Here," he pointed to a parking space, "this is as good a place as any to park. We can walk the rest of the way. You don't mind, do you?"

"Of course not," she chided him softly. "The exercise is good for me. Work off the extra pounds and all . . ." Frowning, she turned to face forward. It had been so long since she'd used that phrase that it sent a chill through her. If anything, she could afford to put *on* a pound or two. Shaking her head, she was out of the car before Chris had reached her side.

As she timed her steps to match his, Arielle pushed all thoughts of her slip from her mind. He hadn't asked about it; perhaps he hadn't noticed. In any event, it was irrelevant to the here and now.

They walked side by side. The downtown area here was much different from its counterpart in Philipsburg. Where the latter consisted of two long streets, Front Street and Back Street, each running parallel to the other, Marigot was a more complex community, small, yet multi-cornered. Mercifully, Chris knew his way.

Open vegetable stands fell behind them as they walked, as did the slew of shops and restaurants. Emerging onto what seemed, by virtue of its length and width, to be the main thoroughfare, they followed it past a drug store, the police station, and a charming restaurant complex. Then, Arielle discovered what it was that Chris had wanted to show her. The school yard — a broad, concrete area, bordered on three sides by the drabbest of cement-fronted buildings and on the fourth by the iron-work bars through which they now peered — was in animated use, a host of small children, black and white intermingled, playing games in small groups.

"Ooooh, my camera," Arielle moaned in a whisper as she leaned against the iron railings and watched the children within. Childhood was a universal reality, yet somehow, perhaps because she herself was on vacation, she hadn't expected to see children at school. The awareness of Chris right beside her gave her a sense of contentment as she watched the children at play. Their speech was French and incomprehensible to her, yet their games were ones that might have been played at any playground, in any country — hopscotch, jump rope, dodge-ball, foursquare.

It was Chris's hand on her shoulder, brief and light and gone before she even knew it, that finally drew her away. "We'll come back another day . . . with cameras," he assured her gently, leading the way back to the car. In what seemed to be far too short a time, he pulled up in front of her cottage to drop her off.

"Thank you, Chris," she offered quietly, downplaying her enthusiasm for what had been, to date, the highlight of her vacation.

His response was as simple. "Thank *you,* Arielle." Then he was off, with no word for the future beyond that soft promise he had given by the school yard.

Yet the atmosphere lingered to infuse the

next few days with its warmth. Their encounters took place primarily on the beach, with its rich offering of sun, sea, and sand. Hesitant at first, Arielle was gradually put at ease by the demonstration of Chris's restraint. He never touched her, save for the occasional grasp of an elbow in support as they climbed over the rocks around the bend in search of shells for Arielle to photograph.

"Why don't you buy a macro lens for that kind of work?" he asked her one afternoon as she struggled to screw on the three layers of close-up filters she had chosen to use.

She shrugged her golden brown shoulders against the thin straps of her suit. "These are easier and less expensive. If I photographed shells for a living, I could justify the cost of a macro, but my kids demand nothing more than the 105-mm I've got back at the cottage." Her slender shape moved in and around the grouping of vari-colored shells she had painstakingly arranged in the sand at the base of a darkly colored piece of volcanic rock. "The light's all wrong," she spoke aloud, but to herself, standing back for a minute to survey the setting from a different angle.

Chris moved to stand beside her. "Wait here a minute." A few long strides took him back to where their towels lay. When he returned, he carried the white T-shirt he had casually discarded on the sand when he had arrived. Draping it deftly across his thigh as he knelt, he positioned himself to allow the shirt to catch the force of the sun and direct it to the spot where it was needed.

"That's perfect!" Arielle beamed excitedly, musing at how limited she had been, with her neat studio setup at home and the children who came to her doorstep, when such a simple thing as a T-shirt could accomplish here what her sturdy white and silver reflectors accomplished at home. "You're very resourceful," she complimented him, curious anew about his work, which he seemed particularly reluctant to discuss. On those occasions when she'd broached the subject he'd answered her questions as succinctly as possible, then changed the subject. In this case, he urged her to action.

"You'll have to be the resourceful one in a minute if you don't hurry it up. My leg is going to get cramped pretty soon. And I'd really like to go for a swim."

Reluctant to lose her prop so quickly, she set to work, photographing the shells from every possible angle. When she was done, they returned to the sandy beach, she to sink down on her towel, he to dive into the waves.

As he swam Arielle reviewed the nature of their relationship as it had evolved over the last few days. To her amazement, she found herself actually liking Christopher Howe, the man whose arrogance and fury had both disgusted and frightened her when she had first arrived in St. Maarten. She trusted him. True to his word as he had given it the other morning in her cottage, he hadn't touched her — at least, not in *that* way. Now, as his bold form wove majestically through the waves, she almost missed his touch. It had been so very beautiful that once; now, with her fear of him held at bay by his promise, she almost wished he would touch her again. But that would be breaking the promise — and she might find herself in worse straits. For she could never forget the pain, the humiliation of that night with Peter Stoddard. It was etched indelibly on her brain, and came forward with each taste of the rapture a man could show a woman. Chris's powers of persuasion had overcome much of it — but only to a point. At that point, the horror of the past had returned. In the final analysis, she could never be quite sure of any man, could she? Chris was now her friend, and as such, she could trust him. But as anything more . . . ?

"Arielle!" he called now from the distance, standing chest-deep in the surf, gesturing for her to join him. "Come on in! It's beautiful!"

Sudden playfulness overcame whatever hesitancies she might otherwise have harbored. With a bound, she was on her feet and running toward the sea, her hair flying, smiling as the water swirled around her ankles, then her knees and thighs. With a huge gasp, she dove in, swimming the final distance to where Chris waited, then surfacing beside him.

"This is divine," she sputtered, floating back to let her hair trail in the water, kicking a splash of saltwater in his direction. With a lunge, he stilled the offending foot, encircling it in his strong hand, flipping her up and over into a half-dive before releasing her. When she surfaced once more her grin was as wide as his. "That was pretty smooth. I almost felt like a dolphin. Very graceful. But only in the water," she added with a laugh, swimming closer toward shore to elude the quizzical glance he gave her. But if she'd hoped to escape him this time, she was mistaken. His strong stroke brought him quickly to her side.

"I wouldn't say that, Arielle. You're a very

graceful person on land. But you don't believe that, do you?" He was clearly puzzled by her lack of self-confidence.

Frightened by the glittering reflection she saw in his eyes, she splashed off toward shore. When those familiar fingers closed around her ankle once more, she geared up for the game, inwardly pleased that he had not let her refusal to discuss the matter come between them.

For a while longer the waves cushioned their romp, swelling gently about them, then leveling off as they reached the shallows. It was invigorating exercise, the game of cat-and-mouse to which they'd resorted, comparable in demand to the lap swimming Arielle tried to do regularly at home. Finally, breathless, she let Chris catch her.

"I can't take any more," she panted, grasping his shoulders for support, resting back against the arm that curved about her waist. "You've worn me out!"

"That was the idea," he crooned softly, his own breathing maddeningly steady, apparently unaffected by their active play. "If I wear you out, you won't fight me."

At the instant when her eyes met his, playfulness dissolved into something quite different. Her breath caught at the intensity of it all; her body became suddenly and acutely aware of his, floating against it. Wet, strong, and masculine, the feel of his body excited her. Perhaps she had wanted this to happen as she'd sat and wondered back there, alone on the beach. Her fingers tightened on his shoulders and a sigh slipped through the moistness of her lips, parting them softly.

"That's a girl," he whispered, sensing her continuing relaxation as he tightened his hold. "I'm only going to kiss you. Nothing else."

That was all he did, but the force of it stole what little breath Arielle had. Her lips opened helplessly to the foray of his; her arms slid to lock around his neck. With barely controlled hunger, his mouth slanted against hers, consuming her with its need before pulling sharply away. Violent flames sparked in his eyes, belied by the gentleness in his tone when he spoke.

"Now, that wasn't so bad, was it?"

Bad? It had been heady and exciting. And she wanted more. But she dared not ask for it. "No." She smiled sheepishly. "It wasn't so bad." Her own response had told him the rest, all that was left unsaid. And the fact that he, too, wanted more had not escaped her heightened sensitivities. The male anatomy held less mystery than its female counterpart. Her grin imparted that knowledge as well.

"Your blush tells all kinds of stories, Arielle," he teased, his hand pressing against the small of her back for one long moment before he gently pushed her away. "Go back to your towel. I'll be out in a minute."

He disappeared into the waves while Arielle swam easily to shore, gratified that he had stopped when he had. There was something about the spell he cast on her, something about the magic of his body, so long and lean and manly, pressed intimately against hers. Though it had been hidden by the constant nudge of the waves when he'd kissed her, the tingling deep within her now expressed its own desire. Tucking her knees up to her chest and watching as Chris swam vigorously, then emerged to join her, she wondered whether it would ever be satisfied.

"I've got to do a little work," he began between gasps as he toweled the salt from his skin. His voice contained a residue of huskiness, suitably concealed by his breathless state. "An hour or two, perhaps. Why don't you join me for supper at the house? *I'm* cooking — steaks." She met his attempt at nonchalance with a similarly nonchalant return.

"Only if I can bring a salad and dessert." He had already treated her to more than his share of meals. This was one way she could feel justified in eating his sirloin — and it was one way she felt she could keep the dinner on a friendly basis.

"Sounds fair enough. Do you know the back way, through the woods?"

Her voice was softer, almost apologetic. "I've never been to your house. I don't know the way through the woods *or* by the road!"

He grinned wickedly. "Right you are. Then I'll come get you. Seven o'clock?" At her nod, he picked up his things. "Oh," he stopped short, then hesitated, choosing his words carefully, "wear something . . . soft."

" 'Soft'?" Her eyes widened in alarm. "What do I need to wear something 'soft' for?" For the first time in days, she felt threatened.

Sensing this, Chris moved closer, wrapping the towel around his neck and tugging at its ends with his hands. "Please trust me, Arielle. We've done well so far, haven't we?" When she merely continued to stare, he repeated the question. "Haven't we?"

"I-I suppose so."

"I want to take a few pictures —"

"No!" Instantly, she was on her feet. "No

pictures!"

"Arielle . . ." The low warning note in his voice was an instant sedative. "You do trust me, don't you?"

"Yes, but . . ." She clutched wildly at straws. "I thought you wanted no part of photographing people . . . like me. This is your vacation. You don't want to waste it taking pictures of me! Wasn't that what that uproar was about that first day on the beach?"

"I didn't know you then, Arielle. I'm beginning to now, even though you totally puzzle me at times." The light in his eyes told her of what times he spoke. He saw that she recognized it and went on. "There are things I see that I would like to capture. They're . . . fleeting. It's a challenge. You're a photographer; surely you understand what I'm trying to say?"

"I suppose so."

"Then indulge me." When she stiffened he quickly qualified his demand. "If you really feel that strongly, I won't push you. But think about it. We'll discuss it again later. OK?" The deep and resonant flow of his words had the soothing effect he'd intended. Arielle's rebellion was short-lived. "OK?" His dark head tilted down, his eyes demanding a response.

"OK," she whispered, "but I won't change my mind. No pictures."

Not about to risk upsetting her again, he let it go at that, studying her closely, trying to find the missing pieces to explain her fear. But her face gave nothing away. "If you say so," he acknowledged. "But, Arielle . . ." Again, he hesitated, before continuing more softly. "Wear something soft . . . for me?"

Terrified and excited, frustrated yet touched, she heard a voice that sounded terribly like her own give in to his wish. "I will," it whispered from some distant body, reverberating through her with awesome confidence. As her deep blue eyes followed the rugged frame that crossed the sand, then disappeared, her lips shaped the words once more. "I will."

FIVE

It had to be the most absurd, potentially dangerous thing she had ever agreed to! Not only did she *not* want to be photographed, she did *not* want to do something "just for" Chris. Something "soft" — hah! What did he want, a flowing gown of lavender organza with a train around and behind? She had nothing "soft" in that sense, save the pale blue silk blouse she'd brought to wear with her white pleated pants.

What she *should* do, she sensed, was to pick up the phone and call the whole thing off. Yes, that was what she *should* do . . . but she wouldn't . . . for one simple reason. It hit her with stunning force: She wanted very much to spend the evening with Chris at his home. She felt an insatiable thirst to know where he lived, how he lived . . . and so much more. Where would it end?

Seven o'clock found her dressed and waiting, slightly edgy, but outwardly composed.

Her pulse, which was already racing, jumped into overdrive at the sound of his knock. Standing, she looked down at herself once more. Her outfit seemed so very ordinary; if only she had had something truly soft to wear, she thought wistfully. With a sigh, she answered the door.

He looked devastating. Dressed in navy slacks, neatly pressed and perfectly molded to his lean frame, and a white shirt, short-sleeved and open to mid-chest, he seemed taller than ever. The tan he had acquired during the past ten days gave him an even more rugged look. Freshly shaven and with moist droplets from a recent shower lingering on his carefully combed hair, he sparkled.

As she examined him, Arielle felt him examining her in turn. His eyes, black and fathomless, touched her, skimming her body from top to toe, at length returning to her face, which was now flushed with embarrassment.

"I'm sorry," she whispered apologetically. "This was the closest I could come to 'soft.'" Ignorant of the complete softness of her features at that moment, she looked away. Strong, warm fingers forced her gaze back to his.

"It's perfect." His voice was velvet-smooth

and deep; his eyes beamed sparks of pleasure through her. "It's *you*."

He could not have said anything nicer,
anything more capable of restoring her
confidence. Her nervousness slowly began
to disintegrate. "I'll be right back." She
spoke softly, turning toward the kitchen.
"Better still, you can give me a hand."

He was right behind her as she removed
the salad from the refrigerator. A faint scent
of aftershave, crisp and utterly masculine,
surrounded him, sending tingles down her
spine. Before she could realize his intent, he
took the salad bowl from her hands and put
it down on the counter, then turned back to
her. She could not have fought him. His
hands, large yet gentle, framed her face, tilting it up toward his. His lips were warm on
hers, coaxing a response that she would
have given freely. She welcomed his tender
exploration, sampling his taste and texture
with her own tongue. The kiss left her
trembling dangerously at its end.

"Are you all right?" he whispered by her
ear, his breath coming in short bursts to
echo hers. She rubbed her temple against
his cheek as she nodded. "Then we'd better
go. This could get out of hand. And neither
of us wants that, do we?" Unable as yet to
pull away from him, she mutely shook her

head, drinking in the smell of him for one last moment before he set her back.

"You broke your promise . . . again," she murmured softly, lifting her sparkling eyes to meet his gaze. There was a shyness there, and rebellion, for she felt both. But, more than either, she felt excitement, pleasure, contentment.

Humor rimmed his eyes for a moment, then they narrowed suspiciously. "Are you sorry? Truly sorry?"

She shook her head. "No."

In mocking relief, he cast a glance skyward. "Thank heavens! Now, the salad . . ." he said, clearing his throat of its hoarseness as he lifted the bowl easily into the crook of his elbow. "And dessert?"

"Oh!" In her passion-dazed state she would have forgotten it. She went to the refrigerator and took out a bowl of fruit marinated in kirsch and topped with fresh coconut shavings. "Very healthy," she explained, leading the way out.

Within minutes the low-growing jungle of trees and shrubs surrounded them, standing thick and dense on either side of the faint trail that paralleled the ocean. "I had debated paving this path at one point," he offered by way of excuse for any low brambles that might graze her ankle, "but it seemed unnecessary, and even wrong. There's something very beautiful about the vegetation here," he went on, looking back over his shoulder at her as he spoke. "Very free and healthy." He laughed at his choice of words. "What we all want in life!"

When they reached his house Arielle was still mulling over those last words. Free and healthy — a noble wish, but could a person really have control over either? Good health could only be ensured by healthy living up to a point. There were those things, such as the illness which had struck Chris's father, which simply happened. Freedom — that was another matter. Both she and Chris had lives which were relatively free — free of responsibilities to others, free of long-term commitments, free of conflict and complication. But was that really what she wanted? She had always thought it so — but now she was beginning to wonder.

"Well, what do you think?" Chris's deep voice shocked her back to reality, which, in this case, was his own house. "Hey, where were you?" Her return had not been fast enough to evade those sharp eyes.

She smiled shyly and answered softly as they entered the villa. "I was off dreaming somewhere, I guess. Something you said . . . ah, it wasn't critical." Her banter, light and meaningless, had given her time to look around. "Oh, Chris, it's great!" What she saw was a living room much like hers in overall structure, but larger, much larger, and with skylights overhead which currently brought in the light of the early Caribbean evening. The furniture was similar to hers, though the color scheme leaned toward browns and blues, crisp and bold against the basic white walls and carpet. There were three bedrooms instead of one, a full-size kitchen, and two baths, all done in a similarly masculine style.

"What, no darkroom?" she teased when the grand tour was over.

His grin sent tremors of delight racing through her veins. "I had intended this place purely as a vacation home. Then," he went on sheepishly, "I discovered that I couldn't get along without one. A compulsion to work, so to speak. So I compromised. There's no formal darkroom, but the third bedroom has a huge closet which backs onto one of the bathrooms. *Voilà* — with an additional door and five minutes of work to set it up, I'm in business."

His intense, smoldering gaze made Arielle tense. Her fading smile was replaced by a look of fear. "You're not going to take pictures of me, Chris," she informed him tentatively, instinctively stepping back.

"Right now, I have no desire to take pictures. Do you know what I'd like to do instead?" The seductiveness of his tone gave him away, replacing one fear with another in Arielle's heart. He gave her no time to answer. "I'd like to make love to you . . . in there." He cocked his dark head back toward the master bedroom, where his dark blue-covered king-size bed awaited. "But you won't let me, will you?"

Her eyes were wide azure saucers, begging for his understanding. The worst of it was that, for the first time, she wasn't quite sure of the answer she wanted to give. It *had* to be no; accordingly, she slowly shook her head. But did it have to be? A jolt shook her as she realized that, if Chris put his mind to it, he could easily woo her right into his bed . . . and she would not resist. To add to her confusion, a now-familiar tingling sparked to life deep within her.

"God, Arielle," Chris exclaimed, covering the distance that separated them and hauling her against the solid wall of his chest. "Don't look at me that way! I can't stand it — you look so lost, so hurt, so confused!" He spoke loudly, crushing her fiercely against him, then suddenly gentling. His voice when he spoke again was soft and low, his breath fanning the dark hair by her ear. "I'll never do anything you don't want, Arielle. You must know that by now. Please trust me. Much as it might kill me, I won't 'ravish' you until you're ready to return the favor." His humor was what they both needed.

Laughing, she wondered for a moment just what Chris's lovemaking might be like. Then saner thoughts triumphed, as she found herself standing on her own once more. "I love your place, Chris. It's . . . you!" She stole his line with a smile, then turned to walk to the glass sliding doors which opened onto the patio.

Dinner was relaxed and friendly, much as all their time together in the past few days had been. "You must eat out most of the time, with the schedule you keep. Do you mind it?" she asked out of pure curiosity.

"I do," he responded with a brief frown, "but I have no choice. It makes staying at home," his gaze lifted meaningfully to hers, "that much more special."

His response emboldened her. "Do you live alone?" The realization of what she'd asked brought a gasp to her lips. "I mean, no housekeeper or anything?" she added quickly, blushing furiously.

His knowing smile curled her toes. "I have

neither housekeeper nor bedmate, if that was what you wanted to know."

"I really didn't." She shook her head.

But he prodded. "Why not? Most women ask that same question —"

"I'm not most women!" she cried impulsively, then recovered herself. "I'm sorry. It came out the wrong way. It's really none of my business."

"That remains to be seen," he murmured quietly, pouring her a glass of wine as she puzzled over his comment. Whatever had he meant?

But the issue was quickly forgotten as Chris, for the first time, spoke at length about his work. Only later did she realize that he had brought it up himself this time, without prompting from her. The warmth that came with that knowledge would fill her for days. Now, however, she sat across from him at the small patio table, sipping her wine, spellbound.

"You *are* very different from most of the women, the people, I deal with every day, Arielle," he began slowly, looking off toward the ocean and a faraway world. "When I discovered photography, I was sixteen. I set my sights on fashion work because it held the money. To be blunt, that meant more to me at the time than anything." It was as

149

though he didn't want to look at her, to see possible disapproval in her soft gaze. "Everything had come hard to us as children; money seemed the only answer." He took a deep breath and Arielle's eye was caught by the mat of dark hair which escaped the confines of his open-necked shirt before she forced her gaze away and back to his face. He was frowning, now, in dissatisfaction.

"I was lucky. There were breaks and offers. I happened to be in the right place at the right time, as the expression goes."

For the first time, she interrupted him. "Surely your talent had something to do with your success," she chided gently.

He flicked a hand to indicate its relative unimportance in his opinion. "Oh, yes, I knew what I was doing. But if you don't have the jobs you go nowhere. Any number of my colleagues are as talented, if not more so, than I am, but for some reason things gelled with me."

Despite his modesty, Arielle could well imagine the package. Given his good looks, the charm of which he was capable, his driving ambition, his sharp intellect, and his superb photographic ability, there was no mystery as to the reason behind his success.

"What is it like — your job?" she asked,

almost timidly. "I mean, what do you do in a day?"

There was a bitter tinge to his laugh. "You really want to know?" He arched one dark brow as he turned to pierce her with his stare. When she nodded, he outlined a typical day in his life. "I get up at four-thirty or five o'clock in the morning to work in my darkroom — not because I don't want to sleep, but because that's the only time of day in which I won't be disturbed." He paused. "This is in New York, mind you. Things are more hectic when we're on location." His tone was cool and businesslike as he continued the description. "The phones start ringing by seven o'clock and I'm at my studio by seven-thirty. The crew will already be there by then, I hope. If not, there are frantic phone calls to be made. If so, we're off. Hair has to be just right, makeup just so, clothing this way or that. God help us if the client himself is in attendance! Things really get rough then. There's no way a lay person can imagine the finished product in the midst of a shooting session. Then there's music." His eyebrow arched again, this time in sarcasm. "These models have very specific tastes, you know. Once you get into the high-priced range like I am, the models have distinct personalities that they feel should be catered to. There's many a time I'd like to tell them to . . . ah, well, but I need them. It's as simple as that."

Disillusioned but fascinated, Arielle listened intently as he went on. "The lights are the simplest matter, as far as I'm concerned. Lights just go on and off. No temperaments. If one doesn't work, you screw in a new bulb. If another doesn't work, you replace it with a third." He took a deep breath. "If we're lucky, we may be shooting by eleven. We'll take a break for lunch by one o'clock then continue for as much of the afternoon as we need until I feel that I've got what I want on film. Some sessions have lasted well into the night, particularly on location, when we have a more rigid deadline to meet."

He had left out a vital part, that of the artist's — his — preconception and planning. Arielle was about to question him on it when he read her mind. "The thinking gets done during times like this" — he spread his arm to indicate that even his vacation was not truly a vacation — "and in the evenings. That's the part I like best — thinking up an approach, visualizing it, letting my imagination run wild." At long last there was a light in his eyes, a spark of enthusiasm for his work which had been noticeably absent up to this point.

"If you had your choice," she began softly, "what would you do? The conceptualization, the inspiration has to be followed through to its resolution. . . ."

Her words trailed into silence as he got up from his chair and strode into the living room, returning moments later with two white, hardbound volumes. "Have you ever read his work?" he asked, putting the volumes on the table before her, then pacing to the edge of the patio to savor the sinking flares of the setting sun.

"*The Daybooks of Edward Weston*?" she read aloud, then looked up, puzzled. "He's one of the pioneers, the grand masters, of photography. His work is magnificent, I've always loved it! But I didn't know he was an author, that these volumes even existed."

"Most people don't." His voice was quieter, as if it came from far off. "They're a kind of diary, kept during the years he spent photographing in Mexico, then California. Read them, Arielle," he urged, turning abruptly to face her. "Read them. They'll tell you what I want. I identify with Weston's dilemma as an artist, that conflict between commercialism and conscience. Perhaps one day, when I have all the money and time in the world to do anything I wish,

I can retire to a secluded little spot and photograph exactly what I want." He paused, leaning toward her, the intensity in his eyes at odds with the softness of his voice. "Until then, I have to save that inspiration for times like these." Hesitating again, he looked deeply into her, stirring her senses with the fire of his gaze. "Will you help me, Arielle?"

Entranced, she opened her mouth to speak, but no words came out and she shut it again. Her gaze slid from his to the strength of his nose, the firmness of his lips, the smooth sheen of his tanned cheek. It was all she could do to keep from reaching out to caress his features, so close, warm, and enticing. "What can *I* do?" she finally whispered, her breath catching as he answered.

"Let me photograph you." The words came so softly that she might have missed them had she not, somewhere deep in her mind, expected it. A reflexive tension crept through her. "No, don't do that to me," he asked, instantly sensing her withdrawal. "I won't hurt you. I just want to take some pictures. Why does that thought upset you?"

Her downcast eyes avoided his. "It's just painful for me . . . to be on . . . that side of the camera. I think that's why I became a photographer myself," she laughed, then sobered. "I just can't."

Chris had knelt beside her chair and now cupped her chin with his fingers and turned her head toward his. "Let me help you. It won't be so bad. It would really mean a lot to me."

For a brief moment she rebelled. It was like wearing something soft, just for him. How could she ever do it? Even now, in anticipation of having that all-seeing lens pointed in her direction, her stomach knotted. "You really don't want this plain and uninteresting face on film, do you?"

"Yes! I do want that face on film, but there's nothing plain or uninteresting about it. Why won't you believe me, Arielle? You have more to offer my camera than any model I've photographed in years."

"But I'm not a model. And I don't want to be one!" she protested, refusing to hear his compliment, yet sensing that, in the end, she would capitulate. Whether he sensed it too, she wasn't sure. But he suddenly changed the subject.

"Come on, let's get some more wine. I'd like to show you some of the things I've done since I've been here."

They spent the next hour side by side on the large living room sofa, wineglasses in hand and the slowly emptying bottle at arm's length, poring through the stack of black-and-white prints he had brought from his makeshift darkroom. There were close-ups of plants, fruits, and vegetables, each captured with its distinct qualities, its unique "personality." Many were photographed in such a way as to imbue them with near-human curves and textures, much, she recalled, as Weston's work had done. There were masterfully executed portraits of natives in their homes, animals in the fields, and sunsets, sunsets, and more sunsets, each more spectacular than the last, each doubly remarkable in that red and gold shards exploded from what was in truth a black-and-white surface.

"They're beautiful," she whispered, awe-struck, one small part of her wishing that she'd had less wine and could discuss them more clearly. But the wine was what she needed . . . if she intended to let Chris photograph her. She made no protest when he removed the prints from her lap and set them on a side table. Her hand was small and unsure within his larger one as he drew her up and led her back onto the patio, lit now by the spill of light from the house and the moon, high overhead. The dimness was soft and comforting, as were the little gestures he offered — the squeeze of her hand as he eased her into a sitting position in one corner of the stone wall, propping her gently against the trunk of a palm, turning her slightly to the side. She was in a spell, and his slow movements wove it more securely around her.

His hand tucked a strand of hair behind her ear, touching her cheek lightly as it withdrew. He spoke quiet words of encouragement as he stood back to admire the scene, then brought out his camera as if from midair. Arielle felt herself floating, buoyed up by the wine and the pleasure of his company. He continually told her how lovely she was, how soft and sensual. The clicking of the lens faded away leaving but the slightest tinge of discomfort in its wake.

"That's it, Arielle," he crooned reassuringly. "You're doing just fine. I want you just to relax; put your head back against the tree . . . that's right, just like that. And close your eyes. Now take deep, deep breaths. . . ."

Fully under his spell, she did as he asked, feeling herself to be the most soft and alluring of creatures, if only for this one night. There was something unreal about it all — the warmth, the peace, the contentment. Inhaling deeply, she felt her inhibitions begin to drift away, off into the balmy air which caressed her cheeks as Chris's fingers had done moments before. His words were soft, gentle, as were the hands which touched her arms, her hips, her shoulders, turning her, molding her, then he stepped back to capture what it was he saw.

The sense of security in which he enveloped her was broken when his fingers touched the top button of her blouse. She jumped, her eyes flying open in alarm to question him as she clamped her hand over his to still his progress.

"Don't do that," she whispered fearfully, but he lifted her hand to his lips for a gentle kiss before placing it in her lap.

"Just one button, honey. I won't hurt you. Just one." His lips touched hers lightly, then brushed against each of her closed eyelids. Mindlessly, she let her head fall back against the tree once more, soothed by the wine and content to listen to his sweet words, to follow his magical commands. The sound of his work-roughened fingers against the soft silk of her blouse was heady, but no more so than the coolness that touched her skin as he released not one, but three buttons, and drew the fabric apart to the waist.

"Chris?" she murmured, as though in a dream, needing his voice, his reassurance. A tingling filtered through her every nerve cell now, a heightened awareness which complemented the pacifying effect of the wine. She felt it shimmer from her toes upward to rest somewhere deep within and radiate an intangible excitement.

"It's all right, honey. Trust me."

She did. Completely. His hands found the front-closing clasp of her bra with ease and deftly released it, easing the lacy cups down and to the side, tucking them out of the way, then arranging her blouse so that it broke over the soft swells of her breasts.

"You should never wear a bra, Arielle. Your breasts are beautiful. You shouldn't hide them." Awareness exploded within her as his fingers brushed those ivory swells, his thumbs, with the touch of twin butterflies, bringing her nipples to rosy ripe peaks. As her heartbeat quickened she opened her eyes to look at him, but he had stepped back and now held the camera before him. On instinct, she raised a slender hand to the vee of contoured skin which his knowing hands had exposed, unaware of the sensuality of her movement.

"That's it, honey. It's you. Just relax now." He moved slowly, with none of the frenzy of the stereotypical photographer. Rather, his pace was one of slow seduction, as though he and his camera were inseparable. Eyes open, Arielle watched him tilt and sway. His hands on the camera were sure and steady, manipulating it from the vertical to the horizontal as skillfully as he had handled her. When he stood up to his full height to shoot down on her she lowered her eyes, stunned by the magnificence of his stature, then peered more shyly at him through the thick fringe of her lashes. When he moved in closer to frame her head and shoulders her tongue circled the dryness of her lips with enticing moistness. When he propped himself against the wall and directed her gaze off toward the house she felt at ease, completely and totally at ease before his lens.

Though he barely touched her, what contact there was electrified her. The eye of the camera was his eye, making warm, passionate love to her as it caressed every curve of her body, inflaming her senses with a molten heat. Her breasts were full, her nipples erect, as the need within her grew and grew. Had she been totally naked she could not have felt more enticing. Had he been nude beside her she could not have felt more aroused.

"Here, honey." He reached out to take her hand. "Let's move over here." Dazed by the sensuality of the moment, she let him lead her to a bed of soft grass and shrubs, where, at his quiet command, she lay down. Her eyes held his as, again, he draped her blouse about her, his fingers searing her heated flesh. For a moment his hands seemed everywhere, on her throat, her breasts, the warm, private spots along her ribcage. And then he stood back and began to shoot, leaving her alive and throbbing. Through heavy-lidded eyes she saw his every move, her mind in a passion-haze now quite distinct from the wine-induced glow.

It took long moments for her to realize that the clicking had stopped, that Chris now sat on the grass by her side, his gaze thick with desire, skimming her face, her chest, the open vee of her blouse, the suggestive outline of her breasts against the silken fabric. The shooting was over, yet she couldn't move; she was held to the spot by the fevered touch of his eyes.

His hand was less than steady when he slid it along the curve of her neck. Her lips parted slightly, softly, awaiting his kiss. When it came, she was ready, returning it with every bit of the passion his masterful persuasion had evoked. Disappointment filled her when he pulled back, but only for an instant. His eyes asked the question, then

161

took their cue from the flame of desire in hers. Slowly, his fingers edged beneath the fabric which rested on her shoulder; slowly, they pushed it back, then eased her arms from the sleeves. Her bra disappeared with the blouse; she was naked to the waist before him.

His eyes drank in her beauty; his voice emerged as a husky whisper. "You're very beautiful, Arielle. Very beautiful." With infinite care his fingers traced every outline, every swell, then moved in to cup the fullness of her breasts in his hands.

Arielle had never known the joy she felt now. In his eyes, his hands, she was a woman, beautiful, sensual, wanted. His touch was heaven and hell all at once, bringing her an exquisite pleasure even as it sparked a craving for more.

Moaning, she reached for him, letting him guide her hands to his chest as he urged her to touch him as he touched her. The past, with its pain and humiliation, was an age away. Nothing that she experienced now even remotely resembled that horror. She felt herself swirling in an eddy of sensual delight, glorying in the feel of his manly chest, with its strong muscles beneath her fingertips, reveling in the thrust of her breasts against his fingers, which now teased the pink buds to an exquisite pebbled hardness.

"Kiss me, Chris," she whispered with a gasp, and he did, devouring her hungrily, then lifting her into his arms and maintaining the embrace as he walked until his footsteps were silenced by the thick pile of his bedroom carpeting. She knew only that she never wanted these heady feelings to end. It was a dream too good to disturb. He had discarded his shirt when he joined her on the bed, the warm breadth of his chest thrilling her anew. He kissed her again, gently but thoroughly, then let his lips trace a fiery path across her cheek to her neck, down to her throat, and finally to her breasts. Instinctively, she arched against him, moaning, whispering his name, burying her fingers in the thickness of his dark brown hair, craving more and more.

When his body moved to cover hers she knew of his need as well. Her hands lowered to trace the leanness of his hips with untold abandon until, in an inexplicably poignant moment, she felt him stiffen. It was as though the steady flow of desire she had felt in him had abruptly ceased. Reaching back, he drew her hands above her head, then levered his body higher.

Stunned and bereft, she raised her eyes to

meet his, which were searching her face relentlessly. He seemed puzzled, expectant, yet she couldn't begin to fathom his thoughts. When his gaze chilled, his strangely harsh words penetrated her haze of rapture.

"Do you know what you're doing, Arielle? Do you know what *we're* doing — what we *will* be doing if I don't stop now? We're approaching that point of no return. You do realize that, don't you?"

It seemed an eternity of heart-stopping silence that he stared at her, awaiting an answer she simply could not produce. His jaw was tight as he shook his head. Was it bitterness, disgust, disdain, or sadness that she saw in his coal-hard eyes?

"I don't understand you!" he finally exploded. "What happened to that fear? That little lost animal look? All of a sudden, you didn't seem frightened anymore. To be blunt, you responded like a pro. Was it the wine, Arielle? Or . . . was it all an act from the start?" Her gasp of outrage caught in her throat. "Are you two-sided, too — just like the other women I've known?"

Paralyzed with hurt and anger, Arielle could do nothing but stare at him. The only thing she wanted, as her clamoring body attested, was a resumption of the kiss, a continuation of this ecstasy-laden lovemaking. But Chris would have no more of it. One lithe movement took him from the bed. He scooped up his shirt from where it had fallen, then stormed from the room, leaving Arielle in a state of shock.

It had been the wine, she concluded later that night, long after she had risen from his bed in a stupor, used shaking fingers to put on her bra and blouse, and stumbled through the darkness to the haven of her own cottage. It had been the wine that had prompted her behavior which had been, in every aspect, totally inexcusable. She hadn't even protested when he'd carried her to his bed! What might have happened, had he not stopped? Hadn't she learned her lesson well enough once?

Waves of self-reproach washed over her as she realized how irresponsibly she'd acted. First the photographs, then his embrace — it was horrible! No wonder he had thought her a fraud! Everything she had once fought, she had given in to willingly. No wonder he had rolled away from her in disgust! In his mind, she *must* have appeared as deceptive as the rest! He had no way of knowing about her past; she had told him only a little, and she still lacked the courage to say more. He had no way of knowing how deeply she'd been affected by the wine he'd plied her with. He'd done it deliberately. She knew that, yet she couldn't fault him for it. He had wanted to photograph her; she understood the compulsion only too well.

In a moment's respite, she smiled, recalling the pleasure of the experience, both before the lens, then later. How divine he was — all sinew and bone, muscle and flesh, every inch a man. Even now, she yearned to touch him again, to have him touch her again. . . .

Appalled, she twisted violently on the bed. Had it been the wine, or was she deluding herself? She might never know for sure. Chris had rejected her soundly. He didn't trust her, yet she couldn't conceive of laying bare her past just to win that trust — if, indeed, she wanted it. If this night had been an example, he would not approach her again. What he wanted was someone with experience, someone from *his* world, someone who didn't need wine to relax.

Sleep eluded her for most of the night, coming only as the first light of day peered from the other side of the island. It was a sleep of pure exhaustion, made deeper by the headiness of wine and loving, hurt and frustration. She had been on the verge of discovering the true depth of her woman-hood. Would she ever find it now?

The last thing she had expected was for Chris to appear on her doorstep the next morning, but there he was. She had been asleep when his knock roused her. Groggy and ill-tempered, she shrugged into her robe and padded to the door.

He looked as awful as she felt — small consolation for what had happened, she mused. A dark growth of beard shadowed his jaw, his shirt was wrinkled, his neat navy slacks had been replaced by a pair of old denims. His gaze, though, was sharp and piercing.

"May I come in?" he asked calmly.

Refusing to play the part of the docile maid once more, she challenged him boldly. "Was there something special you wanted? I'm really not feeling great. I was sleeping."

A flicker of concern crossed his eyes before the faintest of smiles signaled his understanding. "I'm sorry. I just wanted to show you the photographs. I've been up working on them all night."

Anything else and she might have slammed the door in his face. But . . . the photographs . . . the pictures of *her.* The barrier between them disintegrated as conflicting emotions engulfed her. She didn't want to see them, yet she had to see them.

"Whoa," he smiled gently. "They're great. You'll be pleased."

Her eyes were filled with insecurity as she stepped back to allow him entrance. He proceeded directly to the sofa and, without a backward glance, removed the prints from the envelope he'd held under his arm and began to spread them on the floor. Arielle hadn't moved from the door, held rooted to the floor by a last-minute fear.

"Come on!" He gestured gaily, his tone enticing her to join him. Timidly, she looked down, then leaned forward to examine the prints. Blinking several times, she frowned. Was that the way she had looked last night? Was that what Chris had seen?

The Arielle in the prints was indeed a woman, every bit a woman. There was seductiveness in one shot, vulnerability in another, softness in a third, shyness in a fourth. On and on it went, through no less than eighteen prints. Over and over, she studied them, refusing to believe what she saw before her eyes. There was beauty where she had expected none, sophistication where she had expected naiveté, allure where she had expected innocence. After the silence stretched on interminably, Chris finally spoke.

"Well, what do you think?" he asked, his tone deep and expectant.

She gazed down at the prints again, unable to tear her eyes away. "I didn't realize you took so many!" she finally whispered.

"Arielle!" he exclaimed, grabbing her shoulders and turning her to face him. But where she might have expected to see anger or disdain there were only excitement and warmth. "Is that all you have to say? What do you think of the prints?" He brought her down beside him to look at the shots again, his arm sliding across the back of her shoulders to hold her firmly against him. It was as if the moment of triumph were shared.

"They're . . . beautiful." Her voice was choked with emotion; her body was trembling lightly. "I never expected anything like this. Is that really me?" Nearly a whisper, her words expressed her continuing astonishment.

The force of Chris's gaze touched her, but she refused to look up at him. "I've been trying to tell you how very lovely you are. Why don't you believe me? Now you can see for yourself. Do you still want to fight it?" Intermingled with his good-natured

169

chiding was a thread of sternness. Only then did Arielle dare to look at him. In that instant he was her mentor, her protector, her savior. He deserved to know the truth.

"I have to show you something." She spoke softly, but with sudden conviction. Extricating herself from his arm, she stood and disappeared into the bedroom, returning moments later with a small photograph clutched in her hand. When she stood before him she hesitated, looking sadly down at the photograph before taking a breath and turning it to Chris.

His hand reached out and took the small snapshot; his eyes studied it for long moments. Watching him for the slightest reaction, Arielle was only aware of the thudding of her heart, which shook her entire body with its intensity. When he looked up at last, she cringed. But his hand reached out for hers, and he held it tightly. Oddly moved, he spoke in a low murmur. "This explains so much, Arielle. I only wish you had shown it to me sooner."

Her eyes filled with tears which, mercifully, refused to fall. "It's very difficult. I don't think I've ever shown it to more than a handful of people. I'm not proud of the way I looked then; it wasn't the happiest period of my life." Even as she spoke, she felt raw, exposed, vulnerable.

Sensing her pain, he pulled her gently down beside him on the floor. His hand stroked the snarls from her sleep-messed hair, soothing the wayward strands away from her face.

"What I see in this snapshot is a beautiful and vulnerable face encased in an abundance of baby fat. You're grown up now, Arielle. Can't you see that?" He spoke softly, comforting her with his words. "Come, sit against me," he commanded gently, drawing her against his chest, tucking her head into his shoulder, his hand encircling hers. "Tell me about it, Arielle. I want to know. It will help me to understand you better."

Having exposed herself this far, it was not difficult for her to tell him more. This time, when she discussed her childhood, she left out nothing. When she told of those sad and lonely teenage years she elaborated fully. His questions were soft and gentle, directing her on in her tale. By the time she reached her college years, there was little else she could bring herself to tell. Although the prints before her and the tender man beside her had given her the strength to reveal the fact of her extreme unattractiveness in those early years, she had not yet reached the stage where she could reveal the full extent of her folly. That particularly painful scene would remain buried deep within her.

"When did you begin to lose weight?" he asked when she had finally stopped speaking.

"I, ah, I sort of lost it gradually . . . after I . . . graduated from college," she stammered softly.

"Were you in Rockport at that time?"

"No." She shook her head against his chest, gaining strength from the ever-steady beat of his heart. "By the time I took the studio there I had lost most of it. But I'll always think of myself as being fat!"

He squeezed her roughly. "Fatness isn't all that bad. It's what's inside that counts, isn't it?"

A spontaneous groan, then a sly chuckle met his ears. "Ho-hum . . . where have I heard *that* before? You sound just like my parents."

"I hope not." His answer was quick. But his humor reminded her of what had happened last night.

"Chris, about last night —" she began, trying to push herself away from him, but destined to fail as his grip tightened.

"Last night is forgotten, Arielle. You had

too much wine; I had too much moonlight. It's hard, sometimes, for me to remember how inexperienced you really are. When you get going . . ." His words were gentle, yet she cringed. Instantly, he misinterpreted her embarrassment. "No, don't be ashamed of your response to me, Arielle," he crooned softly, hugging her even closer to him. "It's very rare to find a woman with the depth of passion you have. Perhaps that's why I need to photograph you. That combination of innocence and passion — it's quite something."

Guilt swarmed within her. Chris assumed her to be *totally* innocent, and *that* she was not. Though it was a technical distinction, it was a fact. Yet she *was* inexperienced; that, too, was a fact. The passionate side of her nature, which Chris had discovered, was a side no man had come close to awakening before. But . . . a virgin? In her heart, she ached to cry out the truth. Letting Chris live with this belief, technically incorrect as it was, pained her. But she couldn't tell him. She couldn't! The humiliation was too great! Her lips remained still, her voice silent. But when he drew away to look down at her she had no choice but to return his gaze.

"I can't promise it won't happen again,

Arielle. Photographing you — making love to you — the needs are equally strong. That combination of purity and passion —"

"Chris!"

"Shhh." He stilled her short-lived attempt at confession with one finger against her lips. "It's nothing to be ashamed of. It's a very potent combination." He sighed. "I wish I could stay away from you, but I can't. I'll try . . . God knows I'll try . . . until you're ready. But I make no promises. I want you; you know that, don't you?"

Her head dipped in a nod. Yes, she knew that as well as she knew how badly one part of her wanted him. But, having reached this point, there was so much more to consider. Once before she had given herself to a man, only to discover that it had been part of a cruel joke. When she gave herself again, things would have to be different.

When. She gasped silently. *When,* not if — that was a change, just as the pictures on the floor before her were a change from the image she'd held of herself for so many long years. There was so much to be considered — so much! Bewildered, she shook her head.

"I feel so confused." She hadn't realized she'd spoken until the words were out. But no harm was done. Chris hugged her to him again, rocking her gently, his understanding only increasing her sense of guilt.

"Time solves all kinds of problems." He spoke as though to himself. "We'll wait. Perhaps things will seem clearer in time."

But Arielle wondered. There was so much she didn't understand. In one sense, Chris had been right. For someone as inexperienced as she was, even given the encounter he did not know about, she had behaved with wild abandon, with unleashed passion. How had she been capable of such a response? There was only one answer. It was Chris — Chris who held the key to her body, Chris who held the strings of her heart.

The next few days saw a return to the more platonic level of friendship which Arielle had found so pleasant earlier. As each day passed, the memories of their first encounter and of that terrible night grew dimmer and dimmer, prey to the charm and companionability of this other Christopher Howe. The memory of his rage, his violence, seemed foreign to the man she'd come to know. That he sometimes fell to brooding, growing silent for a while before snapping back to conviviality, she had to accept as part of the man. That he was generally in control of his moods, however, she found reassuring. Occasionally she wondered what deep, dark secrets drew him taut, but he always relaxed again before she reached any conclusion. Determinedly, she dismissed these lapses from mind.

She also dismissed all thought of that little catch-phrase — the strings of her heart — or tried to. It was not so easy, however. Something had to explain her attraction to Chris, and she refused to believe that her motivations were purely physical. Yet there was so much more that she had never expected to encounter, that she had never dreamed she'd find when she had left Rockport on that cold, wintry morning nearly two weeks ago, that it boggled her mind. Much as she sought them, solutions were elusive. She only knew that she looked forward to seeing him with growing excitement from one day to the next, that she would truly miss him when her month was up. She *did* forcibly oust this last thought from her mind, bent as she was on enjoying her stay. Anticipation of the future would only cast a shadow of gloom on the present. And the present was too lovely to mar in any way.

Six

Chris continued to photograph her. His camera seemed a natural part of his person as they puttered around the villa, lounged on the beach, drove around the island. They were a threesome, joined on occasion by her own Nikon to make a fourth, but even then Arielle captivated his lens more often than not. After that first instance, particularly when she had seen the results, some of which he had left with her and which she took out each night with disbelief, then pride, her self-consciousness dwindled until she felt as much at ease before his lens as she did before his eyes. This man who had so terrified her at first did so no longer. If he puzzled her with his moods, she had to indulge him. After all, he indulged her her fears and, though he must have felt his share of frustration, he didn't pressure her.

There were no repeats of the intimate dinner at his house; though they dined together nearly every evening, it was either at a restaurant or casually, on the beach, in the kitchen — and, by mutual agreement, without wine. Chris made no further bid to discuss his career or his future with her. Nor did he repeat his suggestion that she study Weston to better understand Howe. Arielle knew where the *Daybooks* were, standing among a host of other photographic volumes on the shelf in his living room. When, and if, she ever wanted to look them over, they were hers.

The more she saw of it, the more Arielle felt at home on St. Maarten. One afternoon she and Chris circled the island in its entirety, crossing back and forth from the French to the Dutch sides with ease. What would have been little over an hour's drive was lengthened by the numerous stops they made — to photograph, to walk, to fight the tropical heat with a cool drink. The roads, though they never had more than a single lane in either direction, were better paved on the Dutch side, where the distinctly American flavor contrasted sharply with the more continental flair maintained by the French.

It was on the French side that she found more of interest to photograph. Narrow roads wove through stretches of orchard land, then straightened out to pass through small settlements before curving into rural- ism once more. She captured the woebegone expression of a flop-eared, sad-eyed dog, mangy and scrawny, seemingly dwarfed by the healthier cluster of goats around it. She crouched by the side of the road to frame the sober march of the cows in search of pastureland to suit their tastes. She photo- graphed the homes of the natives, many not much more than shacks, yet all lushly landscaped by nature. And, to her excite- ment, she found a family to photograph — a mother, father, and four children, none of whom exceeded the age of six.

Chris had been driving at a leisurely pace when she first spotted the group. It was an instantly striking picture, for the family members were perched in the most natural of poses on and around the front porch of their slightly ramshackle home, which was set just back from the road.

"Chris, look! Oh, please stop!" As she pointed, he pulled the car off the road onto the dirt embankment. Arielle was out in an instant. "I'll be right back. This is too tempting to pass up."

Her eyes never left the family as she slowly approached. The smile on her face spoke the international language of friendship which the natives immediately understood and answered in kind. In broken French, she explained her wish to take pictures, holding up her camera and elaborating with sign language when memory failed to produce the proper words.

Still smiling, now in pure delight, she began to photograph. All else fell to the side save that which she saw in her viewfinder. The family as a whole, the parents standing silently together, the children as they lost their fear and began to romp across the overgrown front yard. Of the little ones, one was shyer; this one, she coaxed out with soft words and easy gestures. One was more aggressive; this one she tamed with patience and good-natured indulgence, letting him explore her camera freely until he decided he might allow her to photograph him.

She found them to be beautiful people, proud and giving of their time and faces, yet poor as the poorest of the natives on the island. It was with reluctance and only when she ran out of film — and with repeated gestures of thanks to her subjects — that she finally returned to the car. With mild shock, then, she remembered Chris, sitting, waiting, watching her.

"I'm sorry, Chris! I lost track of the time!" She laughed, breathless, as she pulled her camera in beside her and slammed the car door.

"You were enjoying yourself. I enjoyed watching you."

It was a brief but warm interchange; without further words, Chris started the car and they drove on. Not all such stops were as one-sided. Now that Chris had made the breakthrough, he indulged himself in the luxury of photographing Arielle. He found her growing lack of inhibition enchanting, her poses and concentration, as she herself photographed others, intriguing. When, on occasion, she swung around to shoot him, he mugged magnificently, reducing them both to easy laughter.

Progress on her book, however, had come to a standstill; most of her time was spent out of the cottage, usually with Chris. To her astonishment, given her history of rigid scheduling, she did not mind in the least. The time she spent with him was too enjoyable to spoil with guilt over what had *not* been done; if she didn't look again at those photographs of children she'd diligently brought with her from home, there would be time aplenty to study them when she returned.

There were, very simply, too many other things to do, out in the sun, in the midst of this carefree Caribbean atmosphere. As he had promised, Chris took her back to the school yard in Marigot, where she photographed to her heart's content, with the permission of the school officials. Though the language barrier precluded much communication with the ever-curious children, there was an international language of smiles and gestures and mime which heightened her pleasure. For a short while she was a child herself, returning to the age of her subjects with an enthusiasm that was contagious, inspiring antics which her camera snapped up. While much of her time was spent on her backside, she did her share of climbing as well, bent on finding new angles from which to shoot, new directions, new distances. Through it all, Chris was the contented observer, remaining at times in the background, breaking into a grin or a laugh more at Arielle's expense than that of the children. On more than one occasion she cast him a look of mocking reproach, but, in truth, his presence added something very warm to the experience.

"You're wonderful with children," he complimented her one afternoon as she slung the camera over her shoulder, gave a final wave to the imps in the school yard and joined him back on the sidewalk. "I can see why you're so successful at your work. You would be a wonderful mother."

"Well, now, I'm not so sure about that." She exaggerated her protest by drawing out her words, eager to minimize a potentially uncomfortable topic. "It's one thing to manage children when you know that you can turn around and walk out the door whenever you feel like it. It's another thing to send them home for misbehaving — and to realize that you *are* home!"

Chris laughed softly in understanding, yet apparently he had not entirely relinquished the issue. She felt his tension keenly as they walked side by side toward the harbor and its picturesque display of boats — schooners, yachts, and trawlers.

"Wouldn't you like to have children of your own one day?" he asked finally as he, too, allowed his eye to be drawn by the scene before them.

Arielle's shrug was not so much one of indecision as of helplessness. "I suppose so, but I'm not sure it will ever happen."

She would have liked to leave it at that, but Chris would not. "Why not? You're young, attractive; there must be any number of interesting men in Rockport to choose from."

Refusing to take the bait, she simply

grimaced, murmured a soft-spoken, if indifferent, "I'm sure there are," and walked on.

Chris was at her elbow instantly. "Do you date much?" His voice had deepened to a command; to her dismay, he intended to know.

"No." Her eyes reflected the aqua sea toward which she looked, avoiding his gaze.

"Why not?" Blunt and challenging.

Frowning, she stopped, turned toward the wood railing, painted a bright red, and leaned against it. What could she say? The truth was that not only had all of the men who had approached her in *that* sense either been arrogant, boring, or married, but that each of them had also brought his own form of terror. But this confession would only lead to demands for more, and that much she was not ready for. She evaded the issue instead.

"I have my work and my friends."

"What about Sean?"

Had she been watching Chris's eyes she might have seen the flare that accompanied this mention of her friend. But her gaze was held by a huge yacht that had rounded the rocky barrier and come into sight. The mention of Sean's name brought a spontaneous smile to her lips.

"Sean is a dear." The thought of him

warmed her now, as it always did. She felt so very comfortable with Sean, as comfortable as she now felt with Chris. There was a big difference in the relationships, however. She had never felt the slightest beginnings of desire for Sean, but with Chris it was overwhelming. His touch, his gaze, his silent presence beside her — all could spark the tremor she now felt. But, as she had learned to do, more successfully at some times than others, she fought her response.

"I got a letter from him the other day," she burst out on impulse, turning brightly toward Chris. "A card, actually. He says that all's fine at home. They had a snowstorm; life slowed down for a while, I guess, not that it matters with the kind of artist's life he leads. . . ." She let her words filter into oblivion as she studied the sudden glower that darkened Chris's mien. Was he jealous? Of Sean? The thought seemed preposterous, even as it pleased her. But she and Chris had never discussed their relationship, so she did not dare to challenge him.

"What about you?" She turned the tables instead. "You must have someone back in New York." Michael's words returned to her. According to Tom Kendrick, there was no one special in Chris's life at this point, but plenty of not-so-special somebodies.

When Michael had first relayed this information it had held no import. Now, though, she awaited Chris's response with strange tension.

He stood taller, straighter, as he thrust his hands into the pockets of his well-worn denims. It was a statement of independence, this subtle alteration of stance; he leaned on nothing, on no one. "There are many 'someones' back home, but none of them mean anything to me. My lifestyle doesn't really allow for the luxury of a lasting relationship." The undertone of bitterness was back, but only for a minute. "Are you thirsty?" At the abrupt change of subject he looked down at Arielle's puzzled face.

"Uh-huh. It *is* hot."

"Come on. That corner, over there . . ." Long, bronzed fingers pointed to the corner-front juice stand. Moments later they were both greedily drinking the fresh-squeezed juice — lemonade for Arielle, grapefruit for Chris. The subject of love lives was left behind by mutual and unspoken agreement, though Arielle's mind lingered on it. He was right; with a schedule and a lifestyle like his there was no room for a wife, a family. It was sad; he would have made some woman an exciting husband, some children a devoted father. The recollection of the softness in his eyes when he'd spoken of his horde of nieces and nephews vouched for that fact. Arielle felt saddened, in a much deeper and more baffling way than she was ready to analyze.

Sightseeing, exploring, photographing the island provided a neutral ground for the growth of the friendship between Chris and Arielle. But that neutrality was harder to maintain on their home turf, particularly the beach. As a solution, playfulness became the order of the day when the going got hot, which it frequently did. Try as she might to deny it, Arielle could not ignore the intrinsic sensuality the camera inspired when Chris wielded it in these more private spots. That first night had unfortunately set the tone; the same aura of eroticism, gentle but ever-present, sprang up to encompass her all too often. In most cases she managed to pass these tests of her self-control. It became, however, harder and harder.

Determined to avoid an encounter, Chris was careful when and where he touched, kissed, or embraced her. During these private shooting sprees his behavior was impeccable, verging on the detached, and it became a growing torment to Arielle. Much as she still feared the inevitable outcome of such a move, part of her ached to be closer to him in that most physical of ways. A battle raged within her, one that often left her cranky and restless. Yet, though she had lost so many of her inhibitions before this tall and leanly masculine photographer, she had not reached the point where she could initiate any advances herself. And Chris continued, with maddening consistency, to shun any expressions of outright sexuality — until one particularly hot, particularly heady afternoon on the beach.

It was in the middle of her third week on the island. Together, they had driven into Marigot, where Arielle vanished in search of green peppers, tomatoes, and lettuce, leaving Chris to his own devices. Then he dropped her at her own cottage an hour later with a promise to meet her on the beach as soon as he'd changed. But as she opened the door to hop out of the car, he touched her arm.

"Wait a minute, Arielle." His pause was filled with the same odd tension she'd seen in the past, as he debated some dark internal issue. Finally, with an imperceptible nod of determination, he reached to the floor of the back seat and produced a small plastic bag, brightly illustrated with the insignia of one of Marigot's most exclusive clothing shops, one which Arielle knew to be strictly Parisian and very chic. "Would you wear this?" he asked, dazzling her with his request.

Her eyes lowered to the bag, then returned to his face, questioning. "What is it?"

"A new suit."

"*Bathing* suit? But I already have one! Ah," — her head cocked teasingly as she dropped her thick lashes — "I think you're trying to give me a message, Chris. Is my navy suit so awful?"

He smiled, relieved by her good humor, hoping that it would carry her through the discovery of the bag's contents. "I love your navy one, but this is something different. Please wear it — for the sake of my camera?" His endearing quality, when he feigned pleading like this, won her over every time. He had learned that early on, and resorted to the ploy shamelessly.

She grinned. "I'm beginning to wonder about that camera, Christopher Howe. You know what they say — it's not the camera that makes the picture, but the photographer." Then a new thought hit. "How do you know this will fit? I have to try on ten suits at home to find one that looks good."

His reply was a self-assured drawl. "It'll fit."

They were the last words he spoke before he turned the car around and headed for his own house. His certainty puzzled her . . . until she opened the bag in the privacy of her bedroom. *No wonder he was so sure!* she exclaimed silently. What little there was of the fabric she held in her palm did not *need* to fit — if that was indeed possible. For what she held was the slimmest of bikinis, a rich brown duo of bra and panties. That the make was of the highest quality she had no doubt. Nor did she doubt that the silken pieces would fit her perfectly. But she couldn't — she absolutely couldn't! It would be obscene, she argued, all the while savoring the smoothness of the material. Modesty would have prevented her from even trying on such a daring suit at home; on second thought, she mused, the issue would never have been raised, since the shops at home rarely even carried anything as risqué as this!

She thrust the suit down onto the bed, only to lift it up again an instant later. She couldn't! But what would it look like on? That Chris thought enough of her body to have bought it for her was a supreme compliment. On impulse, she undressed, leaving her clothes in disarray on the floor, and put on — or rather, wrapped herself into —

the bikini.

The mirror above her dresser held a sight for which she was not prepared. Following close on the heels of cameras and scales, mirrors were her archenemy. When most girls had been busy studying their ripening bodies in mirrors on closet doors, Arielle had avoided hers doggedly. Even after the last of the pounds had been shed, she continued to see — she assumed she would always see — pouches and fat-spots and all sorts of other unpleasant imaginings. She had not once, that she could remember, stood nude before a mirror. Nor was she nude now . . . though that was merely a matter of interpretation.

She took in her own slender and feminine shape, her eyes widening in disbelief, softening in pleasure. Was that truly Arielle Pasteur? For some reason, stripped of clothing that related in any way to her past, she saw herself whole for the first time. A tan, which left the paleness of her middle with a vulnerable and delicate look, had glossed her skin lightly, leaving deeper flushes on her cheeks, her chest, and the very long and shapely legs which stretched forever beneath the thinly triangular fabric below her navel. Slowly turning, she twisted to look over her shoulder at the revelations behind. Perhaps she had willed them away, those unattractive lumps and swells; perhaps the graze of the sun had camouflaged them. Or, she smiled, was the mirror an enchanted one?

"Very nice," a deep voice crooned from the door, drawing Arielle's head up with a start. Embarrassed both at wearing so little and at having been caught in a moment of such intent self-examination, she blushed furiously.

"You should have knocked!" she cried, mortified, unsure as to what to cover first, finally flinging her arms into the air in despair. "I can't wear this, Chris! How could you ask me to? It's . . . it's . . ."

Chris, with an air of cool assurance and undeniable pleasure, finished the sentence for her, though not with a word she would have chosen. ". . . stunning. You look stunning, Arielle!"

"There's nothing to it!" Her squeal brought an even broader grin. "I can't wear it!"

Unfolding his long frame from its casual stance against the doorjamb, Chris approached her, lightly resting his hands on the soft and previously unseen, much less touched, flesh at her hips. "There's no reason why you can't wear it now." His eyes freely roamed her curves, sending a tingling through her which the feel of his fingers would have accomplished just as well on their own. "I've seen everything it reveals, anyway, so you needn't feel shy." He stood back for just a minute, shaking his head faintly. "Boy, do you look great!"

An ill-calculated move brought her hands up to rest in protest on the sinewed strength of his forearms. Her fingers felt the hair that grew there, dark and straight and delightful in texture. As though with a will of their own, her hands tightened. And her gaze dropped to take in, for the first time, now that her own embarrassment had peaked, his appearance. Covered by nothing more than his own dark and snug-fitting bathing suit, he was the primitive again, all man from the breadth of his bronzed shoulders to the flatness of his stomach and the muscled strength of his lean legs. His chest was warm and inviting, with its virile tee of hair, powerfully tempting to her fingertips.

"Oh, Chris," she whispered unknowingly as her eyes rose to meet his, finding there a look of torment which mirrored her own. His hands moved to her shoulders, but it was her own momentum which brought her head against his chest, her own arms which slid around his lean waist to lock at his back. The softness of his fine mat of hair feathered beneath her cheek in sweet comfort.

"It's getting worse, isn't it, honey?" he murmured huskily. His meaning was clear, and she nodded. "I'm sorry I can't make it any easier for you —"

"No, *I'm* sorry," she interrupted with a gulp. "If it weren't for —" Swallowing hard, she caught herself before she blurted out that most humiliating revelation. For a brief instant time was suspended, the silence rearing up between them. Then Chris stiffened as he drew his own, incorrect, conclusion. With a shove, he thrust her back, turned, and left the bedroom and the house.

Arielle stood in stunned disbelief, totally ignorant of his misconception, totally puzzled by his anger, totally unsure as to what next to do. As feeling slowly returned to her limbs she wandered into the living room, eyes downcast, lost in thought. His anger seemed unfathomable; she was without a clue as to its cause. Chris had no inkling of what she had been about to say. Why then his reaction? There seemed only one answer — and that could only be her continued resistance to his desire to make her his, completely and totally. Her words, abbreviated as they had been, had indicated without doubt that she was not yet ready for his possession. He had voiced his opinion of rejection quite clearly once before; now he had simply expressed it differently.

The pain inside her was devastating. His discomfort was her own, his hurt hers also. What was she to do? In the short span of these few weeks Chris had come to mean something very special to her. Though she wasn't ready to sleep with him, she could not bear the thought of staying away from him. Her eyes moved restlessly around the room, matching the frantic searchings of her mind. Suddenly, a dark, chrome-edged object drew her attention. His camera! He had stormed out of her presence and forgotten this third hand of his, so upset had he been!

Further thought was unnecessary. Within seconds Arielle was on the patio, then the wooden stairs, the camera in her hand, determination in her mind. She had known he would be here, on the beach where they'd shared such far-flung extremes of emotion. His back was to her as he stood, hands on hips, looking past the gently lapping waves toward the depths of the ocean.

"Chris?" she breathed softly from close behind him, her eyes clinging to the darkness of that thick mane of hair, even longer and fuller now than when he had first arrived. When he made no sign of recognition she took a small step to the side, only to be shaken by the sternness of his profile. That he was angry went without saying. For an instant fear engulfed her in a cruel reminder of that first day when he had terrified her on this same beach. Would he explode now? Would he attack her again? Then she had fought him; would she do so now?

"Please, Chris, talk to me," she pleaded in a whisper, willing her fear away.

"What is it?" Surprisingly, there was no anger in his voice. Rather, Arielle heard an element of defeat, totally uncharacteristic and nearly as upsetting to her as his wrath might have been.

Suddenly, she didn't know what to say. "I, ah, I . . . I brought your camera," she finally stammered feebly, groping, struggling for some way to reach him. "I thought you wanted to take pictures."

His jaw clenched. "You're avoiding the issue."

Letting her gaze drop to the sand, she turned away from his disdain. "I-I don't want to avoid it, Chris. I know it's — it's difficult —"

"Do you?" he burst back, facing her now and directing his attack openly. "You have no idea what I feel, Arielle! I've suffered over the past days, controlling myself — and

I keep asking myself why! Why do you still hold out? I know you feel the chemistry — you respond to it well enough." His eyes narrowed. "So what is it in your head that won't release you from those damned inhibitions?" When she couldn't answer, he goaded her. "Is it Sean you're saving yourself for?" Though she looked up in shock, words still eluded her. "Or some deep-seated morality? You don't know what I'm going through. How can you say you know it's difficult?"

Her dark head swung up, sending her gaze into collision with his, so hard and cold now. "I *know!* I feel those same things, too!"

"You *feel?*" His voice lowered suddenly as he mocked her words sadly. "You *feel* — I was beginning to wonder just how much you *do* feel. You've come a long way from where you were when you first arrived here, Arielle. But suddenly we seem to be back to square one."

As Arielle stared at his dark, handsome face she felt those stirrings which gave the lie to his words. These heady sensations had been unknown to her before she had met Chris. In a moment of abandon, she ached to call to him, "Take me, I'm yours!" The emptiness within craved fulfillment, an emptiness she had been oblivious to for all the years before. Yet she couldn't . . . not yet. There were too many scattered pieces of the puzzle that needed fitting together.

Her voice was a breathy sound, a whisper just above the waves. "No, Chris. We're not way back there. You're right; I have come a long way. Very fast. It overwhelms me sometimes. There are some things I'm not yet ready for. But," she hesitated, recalling his accusations on that very first afternoon, before taking the leap, "I would like you to go on photographing me . . . if you still want to." Silently, she held out his camera, every cell within her begging him to take it, to give her another chance. When his hand reached out to lift the weight from hers she exhaled slowly in relief. But it was short-lived. For his eyes remained the hardest, coldest chunks of coal she had ever seen.

She withstood the desire to crumble before them. When they slowly, and with stark deliberation, trailed down to her chest and touched her breasts, so minimally covered with the exquisite brown suit, she refused to cower. When they returned once more to her face she sensed that she had passed a test of sorts. But the *real* challenge was still to come.

"Take it off." He spoke so softly that she wondered if she had heard correctly. But his eyes confirmed her fears even before he repeated his words. "Take it off. The top."

This was to be her punishment for her continued resistance, and a test of her willingness to please him. She saw it instantly. It was his own very special form of torture; the question was whether she could stand up to it. Her strength of moments before was dwindling rapidly. In its place, fear had begun its familiar coursing through her insides. Would he make her do it? Would he? No, something within said that he would not, *knew* that he would not. But if there was to be any hope for their relationship, she had no choice now. This was the most daring test so far — of her trust in him, of her faith in him. Would she accept the punishment so that there might be peace, once more, between them? Her eyes fell for a final moment as she struggled convulsively to swallow her panic.

Then, with a deep breath, she lifted trembling fingers to the tie at her neck, releasing it first, then the other behind her back. When the fabric fell to the sand the warmth of the sun hit her skin for the first time, a sharp contrast to the chill that seeped from within. Her misted eyes lifted to his face in silent pleading for help. But the gaze which met hers maintained its impassivity. Shivering, she waited for direction.

"Lie down on the sand — over there." He sounded completely calm and dispassionate as she followed the direction of his cocked head toward a smooth section of the sand not far from the water's edge. Quietly, she walked to the spot and lay down on her back, aware that Chris had gone back to the rocks and instantly realizing his purpose. This was to be a vital part of her punishment, her torment, her trial — and she was determined to survive it.

Expecting it as she did, the feel of the cold lotion on her fair skin did not surprise her. It was the touch of Chris's hands, spreading the smooth white cream, which sent shock waves through her. Bending over her on the sand, his broad shoulders kept her in shadow for the moment, enabling her to look directly into his eyes as he proceeded to smoothe the suntan lotion over every inch of her, save for that small patch covered by the remaining swatch of bikini.

His fingers moved in purposely slow, maddeningly designed circles, over her chest, around her breasts, over them, beside them, then over them again. Against her will, her nipples hardened at his touch, her breasts themselves swelled into his hands. Gritting her teeth, she closed her eyes and turned her head to the side. But there was to be no relief in that move. His hands widened to span her ribcage, drawing dangerously light patterns in white across her waist, then moving lower. Her navel captured his attention for but a moment before his fingers crept beyond to skim the dark brown triangle which hid so little. When he lifted the thin strip at her hip and slid his lotion-moistened fingers beneath, she gasped.

"How can you do this to me, Chris?" she whimpered, sinking her teeth into her lower lip.

"I wouldn't want you to get sunburned, especially while I run back to the house to get several things," he quipped lightly. That he was immensely enjoying her frustration, as just payment for his own, was obvious.

But before she could ask him about the things he wanted to get, he was gone, leaving her alone and exposed. Arielle knew that he was watching her even as he jogged easily back, retrieved what he needed, then returned carrying a second, larger-format camera, more film, a tripod, and a long cable release.

She lay as still as possible, drawing on every bit of self-control to keep from squirming beneath his gaze. The sand was soft against her back, the sun warming on her breasts. Perhaps the suntan lotion was a good idea, she mused, even as she knew that, in the end, Chris was not worried about her burning. He had savored that torture, had enjoyed her pain, knowing precisely what frenzy was about to explode within her. And he wanted the moistness — she had to remember that. He was the photographer, the master at work. Her body would shine and glimmer now, she knew, adding an electric quality to his shots.

Adjusting his equipment, he set to work, quietly and dispassionately directing her to turn this way or that, to sit up, to lean back on her elbows, to roll over onto her stomach. From time to time he paused to wipe the sand from her skin and reapply the lotion, as though to remind her that things would not be easy. But they were. To Arielle's astonishment, they were very easy. Once the initial shock of being nearly nude before him had vanished, she began to relax. Even with his great stone face on, he showered her with warmth he could not deny, an appreciation of her body, of her curves and hollows, of her smooth, soft skin and her ultimate vulnerability. Yes, as the minutes passed, it grew easier and easier. When finally it appeared that he was nearly done, she sat up, stood, and wandered to a nearby boulder, sitting on it and curving her knees beneath her as she turned her face to the sun.

Chris studied her naturalness for long moments before readjusting his camera, the larger one, to capture her there. The tripod-mounted black box was beneath her, aimed up to frame her against the sky, now clear and blue and cloudless. Arielle was nearly unaware of his movement toward her until his hands took hold of her face, his long fingers threading through the black sheen of her hair to ease it back from her face. Startled, she opened her eyes and looked up at him questioningly.

"There's a very special look I want," he rasped softly, his voice for the first time reminiscent of the would-be lover. His lips took hers gently, caressing them as his fingers had her body earlier. With the wholeness of her own need, she returned his kiss, opening completely, without reserve, unaware of the action of the camera when he finally drew back. "That's it. Exactly." The tenderness in his face brought tears to her eyes. For a fleeting instant she felt . . . loved. It was strange, new, and unreal in its beauty. And the moment was gone as quickly. "Come on; we both need a swim."

Chris took her hand and helped her off the rock, leading her at a run toward the ocean. "Chris, I'm not wearing a suit!" she cried, then laughed at the foolishness of it all. He didn't answer; no answer was necessary. The coolness of the waves enveloped them, cushioning them from the heat of desire which had flamed moments before. When they finally emerged Arielle reached automatically for her bra.

"Don't put it on." His voice came from directly behind her, drawing her gaze around. "You look so lovely. Leave it off. I'm done photographing; let's just sunbathe for a while." His eyes narrowed mischievously, hiding the hardness that threatened a comeback. "You could get a nice tan, have something to show them — really show them — back home."

"Chris!" she exclaimed, hurt by his implication, then instantly pacified by his smile as it spread, slowly, across his lips. "That's absurd!" was the most she could muster in protest. Yet she lay down again without replacing the top — and thoroughly enjoyed the rest of the morning.

It was a tribute to how far she had indeed come. When she had first arrived on St. Maarten, had first encountered the sharp eye of Christopher Howe, she had cringed and cowered. Now she lay freely and openly beside him on the sand, clad in nothing but the small bottoms of a beautiful brown bikini. And, to her lingering astonishment, she felt perfectly at ease.

The aftermath of that morning was an afternoon of soul-searching as Arielle, alone in her cottage, tried to understand the changes that this vacation had wrought. It was as though the ugly duckling had finally seen her reflection. Though she would never believe herself a true beauty, she did *feel* beautiful — new, wild, and sensuous. Chris had done these things for her, had been her very flattering mirror. Would she once more become that old, very proper self once she returned to Rockport?

Determination that such should not be the case filled her. Impulsively, she climbed behind the wheel of the Chevette and followed the familiar road into Marigot, pulling up before the very shop in which Chris had purchased the bikini. An hour later, when she emerged from the exclusive store, her arms were laden with bundles, her wallet relieved of a number of traveler's checks, and her conscience free of all guilt. Smiling, she felt alive and soaring, a bird winging its way upward on a warm current of air. It seemed that nothing could dim her pleasure . . . until she arrived back at the villa to find a dark and ominous cloud hovering on her doorstep.

"What is it, Chris?" she asked in alarm, jumping from the car and approaching his taut form.

"Where have you been?" he yelled, frustrated and cross, his narrowed gaze a razor-sharp edge.

The smile that had softened her lips throughout the afternoon became a thing of memory. "I was in Marigot," she explained softly, frowning. "What's the matter?" Her whisper carried its share of fear. Though Chris had showed signs of temper from time to time — most recently this very morning — he now seemed unreasonably agitated. If only he would explain.

Straightening, he towered menacingly before her. "I was busy working in my darkroom when the mailman delivered this!" He produced a letter from his back pocket and thrust it into her hand. At a glance, Arielle saw her name on its front. But she quickly looked up at Chris, knowing that there had to be more — which there was. "Not only did I rush to the door and ruin the print I was working on at the time — a very special print, one I'd already spent a good deal of time with — but by the time I returned, there was no water."

"No water?"

"You heard me," he growled as though she were in some way at fault. *No water.*

Her brows drew together in puzzlement. "I don't understand. You mean, the water simply stopped running?"

"That's it!" His unrelenting anger kept her in a state of bewilderment.

"*I* didn't do anything to the water," she offered lamely, shrugging to show her innocence.

"I know that!" he bellowed, raking his fingers through his hair. "But as if it isn't bad enough that you've done nothing but distract me since you arrived, there's this! If it hadn't been for that damned mailman and this damned letter for you I would have been able to finish the print before the water dried up."

"Dried up? Chris, I don't know what you're talking about!" She finally exploded herself. "How could the water simply dry up? Where did it go? Do you mean to say that we're completely without water? No drinks, no showers, no bathrooms, nothing?"

"That's exactly what I do mean." Violently chopping one fist into his other palm, he turned and began his retreat.

"Wait a minute, Chris! Where are you going? I haven't got any water!"

"Damn it! I know that!" He paused, yelling over his shoulder at her. "I'm going to see what I can do! Stay here!"

As his dark and turbulent presence vanished into the thickly verdant path, Arielle stood, mouth agape, in utter astonishment. It took long moments before she recalled the letter in her hand. It was from Sean, as the return address clearly stated. But Sean was the last person she wanted to think about right now. Stuffing the letter into the back pocket of her jeans, she retraced her steps to the car and, distracted now, retrieved her bundles and brought them into the house, depositing them in a heap on her bed before returning to the living room and sinking down onto the sofa.

Why had he been so angry? The letter? The water? The fact that she hadn't been there at the cottage when he'd first arrived? But they had made no plans to spend time with each other this afternoon. He had himself stressed his intention of spending it in his darkroom working on the film he'd exposed that morning. She knew only too well the frustration of being interrupted in the midst of a darkroom session; was that the sole source of his anger?

Then another possibility reared its livid head. Jealousy. Her hand snaked back to her pocket and pulled out the crumbled letter. Was he jealous of Sean? He had directed enough questions at her regarding her relationship with Sean, she realized, to support that possibility. Was he really jealous? Hadn't he accused her of "saving herself" for Sean? But, other than the most obvious physical need, why would it matter so to him? Hadn't he told her himself of his carefree state? Hadn't he bluntly illustrated his disdain for clinging females? What was it he really wanted?

Her mind recalled the pleasure of the past days. If she didn't know better, she might suspect that she was half in love with Chris. It would be easy to lose herself to his charm, his good looks, his magnetism, his virility — even despite his recent moodiness, of which she suspected herself to be, in no small part, a cause. But, no! Not for Arielle! Love did not fit into her game plan. To fall in love with someone as footloose as Christopher Howe would be the greatest folly of all. Love was forever, but there could be no future with Chris. The only things that love for him could bring would be pain, heartache, and loneliness. And a return of those she most certainly did not need.

SEVEN

It seemed hours that she sat, on edge, by the phone, awaiting some word about the water situation. But the phone did not ring, nor did the front door open; there was neither sight nor sound of Chris.

The large brown portfolio, abandoned and neglected in the corner, caught her eye. She thumbed absently through the first of the prints, then thrust them down in disgust when she felt no interest in them at all. Recalling Sean's letter, she opened it and read its contents, feeling nearly as great an apathy toward it as toward the prints. In desperation, she paced to the bedroom and began to unload the packages she'd bought. There were several daring T-shirts, an exquisite silk dress, and two brightly colored, high-styled pairs of French-made jeans, all of which she carefully hung up, none of which evoked the excitement they had earlier, in Marigot.

Restless footsteps carried her from room to room in repeated cycles of aimless pacing. Perplexed now not only by Chris's unpredictable behavior but by her own emotional disquietude, she grew more and more impatient as she awaited some — any — sign of Chris. Brooding, she stalked to the patio, then suddenly pulled herself up short.

"Stay here!" he had commanded, as though she were his personal chattel. What right did he have to order her around? If he didn't have the decency to get back to her with some news, after all this time — though a fleeting glance at her watch told her that it had only been an hour and a half, rather than the three she would have bet on — she owed him no loyalty whatsoever. Certainly, she reasoned, closing her blue-eyed gaze to the image of the dark, handsome, and supremely arrogant photographer, there were better ways to spend her time than waiting idly here.

Determinedly, she changed into a sundress and sandals and headed for Philipsburg, a good old hamburger, a cold drink, and a rest-room. No water meant just that, she rued with a smile of guilt; how easy it was to take so simple a thing as flowing water for granted! The thought that perhaps the water problem extended all the way into town disturbed her momentarily until she realized that she had nothing, after all, to lose. Indeed, whether she found water or not, she might at least find some explanation for the problem at the villa.

Several hours later, when she retraced the route, her physical condition was greatly improved. Philipsburg had had plenty of water, though she did learn that a main had broken on the west side of the island, causing a problem for the homes and hotels there that did not have their own supply and relied, as did the villa, on water from the island's desalination plant. Rumor had it that the water would be restored by later that evening, though skepticism was strong among the other tourists with whom she spoke. For herself, she headed back to the cottage armed with several extra cans of soda to quench any thirst that might arise, a precaution inspired by the skeptics.

Physically, she felt fine. Psychologically, though, she continued to brood despite all her attempts to forget about Chris. The enigma that was Christopher Howe had gotten to her. His behavior that afternoon, the abrupt swing from gentleman to tyrant, was beyond her understanding. And its effects on her enraged her even more. Since he'd accosted her on her return to the cottage this afternoon she'd been unable to push him from mind. Worse, it seemed, in retrospect, the man had monopolized her thoughts since she'd first arrived on the island more than two weeks before. It simply wasn't fair, she cried silently! This was *her* vacation!

Gasping, she repeated the thought, then elaborated on it. Yes, this was her vacation, and it had been, for the most part, a divine experience — thanks to none other than the object of her present rantings. Chris had dominated these days much as she assumed he dominated everything else in his life. When he stood on his good behavior he was more than she could ever have imagined in a man; on bad, he was equally as devastating. It simply wasn't fair!

The repeated blare of a horn immediately behind jolted her from her reverie. Bright headlights in the rear-view mirror, indicating a car directly on her tail, startled her. Instantly, she pulled over to let the impatient driver pass, only to be alarmed when the car pulled in front of her and forced her to stop. Her alarm, however, turned to astonishment when she recognized the man who proceeded to slam from his car and stalk toward hers, then to anger when that man exploded anew.

"I told you to stay at the villa!" The darkness hid much of his wrath, but his tone bore a definite edge of fury. "Where have you been? I've been looking all over the place for you! The least you could have done was to have left a note!"

He now stood directly by her car, his hands tautly gripping her open window, his body bent to bring his head down to her level. The Caribbean moon cast its silvered halo on the dark sheen of his hair, yet there was nothing in the least angelic about him at that moment. He was the dictator once again, and Arielle rebelled.

"The least *you* could have done," she snapped back, "was to have let me know what was going on. I sat there waiting, but you evidently had other, more important, things on your mind." Her sarcasm was thick and uncharacteristic, hiding a deeper hurt. "At least the people in Philipsburg talked with me. You know about the broken water main, don't you?"

Undaunted by her attack, he glowered. "I was on my way to tell you about it when you disappeared. I went into town looking for you but you weren't anywhere that I could see. It's pure luck that I ended up behind you now." He took a breath to say more, then let it out, slowly and with obvious control. When he failed to go on, Arielle prodded.

"Well? Are we going to get our water back or aren't we?"

He straightened, forcing her to look up at him. "Oh, we'll get it back all right, but it may not be until the morning." The worst of the anger was gone, leaving a bad-tempered growl. Arielle watched as, without another word, he stalked back to his car and reached into the back seat for something. Here in the dark he had the same animal quality that she had noticed so many other times. His coiled readiness, his sleekness, his grace of movement — all sent that old tremor of fear through her for a passing moment before her annoyance reasserted itself with his return.

"Here," he barked gruffly, crossing to her passenger door, opening it, and depositing two large plastic bottles on the seat. "Bottled water. Use it! Don't take anything from the tap until I give you the OK." Lit now by the car's overhead light, his face was a tense mask of planes and hollows, as forbidding as it had been on that first afternoon. Stifling a shudder of mourning for that softer, more gentle face she'd seen since, she gripped the steering wheel tightly.

216

"And how long will I have to wait for that?" she asked, softly but sharply.

A muscle worked along his jaw in reaction to her taunt. "You'll wait as long as you have to. I own this villa, and therefore you are my responsibility. You'll drink nothing but what's in those bottles until I say so. Is that understood?"

In place of a salute, she simply stared ahead. "Perhaps you should have provided wine, rather than bottled water!" she snipped impulsively. "At least then I might be able to drink myself into a stupor while I sit around waiting for water!"

The moment she had spoken she regretted both her words and their tone. What *was* it that Chris did to her to make her respond so waspishly? After all, it wasn't his fault that the water main had broken. . . .

He stared at her across the width of the front seat for several long moments before he slammed the door and, without another word, returned to his own car, revved the engine and took off in a cloud of dust. Unable to believe the abruptness of his departure, her eyes followed the red glow of his taillights until they disappeared from sight around a bend in the road. Looking down, she slid a hand onto one of the bottles which he'd placed on the seat beside her.

Her fingers grasped the bottle's neck, which moments earlier his fingers had held. If she sought warmth, there was none. Saddened, and with a strange sense of emptiness, she drove slowly home. Sleep was elusive that night, held at bay by the throng of memories — deep-etched and conflicting — which flooded her consciousness. She recalled the first time she had ever seen Chris when he'd been nothing more to her than a brooding presence on the airplane. She recalled his unleashed fury on the beach that first day, when he had terrified her with his accusations, his strength, his kiss. She recalled the gradually warming episodes — the encounter in Philipsburg when they had talked civilly for the first time, the subsequent occasions when they had seen each other on the beach, the time they'd spent with each other from that point on. She recalled her own loosening, the burgeoning sense of femininity which Chris had drawn from her, the well of emotion within her which attested to that awakening. And she recalled his lips, his hands, his body — which set her to trembling even at the memory. The emptiness within her had never felt as hollow as it did during those early-morning hours when she imagined what it might be like to sleep with Chris, to be lying, right then, beside him. To touch him, to trace the firm contours of his form, to explore the depths of his masculinity, to let him teach her the world of joy which her own sexuality could offer — it was overwhelming.

Furiously, she blinked away the tears that gathered beneath her lids as thoughts of that other Chris, the one filled with anger and disdain who she had seen more than once today, dampened her dream. Did he truly dislike her? It seemed so impossible, yet at times it seemed the only possible answer. Was his only interest in her physical? When she continued to hold him off, did his fury grow? There was still that other time, after dinner at his home, when *he* had been the one to walk away. What had it meant?

Try as she might, she could make no sense of the whole thing: Was it simply her own inexperience that fogged the issue? Her eyes had been open during the past five years. She'd seen affairs going on to her left and right. Women her age thought nothing of it. But *she did!* The evening with Peter Stoddard had been a lapse — a very tragic one — which had been motivated, she now understood, by her need for affection, by her yearning to be wanted, by her helpless drive toward acceptance.

Now, the more mature woman she had

become had outgrown many of those needs, while still clinging reluctantly to others. Yes, she wanted Chris to desire her, to admire her body, to cherish her femininity. She wanted to *feel* herself to be woman, to *look* like a woman, to *act* like a woman. And, with Chris, these needs had come as close to fulfillment as she had yet come in her twenty-seven years. But where did she go from here?

The night was warm, and grew warmer by the hour. Humidity thickened the air as a storm passed overhead, dumping its heavy rain on the cottage before moving on. Arielle tossed and turned, feeling worse by the minute. Throwing back the sheets, she padded to the refrigerator, absently filled a tumbler with the ice-cold lemonade she had mixed earlier that day, then returned to bed. But the ache in her middle persisted, bringing with it recurring thoughts of what she might have if only she was willing to take the first step. Jumping up again, she stomped to the window. Large droplets of rain lingered on the foliage around the cottage, made brilliant now by the return of the moon and a sky full of stars. How simple it would be to walk through the greenery, to cover that faint but distinct path from her cottage to his. Would he be in bed? Might she just slip beneath the covers with him, then gently and seductively waken him with her lips, her arms, her hands, her fingertips?

The hollow within gaped and gnawed, driving her back onto her own bed to curl into a ball of frustration. But frustration swelled into pure misery when, several hours later, she was still awake, now softly cursing the first time she had ever laid eyes on Christopher Howe.

She made her way shakily into the bathroom, took two aspirin tablets, then washed them down with a refill of lemonade. The cool flow of the drink soothed her, though the ache in her stomach persisted. Moaning softly, she returned to bed to await the aspirin's dulling effect. When it didn't come, she grew worried. In fact, the ache in her stomach had increased. Had she eaten something that disagreed with her? Had she picked up a bug or the flu? But how could that be? Paradise was not supposed to have germs, only sweet pineapples, rich coconuts, juicy mangos!

She barely made it to the bathroom in time to lose the contents of her stomach. Then, twice more within the hour, she returned on similar missions, each time feeling weaker, more drained. Her stomach was a mass of writhing pain, cramping over on itself even when it was, at last, totally empty. Dozing intermittently, she sought oblivion from the discomfort.

By dawn the shooting pain had faded to a low, dull ache, leaving a residual trembling and dizziness in its wake. It was a fleeting case of the grippe, she told herself in encouragement, turning over, then dozing again. When she awoke once more the sun was far brighter than her own outlook for the day. Though the pain and nausea had passed she was devoid of strength. It would be, she rued, a day of enforced rest.

Chilled and pale despite the growing warmth of the day and the tan she had so evenly acquired, she put on a pair of jeans and a loose sweater, then padded barefoot out onto the patio to lie on the lounge in the sun in hopes of warming up. It was there that she fell into the deep sleep that had eluded her the night before.

"Arielle! Wake up!" From faraway, his voice assailed her, dragging her back to a reality she wasn't quite sure she wanted. "Come on, Arielle! You're burning up!"

And she was. She slowly rolled over and stretched, finding herself to be drenched in sweat and feeling wretched. Chris was perched on the edge of the lounge by her hip and stared at her with open concern, his dark brows drawn together to make deep creases in his forehead, above which his hair had been recently and neatly combed.

"What is it, honey?" he asked, taking in her pallor. "Are you sick?" It was as if yesterday had never happened; he was all warmth and sincerity.

Her smile was weak, her voice a shaky whisper. "I'm all right."

"What's the matter? You were really zonked out!" Suddenly, his face darkened. "You didn't drink anything last night, did you?"

She shook her head and forced a laugh, unaware that her own anger had vanished with his. "I didn't turn a single faucet. I had a bad night, that's all." Not wishing to recall the details, she left it at that.

"You look terrible!" He lifted his hand to smooth the weight of her bangs from her forehead, now wet and warm. "You're dressed as though you had a chill. Didn't you sleep?"

Sighing, she recognized his determination. "I must have had a touch of the flu. No, I didn't sleep. Not until this morning, at least." Lifting an arm to shield her eyes from the sun, she squirmed in discomfort on the lounge, mindful both of the dull ache that lingered stubbornly in the pit of her stomach and the dampness of her clothing.

Chris caught her grimace. "I'm taking you to a doctor. There's one just down the street at Mullet —"

"No, Chris! Please! I'm all right! I feel much better now. All I need is some sleep."

With surprising gentleness, he pulled her arm from her eyes to better study her. "Are you sure you didn't drink anything other than what I gave you? I'm told that some of the islanders have gotten sick —"

Her headshake interrupted him. "The only thing that's passed my lips since I saw you last night was a glass — no, two — of lemonade, and those came from the 'fridge, not the tap."

"Lemonade?" He sat up, more alert. "When did you make it?"

Arielle frowned. "Yesterday afternoon, before the water main broke. . . . Chris, what are you doing?" His arms had slid beneath her to lift her; only her clutching fingers held her to the lounge.

"I'm taking you to the doctor. You've got to have your stomach pumped! That water was contaminated! All of the water at the end was bad! I told you not to drink *any-thing!*"

As he tightened his grip, Arielle reasoned

quickly. Not only did she feel totally out of sorts, but she was unused to this kind of attention and felt strangely embarrassed. "I don't need my stomach pumped, Chris! There's nothing left in it. Nothing!"

He looked down questioningly at her, then, as understanding dawned, slowly eased his hold. "So *that's* how you spent the night?" His drawl was laced with humor.

"There's nothing at all amusing about it! I can assure you, I'd much rather have been out all night losing my money in the casinos!" Her spirited exertion tired her. As her stomach flickered a final time, she closed her eyes, willing the discomfort away.

Chris's fingers touched, then threaded between, hers. The silence held the hint of all the sparks that had flown between them yesterday, yet they fizzled impotently in the moist late-morning air. She kept her eyes shut when his other hand tenderly brushed streaks of perspiration from her cheeks and neck, enjoying the comfort for as long as he chose to offer it. His skin felt smooth and cool, his touch a balm for all of the harsh words that had been spoken. It was only her half-dazed state, brought on by the last of the attack and a sleepless night, that prevented her from thinking more about his change of face. The moment was to be enjoyed . . . as much as her state of internal discomfort would allow.

"I still think I should take you to the doctor." He spoke softly. "You were really knocked out. If I hadn't come over when I did you might have been badly sunburned. I tried your phone, but there was no answer."

His voice held a concern that touched her. Squeezing his fingers in a feeble gesture of strength, she opened her eyes and looked up into the dark depths of his. This was another side of Christopher Howe, this worried, protective side. It was very pleasing. "I suppose I should have stayed in bed, but I don't think I expected to sleep this soundly, even though I didn't get any sleep last night. I never even *heard* the phone." Perspiration had begun to bead on her upper lip, and she felt distinctly grubby. Nudging him with her knee, she managed to struggle into a seated position. Her fingers plucked at the folds of her sweater, pulling the warm wool from her hot skin.

"I've got to go change," she murmured, pushing herself up and starting across the patio, uncaring of her disheveled appearance. The only thing on her mind at that particular moment was a nice, long, cool shower. Suddenly she stopped in her tracks, realizing the dilemma, and turned. "Oh, no," she moaned softly, lifting a hand to push her hair from her warm cheeks. "There isn't any water." Her eyes sought Chris's in dismay.

"That's why I was trying to reach you in the first place," he responded immediately, standing up and quickly coming to her side. He snaked his fingers through the tangle of hair at the back of her neck, momentarily relieving the moist skin of its heavy and hot weight. "The water should be back on by this afternoon — that's the latest estimate." His disgust with the situation came through clearly. "But I've taken a room for us over at Mullet Bay. They've got their own water supply. I've just had a shower there; if you want, I can take you over now." This was Christopher Howe at his most solicitous; if Arielle hadn't felt so poorly she might have been able to appreciate it. But she merely nodded.

"That would be great. I'll go get my things."

It took longer than she had expected to collect soap, shampoo, fresh clothes, comb, brush, and hair dryer, for she paused every few minutes to sit down on the bed and cope with recurring spells of queasiness.

"Can't I do this, honey?" he asked at one

point from the door, but she shook her head slowly, fighting the wave of weariness which threatened to set her on her ear there and then.

"I'll be with you in a minute," she answered softly, oblivious to the eyes that followed her slight form until she had finished gathering her things together. He stood back from the door when she passed on her way to the living room, then watched as she sank onto the sofa and rested her head against its back, eyes closed, one arm thrown across her brow. "Phew," she whispered in self-disgust. "I feel so weak. . . ."

In her spent state, she never saw him disappear into the bedroom, nor return. Suddenly he was kneeling down in front of her. "Arielle?" he called softly, as though afraid of waking her. The back of his hand grazed her cheek lightly as she opened her eyes. He held a blue-and-white checked cotton blouse that had been hanging in her closet. "Let's get that sweater off. You must be sweltering in it."

Looking down in surprise, she smiled meekly. "I thought I'd changed it already." Forcing herself to sit forward, she didn't resist when Chris's cool hands slid beneath the lower ribbing of the sweater and raised it up, past her shoulders and over her head.

That she wore no bra was inconsequential at that point. She was too weak to care, and Chris appeared too occupied with helping her on with the blouse to notice. Slowly he eased her arms in, then buttoned the buttons one by one. When he had finished he rolled the sleeves up to her elbows, then raised his hands to her cheeks.

"Better?" he asked gently.

"Ummm." Peering at him through heavy-lidded eyes, she acknowledged his comforting gesture. "But I really should be furious at you," she whispered, recalling his behavior when last she'd seen him.

Chris followed her thoughts and lowered his eyes pensively. "Are you?" Some of the old arrogance was in those words, but there were other, more enigmatic elements, as well.

Arielle only knew that she was grateful for his presence, improved temper and all. "No." She shook her head against the back of the sofa, then grinned faintly. "I can't remember being pampered like this in years. Actually, I'm not sure how I've done without you all my life." What had been offered in jest suddenly took on far greater meaning. Even amid her haze, she sat up straighter, then fell back, exhausted. Moaning softly, she closed her eyes, only to be taken into the circle of strong arms and held very, very gently.

"God, Arielle, I wish there was more I could do."

In that instant she recalled a statement he had once made about helplessness, and those people who fought it, who needed to be in control. At the time she had assumed that they were both that type. Now she wondered. For, at this moment, she had no desire to be in control. Rather, she was happy to let Chris take charge, to close her eyes and rest her head against his chest, taking comfort in his nearness.

"Ugh . . . Chris . . ." she whispered against his shirt, "I feel so grubby. . . ." Instinctively, she tried to pull away from him, but he held her tighter.

"You're not, honey. You're very . . . vulnerable . . . for a change. A man likes that sometimes." It was half what he said and half how he said it that Arielle found so soothing. At that moment, she did feel vulnerable, strangely feminine, surprisingly wanted . . . and very, very tired. Of their own volition, her arms stole around his waist and she nestled more comfortably against him. Despite the echo of an ache in her middle, this was a luxury she would not give up. With a contented sigh, she fell asleep.

When she awoke she was curled against Chris in the front seat of his car, which was stopped before a building she didn't recognize. "Wh-where are we?"

"At Mullet. Here's our room. I didn't think you'd want me to carry you in." There was laughter in his voice as his eyes noted her growing awareness.

"How did I get here?" she cried softly. "The last thing I remember, I was sleeping against . . ." A crimson flush painted small dots of color on her pale cheeks as she stopped herself, then glanced guiltily up at Chris. "You carried me?" At his self-satisfied grin, she looked away. "You should have woken me, then. I could have walked."

"What? And miss the only chance I'll get to do something noble? No way!" His voice lowered and he teased seductively, "Unless, of course, you'll let me bathe you . . . ?"

Her "Oh, Chris" was nearly lost in her effort to push herself up and across the seat to the car door. In an instant, he was there to help her out.

Not only was the room clean, modern, and equipped with lushly flowing water, but it was cool. Heavenly cool! For the first time since she'd been in St. Maarten, Arielle felt an intense appreciation of air-conditioning.

After a slow drink of cool water, a primary test of her stomach's staying power, she left Chris lounging on the bed and found solace in the bathroom, where the shower pelted her with its refreshingly cool droplets, rinsing away the worst of her stickiness. The thick shampoo lather slid from her head down her back to her legs, its richness a delight against her skin. When she stepped from the shower, disgracefully but delightfully long minutes later, she felt much better. After dressing in the fresh clothes she had brought, a pair of white shorts and a long, maroon over-blouse, she dried her hair, applied a touch of makeup to hide her pallor, and emerged from the bathroom.

Chris was sound asleep on the king-size bed, his legs crossed at the ankles, one arm bent in relaxation by his side, the other resting lightly on his waist.

The sight of him looking so peaceful caught Arielle's attention even as she felt her own fatigue growing. Barefooted, she tiptoed to the side of the bed on which he lay, staring transfixed at his features. In sleep they were firm yet gentle, commanding yet compassionate, strong yet warm. Dark lashes, whose length and fullness she had not noticed before, fell across the hollow just above his cheekbone. His skin was smooth and sun-grazed, with just the hint of a laugh line at the corners of his mouth. How nice it was to hear him laugh! She cast her mind back to those times when he'd been at ease with her, when he'd treated her to the luxury of that laugh. How rich and warm it had been! How beautiful he was!

With a shuddering sigh, she tiptoed back to the empty side of the bed, debating for just a moment before slowly easing her weight down and curling into a ball on her side, facing Chris. With her stomach finally settled, she felt reasonably comfortable as she let herself drink in the sight of him a little longer. Then, reluctantly, she closed her eyes and fell into a deep sleep.

Soft kisses on her eyelids woke her much, much later, then his touch shifted to her cheeks in gentle nips as she slowly opened her eyes. "How do you feel?" he whispered against the tip of her nose before dropping his head back to the pillow.

For a minute there was confusion in the gaze she cast at him, then understanding, as she recalled where she was and how she had come to be there. "A little better, I think," she replied honestly, unable to muster the strength to move, yet feeling more composed than she had earlier in the day. "What time is it?"

He cocked his dark head, the hair now mussed boyishly, toward his watch. "Five-thirty. We've slept away most of the afternoon. Are you hungry?"

"A little." But she didn't feel like eating. She wanted to stay here, lying on this big bed only inches away from Chris. No, she realized with a start, what she wanted even more was to lie *closer* to him, more intimately. Then she chided herself for letting her groggy state bewitch her mind.

But Chris had seen the light in her eyes moments before and would not relinquish it. His gaze fell to rest on her lips, so moist and soft and open. Slowly, he lowered his head to taste them, barely touching their outline, moving his own lips over them, then, at her gasp, letting his tongue trace their curves. Arielle felt the explosion of desire within her, astonished at its presence, trembling in its wake. With a sigh of delight she closed her eyes and opened her mouth to let her lips partake of the movement. Heady pleasure engulfed her. Instinct took over. Her tongue found its path to his and they touched, creating an electrical spark which shook them both. Instantly Chris withdrew, rolling over and off the bed with one fluid move.

Clearing his throat, he paced to the door, pausing with one hand on its knob. "Ah, food. What would you like? There's a good deli here on the Mullet Bay complex. I'll run over and pick us up something to go. What'll it be?"

Arielle slowly sat up on the edge of the bed. "Anything will be fine," she answered softly. "Not much, though. I don't think I can eat a whole lot." With the bliss of his nearness torn from her, she felt an all-pervading weakness, the legacy of her illness. Helplessly, she rolled back onto the bed and closed her eyes, blotting out Chris's look of concern and his departure moments later.

He returned with sandwiches, chowder and tea and toast. The small round table and two cushioned armchairs were their dining room furniture as they ate in companionable silence. When they had finished and Arielle sat back limply to rest, he offered her the last of the tea. At her headshake, he downed it himself. "Why don't you lie down here while I drive back home to see what the status of the water is there. You could use a little more sleep —"

"No, I can come," she interrupted, suddenly realizing that they were on the verge of sharing this hotel room for the night.

"The ride might do me good," she added quickly. "I really do feel better."

Skepticism was clearly spelled out on his features as he studied her closely. She was still pale and tired, but all her discomfort seemed to have passed. "Are you sure?" At her nod he moved to gather her things together.

On their return to his place they were greeted by a large, hand-scrawled sign on his front door. "Water on, boss. All fixed," it read with native humor. Chris smiled broadly. "Old Ramoa and his wife have been around, it seems." Arielle had learned that the native couple cared for the villas during Chris's absences; it had been the old man's wife who had stocked the kitchen for her before she'd arrived.

She joined him in a grin. "They are a find! You're lucky to have them to keep an eye on things down here." Then, to her chagrin, a wave of weakness returned. "I'd better be getting back to my place," she offered softly, turning to retrieve her things from the car.

"Arielle?" He didn't touch her, but she stopped short and waited. "I'd like you to stay here for the night. You're still feeling very weak, and I'd like you to know that I'm here if you need me. It all *has* to be very innocent, doesn't it? After all, you have been ill."

Good sense was a vital part of Arielle's character, and in this instance what Chris suggested did make good sense — not to mention the fact that her legs felt too weak to even begin the short trek through the tropical growth. Her eye caught his as she turned and spoke softly. "Yes, it does. But . . ." Faintness surrounded her suddenly. "I really do have to lie down . . . quickly. . . ." Chris caught her up in his arms as her knees buckled, carrying her through the house to his big bed, drawing the covers back with one hand, then laying her atop the sheets with infinite care. She was asleep within a few minutes.

The night passed with Arielle dead to the world. She was ignorant of Chris's worried frown, of his second thoughts about taking her to see the doctor. Her tea and toast had stayed where it belonged; he assumed that the morning would see an improvement in her condition. She slept soundly, wearing nothing but the robe which he had carefully wrapped around her after he'd undressed her in an effort to add to her comfort.

She was unaware of the long hours that he sat and stared at her sleeping form. She was unaware of the war of emotions that raged within him. She was unaware of the fear he felt, this big master of a man, as he realized the strength and nature of his own feelings for this lovely waif of a woman. By the time she woke up the next morning he had fallen asleep beside her, his arm thrown protectively across her body, his face buried in her raven-black hair.

It was so natural to awaken this way, she mused with a smile and a feline stretch, as she looked at Chris gratefully. His eyes were suddenly wide open, their black depths unfathomable, though gentle. When his lips curved in a smile, hers mirrored it.

"Hi," he drawled deeply.

"Hi, yourself," she responded lightly, fearful of making too much of the fact that she had just — albeit innocently — spent the night with a man.

"How do you feel?"

"Great!" The clarity of her blue eyes attested to that, as did the return of color to her cheeks.

"Can I get you some breakfast?" His gaze drank in her renewed good health and his pleasure was reflected in his voice.

She noted the shadow of his beard, then reached out impulsively to feel its roughness. "That sounds good," she hummed softly, then yelped when his teeth closed on the finger that had wandered so boldly.

Without another word, he bounded away from her and off the bed.

Arielle was to look on these two days, the one when she'd been so ill and the next, when Chris insisted on doting on her, as nearly perfect. Despite her protest, that second day, that she was feeling practically normal, she was treated like a princess. Her every wish was anticipated and met with a pride on Chris's part that endeared him to her all the more. Both breakfast and lunch were served in bed — his bed — though, to her open amusement, Chris ate more than she from the tray he had so gallantly prepared. When she wandered out to the patio he quickly moved the lounge chair into the shade for her. When she fell asleep there, he guarded her indulgently. As guilty as she felt, in light of her markedly improved state, she savored his attention.

By late afternoon she felt much stronger and, finding Chris in the living room studying some papers, helped herself to the *Daybooks of Edward Weston,* nestled into a comfortable chair, and began to read. Two hours later her eyes finally lifted from the pages — and met the ones that had been studying her for a large part of that time.

"*Are* you like Weston, Chris?" she asked

softly, astonished by what she had read, eager to know Chris's inner feelings at that moment.

His lengthy frame was folded casually into a chair on the opposite side of the room, his face in the shadow of a rhododendron growing just beyond the window. His voice floated smoothly to her. "Weston was a genius, a true artist. He was one of the master photographers of our time. In that sense, I'm a long way from him," he answered with more modesty than Arielle felt was necessary.

"Chris, your work is magnificent and every bit as innovative in this day and age as Weston's was in the early 1900s."

He shrugged. "I don't know about that. But I do identify with many of Weston's ideas." Deep in thought now, he frowned and looked down.

"Such as . . . ?" she prodded, fearful of losing him to his reveries.

His dark head lifted to face her, his intensity reaching her from across the room. "Such as the conflict between commercialism and art. One part of me would like to retire now, to photograph only what I want to photograph. There's something almost base about the lavishly orchestrated shooting sessions I live through most of the year.

It seems so far from art. . . ." Bitterness was noticeably absent from his voice, though sadness was not. She was strangely touched.

"But the end results — aren't they worth it? Your work, as the public sees it, in magazines, on covers, in museums, is recognized by the best as *being* the best. There must be satisfaction in that."

Even before he answered, she knew what he would say. After all, the clues had been before her in the pages she had finished turning. "It's a surface satisfaction, Arielle." He spoke softly, then stood and slowly walked to where she sat. Her head tilted back to hold his gaze, which was filled with confusion. "It pays the bills and butters the bread and earns the praise of critics, for what that's worth. But underneath, that's another story."

Arielle's every instinct urged her to comfort him, to help ease the look of pain which was etched so clearly on his face. But something held her back, and she dropped her gaze. The book lay on her lap, opened now to a magnificent photograph of the woman with whom Weston had lived for many years. It was a portrait of emotion, a symphony of form and feelings, a nude to surpass all others in beauty and sensitivity. Suddenly Arielle knew what Chris wanted, and it frightened her.

His keen gaze pierced into her mind. He hunkered down to her level, his large hands on the arms of her chair, his eyes compelling her to look at him. Timidly, she acquiesced.

"What I really want," he spoke in a near-whisper, deep and low and from the very depths of his being, "is to take photographs that speak to *me* and to me alone. There don't have to be many, just a few here and there. But I want that inner satisfaction, that sense of being true to my own vision for a change." He paused, searching for a hint of her feelings, before continuing slowly. "The pictures I've made of you over the last two weeks have brought me closer to that ideal than I've ever been before. The pictures I took the other morning" — he hesitated long enough to catch the flush on her cheeks — "have meaning and feeling. I was able to capture a person, a heart, a mind. Those photographs did more than just isolate a moment in time; they immortalized a being — you — and the essence of womanhood."

Arielle was deeply affected by the sincerity of his words and the sentiment behind them, and her eyes filled with tears. In that instant, she knew. He had said it himself; he had captured "a person, a heart, a mind." Yes, in that instant, she knew. What she had so steadfastly avoided recognizing in the past few days was, indeed, a fact. She was in love with Chris! Deeply and thoroughly in love! A searing pain rocked her body. She was in love with a man whose only love was for photography, an ideal, an essence. How could she compete with that?

"I've upset you." It was a statement, spoken in the velvet-smooth voice she knew that she would remember forever. His thumbs brushed away the few tears that had escaped before she was able to blink them back.

Yes, he had upset her, but in a way totally different from that which he supposed. "No, I'm fine," she lied, smiling. "It's just that what you said was very . . . beautiful." Indeed it was. Given the fact that Chris couldn't love *her,* his heartfelt devotion to an artistic ideal of which she was now a part was as close as she might ever come to having a place in his heart.

"Do you understand what I'm saying?" he asked, a driving need underlying the gentleness of his question.

Her dark head bobbed in the affirmative as her eyes dropped to the fingers clenched in her lap. "I think so."

Silence hung between them, the last barrier before he tore it, too, down. "Will you be my model, Arielle? There's so much I want to do and so little chance to do it right. We're perfect together. The rapport is there. Please give me this chance to prove something to myself."

Two things became very clear to Arielle in that instant. First, she realized that Chris saw her as a photographic tool and nothing more, save perhaps a warm body beside him in bed, fulfilling his masculine needs as well as his artistic ones. Second, she understood that he wanted to photograph her nude. Both conclusions deepened the pain she felt already, the pain radiating from her heart with the newfound recognition of her love.

Emotion choked all sound from her throat as she forced herself out of the chair and away from Chris. It hurt so much to be near him, to know how much she felt and know how little of it was returned. The ocean, far beyond his window, held her gaze as she struggled to find a small measure of composure.

"Arielle?" His footsteps approached her from behind; his hands gripped her shoulders tentatively.

"I don't know, Chris. I don't know." The words fell out quickly, quietly, expressing the truth.

To her horror, he misunderstood her qualms. "I won't ever commercialize them, if that's what's worrying you. You needn't be afraid of appearing as a centerfold; it would never happen."

"I know that!" She swung to meet his gaze, offended by what he had suggested. It had never occurred to her that he would misuse the negatives, even those he had already taken which, in the wrong hands, could be very compromising. She loved him; she trusted him. She knew intuitively that he would never hurt her in that way. But there was still so much to consider. "I need time . . . to think," she whispered, dropping her chin to her chest, letting the black curtain of her hair fall forward to shield her from his demand.

To her surprise, given his previous outbursts when she had thwarted him, he remained calm, quiet, cool, and compassionate. "That's fair enough. But," he added with more sparkle, "don't wait too long. You leave a week from Sunday, don't you?"

Ten days off! Her departure was only ten days off! The reality of that hit her in the face. In ten days she would return to Rockport, leaving this man — and her heart — behind. What was she to do?

Lost in her own quandary, she missed the tension that had crept through his limbs and his features as his own attempt at lightness backfired. With only ten days left to go there was still so much to be done, so very, very much. Each day was precious and not to be wasted. Did she understand that? he wondered, deeply disturbed himself.

He hadn't seen it for a long time, yet now it was back — that lost look, that cornered look, that look of fear which spoke of her vulnerability. Could he help her to move beyond that? He had coaxed her toward liberation as a woman. He had seen a tremendous change in her. Could he lead her the rest of the way?

EIGHT

Arielle returned to her own cottage that night with plenty to ponder. The very last thing she had expected from her vacation was to fall in love. How ironic it was that, when she had harbored such a fear of the sexual side of men, it was the other, more cerebral, more emotional side which had proved the greater threat. For, had it only been a physical attraction — and she couldn't deny Chris's visceral effect on her — she might have been able to keep her distance. But his attack had been on a higher plane, merely complemented by the physical. As she looked back on it, he had handled her to perfection, reading her every mood, reacting to it in a way calculated to achieve the desired result, *his* desired result. He had opened up to her only as much as was necessary, never making more of a commitment than he cared to make, than suited his purpose.

And she adored him! She adored the way he coaxed her into a softness she hadn't known she possessed. She adored the way he brought her out of herself. She adored the way he made her feel free and beautiful, and, in turn, she adored making him happy. To give joy to him was a joy in itself, though a joy she had only begun to taste. She loved his smile, his eyes, his body. She loved the warmth of him when he came near, the strength of him when he hugged her, the fire of him when he released her passion in answer to his. In his arms, she was unafraid.

As she loved him, she ached to please him — for giving and sharing was a vital part of the love she felt. Yes, one part of her cried for submission to his request, cried for her to pleasure him, to satisfy him. The other part, however, still held — though with weakening threads — to a semblance of resistance, reminding her of what it would be like, what it was going to be like, when she returned, alone once more, to Rockport.

As before, Chris allowed her only enough leeway to give her the impression of controlling her fate as he shaped events to subtly predetermine the end result. For the next few days he was a model of chivalry, courting her without pressing her, forwarding his point of view without a hint of argument, keeping his moodiness at bay, beyond her awareness. It was, however, not far from the surface.

Arielle had, by this point, given up all pretense of working with her own prints. Her mind was far too removed from child photography to venture back for the few, far-interspersed moments that her heart would allow. When Chris called her on it, she managed to hedge.

"I thought you were supposed to be getting your own work done." He eyed her narrowly, several days after she had been sick. "Are you?"

Her guilty grin was an answer in itself, but she joked on. "And when, may I ask, do you give me the time to work?"

"You've got every night," he retorted soberly, lapsing into a moment's anger.

She ignored it, resorting to humor to skirt his mood. "Hah! You run me ragged all day, traipsing all over this island, and you expect me to work? For your information, I sleep like a baby." They both knew it was a lie, she from first-hand information, he from the dark-smudged evidence which lingered beneath her eyes. But he let it go, grabbing her hand suddenly. He always did that, she mused — changed the subject when the going got tough. In this case she was appreciative, rewarding him with a broad smile. "Hey, where are we going?"

But he wouldn't answer, merely drew her alongside him, draping his long, tanned arm over her shoulders as he led her to his car. It took them about half an hour to reach the beach he had in mind. When she eyed him warily, he finally spoke. "I want you to see something."

Curiosity filled her as he took her hand and she fell into step beside his tall form. They both wore shorts and T-shirts, Arielle's one that she had bought that day in Marigot. The dirt path was easily negotiable, taking them winding around and between dunes on the Atlantic Ocean side of the island, finally depositing them on an overlook to the south of a stretch of beach she had never seen before. Unceremoniously, he hauled her down to sit close beside him, letting her look around for herself while his eyes studied the horizon closely.

The beach was different, not as white and soft as the others had been. From where they sat, half hidden by the tall sea grasses, she could see a group of cottages, a handful of sailboats, a few sunbathers and the dark blue of the ocean on this more coarsely pebbled stretch of shore. But something was different, beautiful and different. It took long moments for her to identify the source of that difference; when she did, she gasped.

"Chris?" she half-whispered, "is it really . . . is this . . . why didn't you tell me . . . ?"

Only then did his dark head swivel slowly toward her. "I wanted you to feel what I felt." He studied her face intently. "You did, didn't you?" Uncannily, he knew of the beautiful difference she had sensed. Shyly, she nodded, then hesitantly turned her eyes back to the scene far to their left. "St. Maarten is famous for its nude beach," he explained calmly, turning to follow her gaze. "It's lovely, isn't it?"

"Yes, it is." There was a naturalness about what she saw, a sense of freedom, a raw beauty. "They aren't at all self-conscious, are they?" she asked, resting her chin on her arms which, in turn, rested across her bent knees.

"There's no reason for self-consciousness, Arielle." He was the teacher once again, patient, understanding, filled with conviction. "The human body is a thing of wonder, a very beautiful thing. Clothes are merely the trappings of society, the masks behind which we hide our inner selves. Without clothes, the true person can escape."

"Are you advocating nudism, Mr. Howe?" she quipped to cover her embarrassment.

He turned to look at her. "Not nudism in general. If I felt that way, we'd be down there with those folks, rather than up here hidden by the grasses. But I do believe that the human body is beautiful and free and very personal."

Arielle felt her pulse racing, and had the sense of strange vibrations whirring within her. Never would she have dreamed of having such a conversation, not even with someone as close to her as Sean. Oh, she certainly *had* come a long way, she told herself once more, yet she still had some inhibitions which brought an involuntary blush to her cheeks. In retaliation, she threw back a light jibe. "Are *you* modest, Chris?"

Immediately, his eyes met hers, holding them for infinitely long moments before even blinking. Then, with a deliberate slowness, he moved his hands to the buckle of his belt and began to release it. Realization of his intent brought her own hand out to cover his, clutching the belt closed. "No, don't!" she whispered, her eyes rounded in alarm. But, even as she feared seeing him without benefit of clothes, she knew that her fear was, in truth, of herself. Her fingers, as they gripped the waistband of his shorts, rubbed against the warmly textured skin of his stomach, sending shudders of excitement through her helpless body.

He felt it, too. With a groan, he took his hand from beneath hers and cupped her face, kissing her with a hunger she eagerly matched. Flames of desire exploded with a suddenness that astounded her, banked as they had been for the past few days of innocent camaraderie. Knowing now of her love for him, she was helpless to resist his sensual presence, desirous of giving him pleasure as he gave it in turn.

His lips trailed wildfire across her face as he eased her down on her back in the soft grasses whose height shut off the rest of the world from the passion which existed in this one small hollow. "God, how I need you!" he moaned hoarsely an instant before fastening his lips to hers in a kiss filled with that dire need and desperation.

"Need," he had said. Arielle heard it and felt it. Much as she rebelled against the fact that he merely needed her, she loved him too much to move. His body felt too good against hers, his arms too strong, his lips too heady. She was captivated, a willing prisoner of the steel bands which encircled her.

His hands rubbed her back, then crept

down to the hem of her T-shirt and began an exploration of her skin. Her body arched against him in intuitive response, her arms coiling around his neck with a fierceness belying her limited experience. There was a boiling, a boiling within her, a red-hot bubble threatening to explode.

When he drew back for a minute she was devastated. "Chris?" she whimpered softly, pleading with him not to leave.

"What is it, honey? Tell me what you want. I only want to please you."

She believed him. Even knowing that he didn't love her, she still believed him. He was a thoughtful, generous person. And her need was so very, very great. "I . . . I . . ." she began, unable to verbalize how much she wanted him.

But he knew. With one swift movement his jersey sailed over his head and was discarded on the ground, exposing his broad, bronzed chest to her view. She sat up, driven by the need to touch him, to memorize those muscles, that skin, the mat of hair beneath her fingers, for eternity. Patiently, he let her explore, sensing her desire as he struggled to contain his own. When he could stand no more, she sensed that, too. Pulling back, she lowered her head, took a deep breath, and reached down to pull her own T-shirt up and over her head. Her eyes held his as she released the catch of her bra and let it, too, join the pile. It was she who edged forward, she who wrapped her arms around his middle, she who sidled against him and cried out at the electrical fusion of her rounded breasts against his rough-textured chest. "I want you, Chris." The words came out clearly and spontaneously. She looked up at his face and repeated them, suddenly filled with resolve. "I want you to make love to me. Show me what it can be like. I want you so badly!" It had all been spoken in a whisper, but every word, every last syllable, was heard.

"Do you know what you're saying, Arielle? Are you sure?"

She was more sure of this than she had ever been of anything. She loved Chris and wanted him. There was so little time. If she was destined to spend the rest of her life alone, without him, she had to make the most of every minute now. Nodding, she caught her breath. "Please . . . now . . ." Her entire body trembled with desire, ached for the fulfillment that only his total possession could provide. Yet when she would have confessed her love, she could not. Her tongue was suddenly thick in her mouth, preventing speech beyond the soft sounds of pleasure which floated out as he laid her down again and lowered his firm body on top of her, pinning her thighs with his own, her hands with his. Intuition taught her movements she had never contemplated before as she struggled to get closer to him than the barrier of their shorts would allow. His lips played havoc with hers, then plundered the length of her neck to reach her breasts, where his tongue continued its sweet torment on their pebbled tips, leaving her aflame with desire when he finally stopped.

His eyes were soft, yet dark, his expression sober. "Not here, honey. Not like this. Not the first time."

Desolate with need, she held his gaze beseechingly. "Don't you want me? I thought . . ."

A wicked grin broke through his sternness as he moved his body over hers in a graphically sensuous response. "You thought right. And if I don't get away from you right now" — he rolled off her and sat up with his back toward her, his voice stern once more — "there will be no turning back. But I want it to be right, not stolen in the grasses by the sea." He turned back to her, suddenly even more intense. "Don't you see, when I make love to you it's going to be slow and leisurely. I don't want to look over my shoulder for intruders or worry that your small white bottom will get sunburned." He smiled at her blush, so incongruous in the bare-breasted woman who lay, nearly devoid of inhibition, before him. "Besides which . . ." He paused, debating, looking out to sea before speaking again, ". . . there's the matter of the photographs. You still haven't agreed to model for me."

Arielle froze at his words. *Damn him,* she seethed in a taut blend of anger and frustration. The photographs . . . always the photographs! They were his true love. But then, she had known that already, so why her anger now? As quickly as it had flared up, it died. Sitting up, she reached for her bra.

"No, don't." His hand stopped her. "Wear the T-shirt without it. I may die of desire," he smirked devilishly, "but I want you to feel it, too."

"Chris! I don't believe you!" Her exclamation was one of pure spontaneity and utter frustration. "It's 'yes' one minute and 'no' the next. You drive me wild and then you stop me cold. I should get dressed, then I shouldn't." With a soft oath, she threw her hands into the air. "I give up."

Suddenly Chris was utterly serious, swiveling on his knees to face her more fully. "Don't do that, honey. Please, anything but that. Never give up!"

Totally bewildered, Arielle managed, after long moments of paralysis, to draw on her T-shirt, tucking her bra into a corner of her pocketbook. Chris was right about one thing, she mused, even as she wondered how he knew about it. This braless feeling was new and definitely pleasant! As the car wound slowly over the now-familiar terrain, headed back toward the villa, she savored the feeling and the newness of herself — this Arielle Pasteur who had flowered on the tropical paradise of St. Maarten. Instinctively, she knew that she would never be the same. Once she was back in Rockport the outward order of her life might return to that more normal, more predictable, more steady one she had known before, but within, *within,* she was a different person and always would be.

Sensing her need to work through her thoughts, Chris dropped her at her door with a simple "See you later," then drove off. Arielle let herself into the house, poured a tall glass of soda, then wandered onto the patio and propped herself atop the stone wall that overlooked the ocean. As she had done on that very first day, as she had done nearly every day here, she breathed deeply of the balmy air, appreciating anew the warmth of the sunshine, the solace of the rhythmic flow of the waves far below. With Chris by her side, clear thought was impossible. Now that he had given her room, she took it, settling down with her thoughts in an attempt to sort them out.

That she loved Chris, that she wanted him, she knew for a fact. That he didn't love her she also knew, and the sadness of it brought tears to her eyes and a tightness to her chest. Then another sentiment reared its ugly head, one which had had no cause to appear before. Shame, guilt, mortification . . . As she replayed the events of earlier that day, their near-lovemaking in the high grass, she was engulfed by a wave of humiliation. She had begged Chris to take her, had clearly asked him to make love to her! And she would have gone through with it, even knowing the limits of his feelings for her, knowing that she would never see him again once this vacation was over. She would have gone through with it, driven on by the insatiable hunger that Christopher Howe had stirred in her — and, pathetically, her love for him.

Her stomach churning, she felt the tears

slowly trickle down her cheeks. If only she knew what to do! It seemed an impossible decision which stood before her. There were two things that Chris would demand of her before her time on the island was over. A jolt shook her as she recalled his angry words that very first afternoon, his accusation that she was but another of the women who wanted him to either photograph them . . . or bed them. Bile rose in her throat at the realization that he intended, in his own slow but sure way, to do both. Why hadn't she seen it sooner? Had she been that blinded by her growing love that she hadn't seen precisely what he wanted? And then what? When it was done, would she simply be discarded, like a torn pair of rubber gloves in his darkroom?

"No!" she cried aloud, jumping up stiffly and stumbling into the cottage. She would leave! There seemed to be no other choice. She would leave this very afternoon on the first flight off the island! The prospect of a future without Chris was bad enough, but to be used and discarded as he obviously intended to do was unthinkable! She would leave before the worst could happen.

Frantically, she tossed her suitcases on the bed, threw her clothes haphazardly into them, then headed for the bathroom and the rest of her things. One glance at herself in the mirror was enough to set her knees to shaking again. Tears streaked down her face, smudging the faint coat of mascara which she had put on to see Chris earlier. Reaching for a washcloth, she repaired the worst of the damage. The decision was made; there was no point in tears. They might come later, in the privacy of her bedroom above the studio in Rockport, but for now, there was only her packing to do and a plane to catch.

She stored her photographic equipment and prints cautiously, including the pictures Chris had taken of her that first time at his house, the prints she would always cherish, despite the pain they might evoke. They were him, they were her — a poignant symbol of so much that might have been. Sadly, she changed into a sedate skirt and blouse, gathered her things together and piled them into the car. Then, turning back, her eye fell on the cottage, now closed up once more. She would always remember it and the lovely things that had happened to her here. She would always remember. . . .

Tears flowed afresh as she swore beneath her breath, ducked into the car before she could change her mind, and bolted out of the drive and onto the main road that led to the airport. The loudest voice in her mind told her she was doing the right thing. Those smaller voices, with their chant — what about Chris? what about Chris? what about Chris? — were doggedly ignored.

It was late afternoon, and the airport was ominously quiet. There was none of the hubbub of the arrivals and departures that had characterized the small group of buildings when she had landed on the island. Determined not to get sidetracked from her intent by mindless daydreams, she pulled up before the rental office, returned her car, then shouldered her bags and entered the main terminal. It, too, was noticeably empty of the activity she would have expected to find.

Moments later, she discovered why. "I'm sorry, miss," the rather disinterested man behind the counter informed her flatly, eyeing her as though she were crazy, "there are no more flights scheduled until the morning."

"The morning?" she shrieked in a panic. "I can't wait until the morning! I've got to leave now!"

Hard gray eyes challenged her to defy him. "You can hire your own pilot if you want; he might take you to one of the other islands. But it would take just as much time as if you were to wait, just like all the others." The last had been added with a pointed edge; she felt its mark.

Wordlessly, she left the ticket counter and sank into the nearest seat. The morning . . . not another flight out until then? It couldn't be, not after all of her hard-fought-for determination! Hire a pilot? Hah! She didn't have the money or desire to do that. All she wanted was to be back in Rockport with Sean and her friends and her studio. Distraught, she began to cry again, this time slowly and silently, in confusion and heartache. She didn't even think to reach for a tissue in her bag, but sat with one arm hugging her waist, the other bent at the elbow and shading her eyes from the world. What was she going to do now? She'd returned her car, locked up the cottage, made the emotional break. To return would be pure torture.

From within the maelstrom of her thoughts she managed to hear the growl by her ear seconds before a hand clamped around her arm. "Just stand up, Arielle. You're coming with me!" When she tried to pull her arm from his grip, he tightened it painfully. "Don't yell or make a scene. You still have my photographs. I'll accuse you of theft."

"You wouldn't!" she cried softly, only then lifting her eyes to his. And she gasped in agony. For, in that instant, the three weeks of building a relationship vanished. Before her stood the same enraged primitive, though dressed quite properly now in slacks and a shirt, who had assaulted her on the beach that first day. And she knew without a doubt that he would have no qualms about turning her over to the local authorities. Never had she seen such hatred. Never had she seen such raw, barely leashed fury as she saw now on those ruggedly handsome features, in those compelling black eyes.

Panic erupted within her, sending shock waves through her system. There was no time to think, however, as the hand which nearly stemmed her circulation drew her forcibly out of her chair. The shoulder straps of her carry-on bags had remained in place as she sat. Now Chris scooped up the other bag which stood by her feet and, without lessening his grip in the least, led her toward the door.

"You're hurting me, Chris," she pleaded softly, willing her legs to carry her with as much dignity as was possible under the circumstances.

His breath was against her ear, hauntingly intimate. "I don't really give a damn at this point. And I'll hurt you even more if you don't keep still. *I'll* tell you when to talk."

Terrified, she allowed herself to be briskly escorted to his car, then slid onto the front seat at his command. Her luggage was tossed in back. Now, as she waited for him to join her, she huddled deeper into herself and into the corner nearest the door, farthest from where he would be. It was worse than she expected when his presence filled the car, however. An awesome darkness hovered about him; that same coiled readiness she had admired in his body now threatened to pounce on her and crush her. Yet he said nothing. The sound of the engine cut through the thickness of the silence, and the car moved out into the easy traffic and onward to a hell she could not fathom.

With her eyes glued to the roadway but seeing nothing, she steadfastly avoided looking at him, concentrating only on calming the knotting of her insides, on stilling the trembling of her limbs. There was no doubt as to where they were headed. When he pulled up before his villa she took a deep breath and sat back in her seat.

"Why have you brought me here?" Her voice was even and calm, as she had ordered it to be. He must never know of her weakness, her terror . . . or her love. Never!

"You'll be staying here until your scheduled flight takes off on Sunday. You'll be on *that* flight — not on any earlier!" The chill of his tone spread to her bones, sending a shiver of apprehension through her.

"I can't stay here, Chris," she protested in an attempt to reason with him. "This is your house. I won't stay here with you. In the first place, my own place is still available. In the second, I have *every* intention of being on the first flight out in the morning." What had prompted such open defiance, she could hardly guess. But the resurgence of her old, independent self brought a glimmer of hope to her taut features. It was gone as soon as Chris's anger tore into her.

"You're not going anywhere except into my house," he bellowed darkly. "Now, let's go!" Before she could argue he slid from the driver's seat, rounded the car, opened her door, and gripped her arm. Oblivious to her wince of pain, he led her through the front door, shoved her toward a chair, then returned to the car for her bags.

Arielle watched in disbelief, unable to comprehend what was happening and why. Chris found her that way when he reentered the cottage, easily carrying all of her bags under one arm, taking them directly through to one of the spare bedrooms.

"You'll be staying in there." He came back toward her and cocked his head in the direction from which he'd come. "If you want, you can go in and change." The muscle that jerked at his jaw betrayed a depth of emotion she could only imagine. "I'm going to put something on for dinner. We'll talk later."

It seemed her last chance before total surrender. "I'm not staying, Chris." She shook her head to reinforce her words. "There's absolutely no reason for me to stay —"

"We have unfinished business," he interrupted sharply.

"I don't know what you're talking about!" she protested, though her imagination suspected that she did. "And even if there was a reason for me to stay on the island until Sunday, I wouldn't stay here in your house. I won't have dinner with you and I don't want to talk. You can't keep me here against my will." She rose from her chair and faced him as firmly as she could.

For a breathstopping moment the flare of fury was so strong in his eyes that she wondered if he would hit her. Then, to her astonishment, his gaze narrowed and his features relaxed. His voice, when he spoke, held an almost silken sheen. "I would never keep you here against your will, Arielle." He pulled himself up straighter, emphasizing the differences in their heights in case she should think of trying to outrun him, then he slowly approached her, one long stride at a time. Her heart thudded against the wall of her chest, threatening to explode. She took a step back, but there was nowhere to go. His eyes held hers; she couldn't look away. "All I have to do is to kiss you," he murmured, barely a step away now, "and you would forget about running. I seem to remember those lips saying some very provocative things to me just this morning. . . ."

Her protest came in a mortified whisper made all the more poignant by the truth of his words. "No . . . please, don't . . ."

"Oh, I won't take you now, Arielle. That would be too easy." He grinned savagely. "We have plenty of time. I'd like to hear you ask me again, sweet and urgent, like before. . . ."

"You're despicable!"

"No, simply hungry. Very, very hungry. Now, would you like to change, or would you rather come into the kitchen and watch me work?" It was a question laced with smugness. Arrogance reigned in his step as he turned and walked toward the kitchen, confident that she would go nowhere.

How long she stood and stared at him, the man she loved, the man she momentarily hated, Arielle didn't know. Finally, feeling drained of all emotion and weak in the knees, she retreated to the room that was, by his designation, to be hers for the duration of her stay. It was decorated in much the way her room in the cottage had been, heavy on the blues, greens, and whites. A cry of anguish slipped softly through her lips as she crumbled onto the bed, reluctant to think, to feel, to reason. Things had come full circle with Chris. This might have been the aftermath of that first day had it not been for all of the glorious times in between. What about those? Could Chris forget them? Or had they all been part of his plan from the start?

It had happened all over again, she quietly, soulfully, told herself. This was no different from that dreadful game between Peter Stoddard and his friends. They had toyed with her for their own crude pleasure then, just as Christopher Howe was toying with her for his own unique pleasure now. How could she extricate herself from this horrifying situation? *How?*

She was no closer to discovering a solution when, sometime later, Chris walked boldly into the room. She moved reflexively to the head of the bed, leaning rigidly against it. He stopped, eyed her with strange puzzlement and a hint of disturbance, then spoke. "I've got dinner ready. Are you hungry?" His anger had waned, leaving a dispassionate tone in his voice.

She shook her head, not taking her eyes from him for a minute. If he tried to come closer, to touch her, she would kick. . . . But he did nothing, simply stared intently at her.

"You needn't be frightened, Arielle. I won't hurt you."

"You threatened —"

"I was angry! Just when I felt you had begun to trust me, you disappeared. Ran. Took off." He illustrated that last with a broad sweep of his arm, which then dropped to his side. "Why, Arielle? Why did you leave?" Just when she was prepared to detest him, to ignore anything he had to say to her, Arielle saw desperation in his eyes, a sign which confused her all the more. When he took a step forward, she cringed. "I won't hurt you," he repeated slowly, as though talking to a frightened child. "I just want to talk. I have to know. Why did you leave?"

What could she say? That she had left because she loved him and couldn't bear to humble herself further, as she knew she would if she remained in his presence? No, she couldn't possibly tell him that. Yet, knowing him as she did, he would stand here until she answered.

Her voice was an unsteady whisper, her eyes deep blue pools. "I . . . I . . . thought it best that I left." Her words were nothing more than an evasion; he knew it as well as she did.

"Why, Arielle? Tell me the truth."

The truth . . . was it always as painful as at that moment? Perhaps an offshoot of the truth would satisfy him. Grasping at straws, she spoke quietly, more surely. "I was frightened."

"Of me?"

She shook her head. "No, of me."

"You?" Disbelief coated his low reply. "What are you talking about?"

No longer able to hold his gaze, she looked down to study her fingers. "I felt that . . . after this afternoon . . . I couldn't trust myself."

The long minutes of silence that ensued were thick with anticipation. Would he understand? Would he let her alone now in her embarrassment? Or would he make her further humiliate herself with other, deeper, confessions? At least she hadn't lied. What she'd said had been the truth. For that much she could be grateful. She had not compromised herself as yet. But there were greater tests to come.

His tall form came closer as his deep voice prodded her. "What couldn't you trust yourself about?"

"You." It was a wispy murmur.

"What about me?" She was not to be let off the hook as easily as she would have liked, she realized with a pang of dread. He stood now very close to the side of the bed on which she sat, his dark clothing, jeans and a shirt, emphasizing the unfathomable puzzle he presented to her. The sound of his voice, when it came again more sharply, made her jump. "*What* about me, Arielle?"

Her eyes flew to his face in alarm, widening to take in the evidence of his anger. Then she lowered her head to her upraised knees and buried her eyes from his gaze. Her voice was muffled, though audible. "You do strange things to me, Chris. I seem to . . . lose control when you come near. It was shameless of me to beg you the way I did this afternoon. If I stay, it will only get worse." Again she had said nothing more or less than the truth. Her breathing quickened with tension as she awaited his verdict. Would he believe her?

"It's called chemical attraction." He spoke clearly and with resignation, as though he were making his own reluctant confession. "And it's not one-sided, Arielle. Do you know how hard it's been for me to keep my hands, my body, off you this long? Don't I deserve a little credit for that? You know, you can beg me as much as you want," he added, arching an eyebrow in derision, "but unless I'm a willing participant, you get nothing!"

Arielle raised her eyes for a brief moment to scowl at him. "That's crude!"

"That's a fact!" he snarled with a vehemence that made her recoil. "And it's another fact that very few women nowadays reach the age of twenty-seven with such a fear of lovemaking. What's your excuse?" A dark swatch of hair fell across his forehead as he leaned forward menacingly, placing both hands on the bed not far from her curled legs. In a gesture of self-defense, she angled sideways, away from him. "Well, what is it? Why the holdout, Arielle? Why is it so important to stay out of my bed? Why can't you just give in to it, this chemical attraction that exists between us? You may never find anything like it again!"

The cruelty of his words brought a sick feeling to her stomach. But the last . . . the last brought a return of her tears. It *was* true, though Chris had only spoken the half of it. She loved him; never would she find a love like this again! And *that* she knew for fact!

Unable to answer him, she knew only that she needed to escape. With a speed that belied the trembling of her legs, she bounded off the bed and attempted to circle Chris. His hand stopped her. "Where do you think you're going now?" he growled, his face a cold mask.

Her eyes darted toward the door of the adjoining bathroom as she whispered, "I feel sick." Something in her expression convinced him. In an instant her arm was freed and she ran on into the small room, shutting the door firmly behind her, leaning against it as she inhaled deeply and tried to calm her queasiness. It worked; within moments she felt sufficiently revived to wash her face and mouth with cold water and return to the room.

Chris stood with his back to her, staring broodingly at the tropical vista beyond, but he turned when he heard her emerge and watched her closely as she returned to the bed and lay down, facing away from him. Weak and totally drained emotionally, she closed her eyes, unable to face anything more for the moment. If Chris wanted to stand there and stare at her, she decided, let him! She was simply too numbed by all that had happened to care.

It was pure escapism, the sleep that cast its web of oblivion over her. Pure escapism . . . and delightful! There were dreams, one more pleasurable than the last. There was a surprisingly deep relaxation considering the circumstances which had brought her here. And there was a momentary warmth when the gentle stroke of a hand on her cheek brought her back to a reality that turned instantly harsh. Involuntarily, she flinched from the hand that had touched her so softly. That hand, large and strong, quickly withdrew.

"What do you want?" she whispered fearfully, her eyes losing all grogginess in the suddenness of her awakening. She wondered whether he had been there throughout her sleep, and noted that the only light in the room came from the dim lamp on the dresser. It was completely dark outside.

"You've been sleeping for several hours; it's very late. I thought you might want to get undressed; you'll be more comfortable."

"What I really want is to go back to my cottage. This is absolutely absurd! You can't treat me as some kind of captive. . . ."

He glared at her, long and hard, daring her to cower. When he finally spoke, however, it was with a surprising note of resignation. "Actually, this has turned into quite a farce."

"A farce! That's an understatement!"

"Watch yourself," he growled in warning, growing angry once more. "I'm in no mood for this."

"Then let me return to my place."

"No."

"Why not?"

"I can't."

"That's ridiculous!" She ignored his warning. "It's sitting right over there, through the bushes, waiting —"

"It's taken."

For a minute she wasn't sure she had heard him correctly. "What?"

"I said," he repeated, irritated, "it's taken."

"How can it be taken? I booked it for the month, and that carries through until Sunday. This is incredible; I was there myself only this afternoon! It can't be 'taken'!"

A flicker of what might have been sheepishness, if not guilt, passed across his face. "That's what I meant by 'farce.' After this afternoon," his gaze bore into her with meaningful intensity, "I more or less assumed that you'd choose to stay here. After

I dropped you off, I received a call from some people, vague acquaintances, who had been able to catch a plane down here several days earlier than they had originally planned. Their hotel couldn't accommodate them —"

"So you did." To her chagrin, it was all too clear. "And *my* cottage is no longer *my* cottage . . . ?"

"I'm glad you finally understand the situation," he growled sarcastically. "When I went to tell you about the rearrangement, you had already left. I went directly to the airport. My friends have long since settled in."

Arielle looked away, grasping at straws. "What about a hotel? Why can't I stay in one?"

"If my friends couldn't get a room, you never will."

"Then I'll leave early tomorrow."

"No!" Abruptly, he stood up, then forced himself to lower his voice. "You'll stay until Sunday. Now," he dismissed the issue, breathing deeply, drawing himself up straighter, "if you're hungry —"

"I'm not."

"Then I'll leave you. Good night, Arielle."

To her astonishment, he left. As she released the breath she had unconsciously held, Arielle's eyes clouded in puzzlement. Something had been different about him just then. Something very odd had been in his expression, something she had never seen there before. The anger was gone, as was the disdain. And there was neither humor nor mockery. What *was* there, then? There was warmth, quiet, and a very subdued element in him, and its cause was totally unfathomable to her. Slowly, she sat up and looked around for her bags. Her eyes flew to the closet and a quick glance inside confirmed what she had suspected. He *had* stayed here while she had slept, at least long enough to unpack her things and put them neatly away. The dresser held her nightgowns and underthings. Withdrawing a pale blue cotton gown, she let her mind wander as she undressed and slipped the gown over her head, tying its ribbon in a looping bow beneath the firm swell of her breasts. Then she clicked off the light and climbed into bed.

Perhaps it was the darkness, made magical by interwoven threads of silvered moonlight. Perhaps it was the peace that lingered from the sleep she'd had. Perhaps it was simply resignation, acceptance of a situation which she was momentarily helpless to alter. In any case, she felt strangely calm herself, warmed, quiet, and subdued, much as Chris had been. Her earlier fear had mysteriously vanished, as had her resentment and indignation. It was as though there was no place else she would rather be than this spot at this time. Then she corrected herself with a sad headshake. The place she *truly* wanted to be was across the hall, in Chris's bed, in Chris's arms. Anything else was second best.

How strange it was to think that, had things gone as she had originally planned, she would right now have been back in Rockport in her own bed, safe and sound, far from the perils of the world! Safe and sound . . . and very lonely. For, while there was loneliness in this other bed of hers, there was also the knowledge that Chris was nearby, that she would see him tomorrow, that there would be five more tomorrows before she actually was alone. Several hours earlier, this knowledge had overwhelmed her. She recalled her fury when Chris had brought her back here, then forced her to stay — only much later explaining that there was, in fact, no other option, that she had no other place to sleep.

Fury was only a memory now, replaced by the solace of Chris's nearness. There would be time to pay the piper in the days to come. Indeed, she might soon wish herself safely back home. For now, however, she let the fact of his presence soothe and comfort her as she fell into a peaceful sleep.

NINE

The rich aroma of freshly brewed coffee awakened Arielle the next morning. Very slowly, her thick dark lashes fluttered up, then narrowed against the brightness of the sunlight as it poured through the screens. As she recalled the events of yesterday and their unexpectedly placid conclusion she rolled out of bed. Moments later, freshly scrubbed and wearing a simple white blouse and jeans, she ventured toward the kitchen.

Barefoot and silent, her arrival did not catch Chris's immediate attention, bent as he was on frying the bacon and eggs to perfection. For long moments she stared at him, marveling once more — as she would do every morning, if given the chance — at his height, his power, his lean muscularity, his enigmatic darkness. But the face that finally turned toward her was anything but dark. Rather, it shone with a sense of satisfaction, subdued but undeniable.

"How did you sleep?" he asked softly, his gaze perusing her freshness before dropping once more to the frying pan.

"Well." The simplicity of her response was a sign of her mood. The night had done its job, as had the words which Chris had thrown at her last evening. She was tired of fighting him, his moods, her own past, her own desires. This was, after all, her vacation. From now on she would live and enjoy each moment for its own sake. Next week would bring what it would. For the first time that she could remember, Arielle released the reins and surrendered control of her life to another.

By mutual and unspoken consent there was no mention of plane schedules or departures. Nor was there a rehashing of the events of the evening before. Almost in passing, Chris informed her that he had arranged for his friends to pass her calls along and that any mail she received would be delivered here.

From Arielle's point of view it all seemed perfectly natural. It was like playing house, pretending what it might be like to be Chris's wife, and she adapted to it easily. Though his outward behavior was very proper and markedly controlled, he reestablished an attitude of warmth and caring to accompany the sense of quiet companionship which characterized their relationship.

Had she tried to stop and analyze what had evolved between them she would have been stymied. But she was content to accept this very pleasant coexistence blindly. Chris made no move to approach her sexually, for which she appreciated him all the more. And, despite her constant awareness of him as a man, she managed to keep her own desires in check.

The next few days passed in idyllic harmony, exactly as Arielle had originally planned for her vacation. There was the sun and the beach, the surf and true relaxation. There was good food — some to her credit, some to his, some to the chefs of the various restaurants they visited. Under Chris's urging she labored over her prints, brooding, examining, shifting them around in order, pensively pacing the floor around them. Her search was for a pattern, a thread, a germ of a theme, yet it continued to elude her. If Chris had his suggestions, he kept them to himself. He studied the prints, though his appreciation of them was on a very different level. He made no comment, applied no pressure, when each day she returned them to their portfolio in defeat. Yet he always had some new adventure to lead her on immediately after, allowing her no time to be discouraged.

On Wednesday Chris bounded in from an afternoon's absence with an enthusiastic announcement. "I just came from Marigot. We have reservations at La Nadaillac for eight-thirty. It's one of the finest restaurants on the island, so I hope you're hungry." His teasing was accompanied by a devastatingly roguish grin. She couldn't deny its force.

"I will be. But . . . La Nadaillac. Isn't that very dressy?"

He shrugged. "Not really. I bought you something, though, just in case."

"You *bought* me something?" she burst out in disbelief. "Is that how you let off steam — making dinner reservations, buying things for women? I don't know. . . ." With mock concern for his sanity, she shook her head. Then she sobered. "I can't take gifts from you, Chris. You've already bought me that bikini." *Not to mention all the other things you've given me,* she added silently, thinking foremost of her new awareness of herself as a woman.

The barest hint of worry in his tone alerted her instantly. "Don't say anything until you've seen it, Arielle. You may not even *want* it!" Doubting that that could possibly be the case, she looked around for a dress box. What she saw, instead, was a small bag resting atop the living room end table.

"There?" she asked as she raised her eyebrows in speculation.

"Take a look."

As she walked past him toward the bag, he swiveled to lean against the door frame, following her progress with controlled anticipation. Her breathy cry of delight brought a relieved smile to his face.

"Do you like it?"

"Oh, Chris, it's beautiful! I've seen *pareus* in the stores, but I never imagined myself wearing one." Suddenly disturbed, she tore her attention from the green-and-blue-shaded piece of silk in her hand to the silky black eyes across the room. "I can't wear this, Chris! I don't have the kind of figure —"

"Arielle!" he barked, then instantly gentled as he approached her. "Haven't you learned *anything* in the month you've been here? Didn't that bikini teach you anything? Hasn't my work taught you anything?" He shook his head in exasperation. "If you don't know by now —"

"Oh, I know, Chris," she interrupted softly, looking down at the exquisite fabric once more by way of escape from the sharp-

285

ness of his gaze. "But it's one thing to 'know,' another to feel and believe. It just kind of . . . comes and goes . . ." Her words trailed off in a wave of embarrassment.

"Well, it's coming now. Do you know how to wear that thing?"

"I don't think so." Impishly, she crinkled up her nose, drawing a deep laugh from the depths of his throat.

"Well, between the two of us, we should be able to get it to stay up!"

As she showered and carefully applied her makeup, Arielle marveled at Chris's improved temperament. This was how she loved him. No, she corrected herself soundly, she loved him *any* way. This way was simply . . . less painful.

By the time she had finished using her small traveling hair dryer, her raven tresses shimmered with every move of her head. A second application of mascara and an additional touch of eyeliner gave her eyes the look of brilliant delft-work framed in soft charcoal. What with blusher and lipstick and the natural bronzed sheen she had built up over her days in the sun, her image was one of health, youth, vitality, and . . . yes, beauty. As she stood before the bathroom mirror she let the robe slip from her shoulders, leaving her dressed in nothing but the silken panties she would wear beneath the *pareu*. Pleased with what she saw, yet uncomfortable with her narcissism, she returned to the bedroom . . . to find Chris waiting there, lounging casually in the armchair. A purely reflexive move brought her hands up to cross over her breasts. Even the knowledge that Chris had seen her in as little before did not ease the modesty she felt. Posing for his camera in the near-nude was one thing — parading around that way was another. Perhaps if she were married to the man . . . Her breath caught at the unwanted intrusion of what-ifs into her thoughts. She was *not* married to him, would *never* be married to him. It did no good to entertain that preposterous notion even in passing.

"Do you need my help?" he asked gently, sensing her disturbance without quite understanding its cause.

"Ah . . . I . . . I may . . ." she stammered in embarrassment, snapping back to the problem at hand and reaching for the *pareu*. As it happened, the moments she had spent one afternoon in Marigot watching a saleswoman demonstrating the correct method of wrapping and securing the silk stood her in good stead. Before her own audience, no less, she repeated the process, step by step, until she stood back with a grin of satisfaction to invite his reaction.

He gave out a smooth wolf whistle seconds before he uncoiled his frame from the chair and covered the small distance which separated them. With his hands resting lightly on her bare shoulders, he smiled broadly. "It looks fantastic!" His dark eyes were as bright, at that moment, as she had ever seen them, his features as uncompromisingly open. It was a delight more heady than the nearness of him, though that had already set her pulse to racing.

Stepping back, she let her eyes wander leisurely over his own attire for the first time, now that she was suitably — if negligibly — covered. He wore tan-colored pants of a linen material, stylishly and subtly pleated in front, but cut loosely to cover his lean hips and muscled legs to perfection. His shirt was of a dark blue silk, tailored and crisp, open to the midpoint of his chest. He looked clean and fresh and smelled of man and aftershave, a devastating combination in Arielle's very biased judgment. "*You* look fantastic!" she exclaimed in return, offering the compliment with a lack of restraint and an open admiration.

"I thank you, miss." He dipped his head in smooth acknowledgment, then promptly took her arm. "Are we ready to go?"

"Ah," she hesitated, looking around the room quickly, "just a minute." At the closet she stepped into a pair of high-heeled sandals and withdrew a lightweight shawl, one whose style went with her skirts and pants as well as with this dressier *pareu,* and which might come in handy should the evening chill, as it had, on occasion, done. "*Now* we're ready to go!" she exclaimed with a smile, taking the arm that was gallantly offered and letting Chris lead her where he would.

Dinner at La Nadaillac was the most elegant meal she'd eaten on the island. The atmosphere was as French as the food, and both were superb. The small table which she shared with Chris overlooked the harbor of Marigot, smaller and less commercial than that of Philipsburg, with the air of a Nice or a Cannes. The owner was French, as were the waiters, whose attempts to converse in English were fast overridden by Chris, who managed quite beautifully in their native tongue. Not only was the duck she ate cooked and crisped to perfection in its orange sauce, but the accompanying vegetables were served in arrangements such as she had never seen before. Fresh green beans, firm and sliced on the bias, were offered in a miniature basket on her plate, a basket — she was soon to discover — made of slivered potatoes. A salad of tomato and watercress added color to the dish, with delicately scalloped peach slices garnishing the duck. Chris was just as pleased with his veal Parisiene, offering her samples from his own fork with an intimacy which warmed her as much as the wine which they sipped very, very slowly.

Following the meal they walked, arm in arm, down quiet streets now stripped of tourists and natives alike. "Where have they all gone?" she asked, tilting her head up toward the squared-off strength of his jaw.

"Oh, I suppose the natives are asleep. Tomorrow is a working day for them, as usual. And as for the tourists, most of the restaurants are closing. That leaves only the casinos." The darkness hid his expression from her. "You haven't been to a casino yet, have you?" She shook her head against his shoulder, enjoying its sinewed protection. "Are you sorry?"

"No. I don't gamble."

"At all?"

"Nope! I'm a very staid and proper woman. Very conservative."

His growl was deep against the bangs of her forehead. "You don't look very staid and proper in that *pareu*. It doesn't leave a hell of a lot to the imagination."

"Is that a complaint?" she teased him back, feeling deliciously light-headed and very bold, neither of which feeling had anything to do with the small amount of wine to which she had quite consciously and carefully limited herself.

"Uh-uh," he denied, hugging her closer to the leanness of his lines, "just an observation." His eyes underscored that observation, warming her everywhere they touched. They walked in silence for a block before he spoke quietly and more seriously. "A penny for your thoughts?"

She smiled at the innocence of the expression, then yielded easily to its request. "I was just thinking how much I'll miss St. Maarten when I leave on Sunday. After being here a month, I feel very much at home." It was the truth, the very *general* truth. There was much more to her feelings that she could confess, if she had wished to open herself completely, which she did not. As it was, however, she was all too vulnerable.

"What is it you like best about the island?" They rounded a corner and came within sight of the car.

"Best?" she echoed, knowing that she would have to fudge the issue. "Oh, for starters, the weather is ideal. I've never done this type of thing before — you know, gone to a totally different climate for a vacation. In the winter we went skiing, in the summer we went to the beach. This is positively divine, this sun and warmth in the dead middle of the winter. I don't relish the thought of putting on boots and a parka again." The thought brought an anticipatory shudder and Chris squeezed her arm in consolation.

"What else?"

"Mmmmmm, I guess the leisure of it all would have to place pretty high. I've never lived so lazily for so long. It's kind of nice, even though I would probably be bored with it after another week or so," she lied. She knew that if Chris pushed her much further, uncomfortably personal feelings might come out, so she threw the ball back to him. "What about you? How much longer will you be staying?" They had stopped beside the car and Chris made a point of fumbling in his pants pocket for the keys.

"I have another two weeks before I'm due back in New York."

He opened the door for her and she turned, moments before sliding in, to offer, "Won't it be nice to have the whole place to yourself for a change? You can think of me, freezing my toes off back up there while you're basking in the sun down here." In her heart Arielle wanted him to refute her suggestion. She would have liked nothing more than to hear him deny how much he would enjoy the solitude. But he did not. His expression was unfathomable in the darkness, his very lack of response a statement in itself. In an effort to ease the awkwardness she slid into the car as smoothly as the snugly wrapped *pareu* would allow, then concentrated on the view of the harbor ahead while Chris slammed the door, walked to the driver's side, and joined her in the car.

They said little during the ride home. Arielle's thoughts were on her imminent departure and on how very much she wanted to do and to feel, to give and to experience before she left. A month had been a long time, yet there was so much left undone. Whether Chris's mind ran a parallel course she didn't know. When they reached the villa he seemed more aloof than he'd been in days. His anger was one thing, his charm another, but Arielle felt better able to cope with either one than with the noncommittal attitude she was faced with now.

Bathed in the light of reality once they had entered the house, she felt even more perplexed. How could she approach him? How should she do it?

"Good night, Arielle," he said quietly, crossing the living room to stand before her. He seemed strangely distant, uncharacteristically preoccupied, almost melancholy. Lifting one hand to stroke the smooth hollow of her cheek, he smiled sadly. "It was a lovely evening. Sleep well."

Arielle had barely opened her mouth to speak when he turned and left the room, heading for his bedroom and clicking the door shut behind him. Why hadn't he offered an invitation? Why hadn't he pushed his cause? Why had he done nothing, but say a bittersweet 'sleep well'? Had he rejected her once more? Or was this delaying tactic part of his plan to make her beg?

Stunned and dissatisfied, she retreated to her own room, kicking off her sandals, then padding to the window to stare blindly into the night. The knot of tension deep within her was a poignant reminder of how much she wanted Chris. The sense of emptiness which shrouded her heart told her how very much she would miss him when she returned to Rockport. Even his inexplicable retreat moments before could not alter her feelings. She could feel neither bitterness nor resentment for him, only love.

She felt herself to be on the verge of an unexpected crisis, a change in her life.

Having successfully willed the previous night's tension and frustration away, she was bent on savoring the new day when she awoke. Only the most pleasant of memories from the evening's dinner remained, leaving her feeling almost light-headed. She and Chris spent the morning on the beach, then returned to the villa at midday to clean up. Sidetracked by the sight of a large luxury yacht passing from St. Maarten to nearby St. Barth's, Arielle lingered on the patio while Chris showered. Only when he announced his intention of picking up some groceries at the market on the road to Philipsburg did she abandon her Caribbean vista.

"I won't be long," he called from the car just before setting out. After waving him off she entered the house, musing at the pleasantness of his humor and her own frame of mind. A long, hot shower washed the salt and sand from her skin. Her thick black hair squeaked between her fingers. She felt calm, relaxed, and very content as she wrapped a dry towel around her head turban-style, enfolded her body in a thick blue bath sheet and padded toward the living room. Assuming that Chris would be gone awhile longer, she dropped into the armchair in the corner, slouched down until her toweled head rested against its back, stretched her bare arms out full length over the wicker arms of the chair, and crossed her legs at the knees. It was a whimsical pose, an instant of carefree indulgence. She pretended to herself that she was the embodiment of feminine grandeur, but she sadly underestimated the time that Chris would be gone as she was lost in thought.

He found her like that, her eyes closed in an attitude of utter peace and purring contentment, when he opened the front door, his arms laden with grocery bags. Lazily, she opened an eye to identify the source of this interruption of her silent bliss, then closed it again as he passed through to unload the bundles. Her ear followed his activity, heard him open and shut the refrigerator door, rattle bottles against one another, slam a cabinet, until there was silence once more. Only then did she peek again.

Quickly, her eyes widened. Chris stood before her, tall and alert, camera in hand, photography in mind. In her state of confidence, built up steadily over the past few days, she made no move to escape him. He had photographed her before; this would be no different.

It was not . . . at first. He squatted to her level for the first few frames, moving from left to right, directing her softly. Then he moved in closer, exposing film as he moved, smoothly, calmly, intently. With the camera placed temporarily on the floor by the leg of the chair he stood and leaned toward her, removing the turban from her head, combing her damp hair with his fingers, arranging it tenderly around her face. Click. Whirr. Click. Whirr. She was the model, warm, soft, and sensuous. His whispered murmurs reflected her mood, then augmented it, evoking a sensuality from her in his uniquely powerful way. For the first time that week there was a growing headiness between them, thick in the air yet played out only for the lens of the camera.

When he reached the end of the roll he straightened, studying her softened features for long moments, then turned to reload the film. As though she had been released from an invisible wire, Arielle let her head fall back. Eyes closed once more, she felt herself relax muscles she hadn't even realized were tense. But it had been tangible, that air of awakening; it was real, much as she struggled to dismiss it. Held in abeyance all week, it had been destined to re-appear.

Her breathing had barely begun to steady when she felt the warmth of his fingers against her skin near the towel, at the point over her breast where she had tightly tucked it in. Her hand flew to cover and stop his instantly, her eyes widening as they shot to his face. There was no question as to what he wanted to do, nor was there any doubt in her mind, so far had she come in trusting him, that he would abandon the idea at her say-so. It was perhaps this knowledge that silenced her protest. The deep black abyss which drew her in grew more awesome by the minute, yet she could not pull back from it. She saw that same unfathomable element in his eyes now, strange and bewildering, bidding her to open herself to him. There was a hint of pleading, then it was gone, willed away by a man who would not resort to such tactics. And her pride matched his when, slowly and deliberately, she removed her hand and let it fall to her side.

She felt the air touch her skin as he gently pulled the towel apart and draped it softly by her hips. Her eyes never left his, follow-ing their examination of her fully revealed curves with only the slightest embarrass-ment, to which the flush on her cheeks and the quickening of her breath attested. Before she could squirm he met her gaze, leaning over the chair, bracing himself with his hands beside her elbows.

"You're not frightened, are you?" he whispered softly, his breath a sweet aphrodisiac to her tingling senses. With words a seemingly elusive commodity, she simply shook her head. His smile was gentle, his fingers, as he lifted them to her lips, even more so. "Good. Just remember that I won't hurt you. OK?" At her nod, he placed his lips where his fingers had been, tenderly coaxing hers into response, parting them softly, then backing off and lifting his camera.

It began slowly, the intermingling of quiet words of encouragement and the clicking of the camera as Chris guided her masterfully through the preliminaries. He knew what he wanted and how to get it, positioning her just so, then moving himself around before her. His fingers touched her from time to time, searing her, branding her, drawing from her the response he desired. When her dormant hesitancy erupted into her consciousness she had only to look into his face to find the reassurance she needed. For he was in his element, his eyes glittering with the pleasure of his art, his lips gentle but still in concentration. There was an eagerness in his quiet movements that told her of the joy she had, by her acquiescence, given him. The knowledge of that joy was enough to ease her past any lingering unsureness. In the eyes of Chris and his camera she was a very desirable woman; that was more than enough for the time being.

Her curious eyes followed his lithely athletic form as he lifted the sofa and carried it to the window. When he stood back to study the scene with the critical eye of the photographer she did the same, noting the gentle flow of golden sunlight as it penetrated the screen to cascade over the sofa. It was idyllic and tropical, the bright splash of color waiting only for the more neutral tones of her flesh to give it focus.

"How're you doing?" he asked softly as he returned to her and squatted down to her level.

Her answering whisper was from the heart. "I'm fine."

A rewarding smile welcomed her as she raised her arms to be lifted into the cradle of his and carried to the sofa, where he put her down very, very gently in the pose he wanted. The sun-warmed cushions cradled her back, but the rays themselves caressed her, sending a flush of pleasure pulsing steadily through her nerve ends. Helplessly content, she held the pose, then stretched and purred to the tune of the camera's rhythmically percussive beat, lost in a cocoon of warmth, floating in a sea of sensual delight. It was a vortex of passion into which she was swept, carrying her higher and higher and higher . . . and then no more. When the sound of the camera ceased she tumbled back, breathless, to the reality of awesome unfulfillment and agonized frustration.

"Now, that wasn't so bad, was it?" His voice was thick despite its teasing tone, startling Arielle. She had thought him too caught up in his photographing to be susceptible to the arousal he had himself created in her. Yet his gaze held hers, mirroring the pain she felt. Had his own supposed professional detachment been faulty?

The ache within her grew even greater with each passing minute. In spite of everything that had come before — perhaps *because* of everything that had come before — she would have gone to him willingly had he but held out his hand to her. She loved him and needed him. That was all that mattered!

But rather than offer the welcoming hand she craved he turned his back to her with a low-growled oath. "Damn it, Arielle!" His feet hit the floor with the force of his anger, one crisp explosion after the other, as he went to retrieve the towel and threw it at her with a glare. "Why do you do that?" he boomed.

"Do what?" she shuddered, clutching the towel to her, reeling in the aftermath of his abrupt emotional turnabout.

"Look at me with that very open invitation written all over your face. Damn it, I've fought to control myself for *your* sake. I can't hold off much longer. . . ." His head dipped, eyes shut tightly, in a firm bid to contain the emotion raging within him. It was with deliberate control that he finally turned to her and raised his eyes.

"Let me love you," he ordered softly.

It was the moment of truth for Arielle. Heart pounding in betrayal of last-minute fears, she looked longingly at the man she loved. Once she had sworn to herself that this would never happen again. Now she was going into it open-eyed. There was no question in her mind as to Chris's motive . . . or her own. In the end, there was no decision to be made.

Her low-whispered "yes" was barely audible, but her lips formed the word and Chris understood it.

"Are you sure? I won't have you hating me —"

"I'm sure." She was very, very sure.

There was no going back. Chris crossed the short distance that separated them, perching on the edge of the sofa, his strong arms circling her shoulders and gathering her to him. He felt her tremble and sought to reassure her. "I won't hurt you. It will be very beautiful." And then he kissed her, repeating with his lips what his words had meant to convey.

Arielle gave herself up to the power of him, holding nothing back in her response to the slow and sensual lovemaking he showed her. His lips drugged her; his hands lifted her above the realm of reality, stoking fires within that only he could feed. Her body became an instrument of rapture beneath his skilled fingers, allowing no thought in her mind but that of the ecstasy toward which he led her.

Somehow, at some unknown point, the towel fell to the floor. When Chris lifted her into his arms and carried her to his bed, her flesh burned against him. Very gently, he laid her down, pulling the blankets back so that she rested on the cool, crisp sheets. Then he stood back and drank in her nakedness. It was as though the images he had captured on film did not exist, as though he had never before seen her like this. Then she had been a model; now she was a woman.

Her body tingled with excitement and anticipation as her blue eyes followed his movements. His hands removed his belt, then moved to the zipper of his pants. When he paused, she felt a split second of panic. Would he spurn her now? Was it possible?

"Are you absolutely sure, Arielle?" he whispered, sinking down onto the bed beside her without undressing further. "I won't let you change your mind, once we get past this point. . . ."

Her answer was to lever herself up and slide her arms around his neck, drawing herself against him. The feel of his textured chest against her breasts inflamed her, bringing a cry to her lips. "Please, Chris, don't stop . . . don't ever stop. . . ." She had whispered urgently for him, as he had wanted, but was too drunk with desire to regret it. Her hand slid down his chest, over the flat plane of his middle to the line where his pants began, and her fingers inched them lower. With a sharp intake of breath Chris stood and stepped out of the pants, then his briefs, finally coming to her in raw, manly splendor. It was the first time she had seen him naked; she was mesmerized by the animal beauty of him. The thread of fear that his arousal inspired was secondary to the primal instinct which erupted within her.

As he came down to her on the bed he murmured soft words of encouragement in her ear, then began a sensual attack with his lips and his fingers, finding her secret pleasure places and making them his, preparing her for him as she had never been readied before. When she could stand no more of the sweet, sweet torment she begged him for release. One last time, he kissed her, long and deep, then left her no time to fear, consummating their union with a throbbing possession that brought a cry of ecstasy to her passion-moist lips. Even when he stilled for an awful, awe-filled moment, the beauty of ultimate fulfillment was there. Awash in the wave of his sexual mastery, she was oblivious to the tightening of his body, to the losing battle he fought, to his reluctant and inevitable capitulation to the flame that raged through him with incendiary force.

Pure instinct guided her in the art of pleasing as she stroked the flexing muscles of his back, then gripped the lean flesh at his hips and timed her thrusts to his. Together their fires soared to dizzying heights, eclipsing one another, again and again, until, at last, the explosion, the summit, the ultimate was reached. It was a moment, for all her previous imaginings, that Arielle would not have believed possible, a moment of rare and exquisite beauty to last in her memory forever.

Slowly, very slowly, they relaxed against one another and their breathing steadied. All was silent. For Arielle there were no words to express what she had felt. She could only savor the deep beat of Chris's heart, the dampness of his body now stretched to full length by her side, the weight of his hand as it rested heavily on the warmth of her stomach. His head was turned away from her, his hair thick and dark against the pillow.

And then he was gone. In one fluid motion he was off the bed and walking away. Her hand reached instinctively to cover the spot where he had lain moments before.

"Chris?"

His only response was the rustle of clothing as he got dressed. Shafts of fear, bordering on deep-seated terror, coursed through her suddenly chilled veins.

"Chris . . . ?"

Struggling to force herself into action, she managed to sit up and pull herself to the side of the bed from which he had so abruptly charged.

"What is it, Chris? Where are you going?"

But her frantic words fell into empty space, for he was gone in the instant, stalking through the hall and the living room to the front door, which banged shut with heartrending finality behind him. When she heard the sound of the car motor she curled into a ball of misery and wept, wept as she had not done since that awful, awful night so long ago when Peter Stoddard had taken her virginity and laughed.

Torrents of emotion shook her, devastating the body which had so recently been alive and glorying in love. She had known there was no future with Chris, but to be reminded so starkly of the fact, to be robbed of the afterglow of the most precious thing she had ever, in her life, experienced, was totally heartbreaking. Tears wet the pillow she hugged, until, finally, bereft, she fell into an exhausted sleep.

When she awoke the bed was as crushingly empty as it had been that afternoon. The orange-red glow which trickled across it announced the day's denouement, echoing that deadening deep within her. Unable to dwell longer on that which she could neither understand nor accept, Arielle crawled from the bed and returned to her room. It was only when she was fully dressed that she took a deep breath and dared to explore the house, looking for signs of Chris. There were none. Silence hung in the air like an ominous storm cloud, calm, still, and stiflingly heavy.

Her watch read nearly seven o'clock. Where was he? Sinking down onto the sofa, she leaned forward, burying her face against her knees. She should have known; she should have expected it. Perhaps it had been her secret hope that, by giving herself, body and soul, to him, she could stir his affection. During dinner last evening — indeed, so many times during the past weeks — he had been warm and compassionate. How could he have been so cruel as to have left her the way he had? It simply did not fit with what she wanted to believe!

But what she *wanted* to believe had little to do with reality. Chris had fancied her body — to photograph and to bed. Having had his way, there was no more he required, or desired, of her. His conquest was complete. It was as plain as that. Crude . . . blunt . . . obvious. Her vacation was over.

When she finally raised her eyes and caught sight of the pair of envelopes in a prominent spot on the coffee table, with her name printed in bold letters on the smaller, topmost one, she was only marginally interested. The discovery that Chris had exchanged her airline ticket for the first flight out in the morning did not surprise her. After all, she had been the one who had wanted to leave; now he had given her her walking papers.

As for the second envelope, the larger one, which she assumed contained prints of her, she could not find the courage even to open it, but simply tucked it in with her own prints in her brown portfolio. A state of numbness descended upon her, protecting her through the evening. Chris never returned. But then, she had doubted he would. Come morning, she blindly packed her clothes and toiletries. When a taxi appeared at the door to drive her to the airport, she wasn't even surprised; she had half-expected it. A final look around the villa was all she allowed herself as the cabbie put her bags into the trunk. But when he held the door for her, she balked.

"Just a minute," she whispered hoarsely, then ran back into the house. Grabbing the first thing she could find in her purse, the red envelope in which her airline ticket had been tucked, she scrawled her brief message, those three simple words, across it and dropped the envelope on the coffee table. Then, crying silently, she left. Within the hour she was airborne, headed back to Boston.

TEN

It was an azure cameo, simple in its beauty, beautiful in its simplicity. It was a portrait of two faces in profile, one a breath away from the other, one above and beaming down on the other's upturned gaze, one very male, the other distinctly female. It was a medley of skin tones set against a clear, azure sky. It was an image of . . . love.

"No! Oh, no!" Arielle's soulful cry pierced the silence of the bedroom where she sat huddled in misery, wrapped in her large patchwork quilt, staring at the photograph. Two days had passed since her return. This was Sunday, when life all around was quiet, particularly since Rockport was buried beneath eighteen inches of snow. This was the day she *would* have been returning from St. Maarten had it not been for the fact of one Christopher Howe, photographer extraordinaire.

It had taken her this long to fortify herself

before examining the prints Chris had left her. Now the rush of pain stabbed her as violently as it had on that first day when she'd stepped from the plane into the frigid beginnings of a Nor'easter and had indifferently splurged on a taxi to make the hazardous trip through the mounting snow to Rockport and, finally, had let herself into her studio, her apartment, her home. She had cried then, and cried some more, long after the tears should have been spent. At nightfall, when the lights of her apartment announced her return to the world, Sean discovered her, tired and heartsick and badly in need of his shoulder. He provided it with the compassion he'd always shown, hearing her long story with neither approval nor reproach, holding her tightly until she had finally quieted, only then venturing words of hope for the future.

"You'll get over it, Arielle," he told her.

But she doubted it. For the gross injustice of her love, coupled with her total lack of understanding of that final night, nagged at her relentlessly. And then, to open the envelope from Chris and find this immortalization of everything she had become during her stay in St. Maarten — her love, her folly . . . It was nearly too much to bear. Yet she could not look away. Try as she might to avert them, her eyes held to the image before her. They seemed the perfect couple, she and Chris; as captured by the eye of the camera they shared a unity of body and mind that could not be denied.

She recalled the day the picture had been taken. Chris had given her the bikini then, the silken smooth bits of fabric, now tucked safely away and out of sight. They had argued, more accurately, they had failed to communicate. He had thought, at the time, that she was purposely holding out on him, saving herself for another, for Sean, perhaps. Why hadn't she blurted out the truth? Why had their fallings-out always ended with one of them storming away from the other? Why had their reconciliations always avoided the crux of the problem? Why hadn't she screamed and yelled, as she was close to doing now? But then . . . would it have made any difference to the final outcome? Chris was a man of the world, knowing what he wanted, knowing how to get it. He had never whispered words of love, not even during that last, eventful night. He had never promised her anything — only that he would never hurt her. Physically, there was now, there had been then, no pain. It was in the emotional arena that the agony existed. Had Chris anticipated that? No, he hadn't known of her love for him; he couldn't be held at fault.

Her tear-filled eyes fell again to the image of the two of them on the beach. She wore no covering save the small bikini panty, yet it showed nothing to embarrass her. It had been taken with the self-timer, she realized now, chewing on her thumbnail as she recalled the very moment. He had kissed her; he had said he wanted a "very special" look. Was this the look, this look of love? *Impossible,* she declared vehemently! Yet why did his own features bear that soft, caring . . . yes, loving, expression? Had it been a cruel hoax on his part, a stunt for the sake of the camera?

Whatever it had been, its effect on Arielle now was devastating, reducing her to a shuddering mass of desolation. Helplessly, she studied every inch of the picture as though to find a clue to the mystery surrounding it. She traced the profiles, one flowing toward the other, her eye moving down the strong column of his neck to his tautly muscled shoulder and corded arm, which swung toward her own body and touched lightly at her back. His forearm made a sedate covering for her breasts, its deep tan and dark furring a sharp contrast to the creamy smoothness of her own clear skin. They were man and woman, night and day, dark and light — yet every element of one blended with the other in eternal harmony.

The bodies blurred more fully into one another as she began to cry again. Then, in a burst of self-disgust, she thrust the photograph back into its envelope and buried it in a pile of other prints, determined never to look at it again. When the doorbell rang it was a welcome relief. Brushing the tears from her cheeks, she let Sean in.

His cheeks were ruddy, what little of them showed above the tidy beard he wore. Snow lingered on his heavy wool jacket and the legs of his jeans, and his boots were saturated. But his smile, as ever, was warm.

"You're all shoveled out, babe." He winked, then sobered instantly. "Uh-oh, you've been at it again." His eyes did not leave her face for a moment as he stepped out of his boots.

Arielle could only muster a guilty smile. "I'm trying, Sean. Honestly I am. But it doesn't s-seem to h-help. . . ." Turning from him, she hunched her shoulders and found herself reduced to tears all over again. "I j-just don't know wh-what to d-do!"

Sean tossed his jacket on the hook at the back of the door, then came to her, pulling her around and against him. "You'll do just fine, babe. Let it all out. That's a girl!"

He was such a wonderful friend, she mused through her tears. If only she could have fallen in love with *him.* But there was nothing physical between them, nothing at all. It had been precisely this fact that had allowed them to become such close friends in the first place.

"Oh, Sean! What am I going to do? I can't concentrate, much less think about getting back to work. I can't even get myself to shovel my own walk. This is ridiculous! All I want to do is to sit here and . . . cry. . . ." For several moments more she did just that, finally drawing away and sniffling loudly. "You must think I'm foolish. . . ." Her eyes, as she raised them reluctantly to his, held the shame she felt.

Sean was quick to reassure her. "You're not foolish, babe. Just in love. Maybe they're one and the same; I'll never know. You'll get over it, though. It just takes time."

"Time . . . time . . . How much time do I have to suffer through? What do I do in the meantime?" She hugged herself protectively as she turned beseeching eyes to Sean.

"You work and go about your business, just as you did before you left. Life goes on, Arielle. You can't let this past month change all that."

"But it did change all that!" she argued softly, retreating into a corner of the window seat that overlooked the frosted white street. "*I've* changed. *He* changed me." The leisurely movement of pedestrians, their clothing bright and vivid against the snow's white monotony, caught her eye and held it as she talked as much to herself as to Sean. "I became aware of things and feelings inside me that I'd never known existed. I felt loose and free and . . . and . . ."

". . . feminine?"

Her gaze shot toward the insightful artist. "How did you know what I was thinking?"

"I know *you,* babe. I could see it right away. You *have* changed. Oh, you've always been feminine, in the most obvious sense. But now, for the first time, you seem aware of it — and confident of it. And there's a softness about you that wasn't there before. And a vulnerability, but different from the hurt you felt when I first met you five years ago." He stood by her side, looking down at her, his brotherly eyes surveying her features. "And you're still tanned . . ." he ended with a mischievous smile.

"I look horrible!" she argued, knowing how much more tanned she had looked before the pallor had set in, knowing how

317

deeply sunken her eyes had looked this very morning, knowing how . . . plain she looked in her heavy wool pullover and jeans. But Sean was right. . . . Despite her every argument, she had an inner beauty which the experience of love had brought to the surface. There was a depth to her features that had not been there before, a softness that would now be a permanent part of her.

He stroked the back of her hair in a gesture of comfort. "You don't look horrible! And you're going to feel better with each day that passes. Once the worst of the snow is plowed, you'll get back to work. That'll help."

After long moments of thought, she simply murmured, "I hope so." There was no further point to this discussion. After all, nothing she could do would alter the situation. It was a matter of learning to live with it . . . heartache and all.

Within limits, Sean's prediction proved to be true. She took some solace from her work, and she pushed herself harder than ever. Fortunately, clients had been awaiting her return. In addition, there were prints from the island to be processed and printed — a bittersweet business that she insisted on finishing herself, despite Sean's suggestion that she send them out for commercial processing. It was a test she had set for herself, one she passed, but only with numerous new onslaughts of tears.

Then there was the matter of her book, which she had so neglected during the month in St. Maarten. After a week of nonstop photographing in her studio, she laid the prints out once more, early on a Sunday morning when she could have the entire day to study them. For several hours she labored over them, staring, rearranging, pacing, then contemplating them anew. But her concentration was sadly broken by thoughts of Chris and the relationship they had built over the course of her four weeks in his company. Back and forth, from her photographs to Chris, her mind oscillated. Then, suddenly, in a meld of the two subjects, it came. In a flurry of movement, she arranged the prints a final time, then stood back and breathed a long sigh of satisfaction, knowing that, at last, she had found her theme.

It began with infancy and a total, blissful obliviousness to the world around. Her handful of prints of newborns illustrated just that self-contained existence. Then, with the prints of toddlers, came the germs of awareness, ranging from initial caution and skepticism to more open wariness and, in two notable cases, rebellion. But trust was fast to bloom as the subject grew accustomed to the camera, allowing moments of open enjoyment to penetrate the more alert veneer. Solid trust came later, exemplified in several of her favorite prints; in these instances, she had captured the *real* self of her subject, well beyond the surface impression. And, finally, there was the culmination of the relationship, with the camera disappearing completely as a tool. In this stage a oneness existed between the photographer and the subject so that something more, something even greater, existed in the photograph than, perhaps, existed even in life.

That she should make parallels between these steps and her own relationship with Chris was inevitable. From her virtual ignorance of his existence that first day to the emotional upheaval she had suffered on the beach, when a wariness had sprung up, a resistance to be worn down only gradually as the days had passed. Trust, elusive at the start, had grown slowly, culminating in the beauty of their relationship in those final days. For, regardless of Chris's apparent lack of emotional involvement, Arielle did see a beauty to what they had shared. It was something she could never have known alone, something she would always remember. It was a sense of fulfillment, of wholeness and completion that, together, they had produced. In its own way, it was sacred.

This discovery settled something within Arielle. The ache, the hollowness, the loneliness were all still there. But they were joined by a kind of acceptance of life as it was. In her heart she knew that she had experienced something that many people never did. For that, despite the resultant heartache, she was grateful. And life did go on.

Work kept her busy, as did get-togethers with friends, most of whom wanted to know, as had her family, all about the trip, most of whom, however, were too considerate to prod her to go beyond what she freely offered. That they noticed the change in her was obvious from the recurrent questions along the line of, "That trip really *did* mean a lot to you, didn't it?" and, "You seem to have found yourself, haven't you?"

Sean kept a close watch on her, making a point to pop in on her practically every day, bolstering her, encouraging her, comforting her, much as he had done when they had first met. It *was* a comfort, knowing he was there; only *he* knew the entire story.

For Arielle, as the days merged into weeks, the greatest challenge was reconciling the woman she had become with the one she had been. It took courage on her part to realize that she did not want to revert to that shy, aloof, and conservative maiden. Though she would never know Chris's love, she would always know what he had taught her. Now she knew that she had nothing to fear from any man. For she was her own woman, with a sense of strength derived from that knowledge.

Within the month she totally renovated her wardrobe in a continuation of the shopping spree she'd taken in Marigot. This time, the pavement of Boston's chic Newbury Street passed beneath the heels of her new leather boots as she made her choices. When she returned home after a full day of pounding the pavement she felt the totally modern woman, stylish and attractive and admirably slim. For the first time in her life she was truly proud of her looks. For the first time in these everyday surroundings she shed the mantle of the stay-at-home, venturing out much more — in large part to escape the myriad daydreams that assailed her — than she had ever done. Before, she had preferred the security of her own studio for shooting sessions; now she flexed her creative instincts and shot in different settings: a home, a school, a snow-packed park. Her work reflected this new maturity and her business, in turn, prospered.

It was only at night, alone in the dark, with nothing at all to divert her innermost thoughts from their cravings, that she thought of Chris. It had been a month, yet the pain of missing him was no less. He would have been back to New York and at work long since, surely having totally forgotten about the nuisance he'd found on his private beach that afternoon in St. Maarten. But forgetfulness was a luxury *she* was not to be afforded. Against her better judgment, the viewing of the azure cameo, as she had come to call it, became a nightly ritual, inevitably bringing fresh tears to her eyes and a tight knot to her throat, but just as inevitably bringing a strange kind of comfort. It was a piece of Chris, only paper and vulnerable to light and time, but a piece of him nonetheless. And it was very precious to her. If she was never to see him again, she realized, this was all she would have.

It was a Sunday morning, just over a month after her return. The first of the April showers had washed the last of the snow from her walk, and she had decided to bundle up against the wind and take a walk in the rain, a totally carefree and delightfully irresponsible way to pass an hour or two. Or three, it turned out, when she finally returned, having walked along the beach, stopped for coffee at a small shop owned by some friends, then returned along the shore road. She thought nothing of the sleek gray Porsche, its sides spattered with mud, which was parked just beyond her house. Rockport attracted any number of visitors; this was but another.

Rain dripped from the visor of her bright yellow slicker as she paused at her front door to scrape the mud from her boots. Head bent, she did not see the tall form emerge from the Porsche, stare at her for long moments, then determinedly approach. Her hand was on the doorknob when he called.

"Arielle!"

She turned and jerked her head up in time to see him bound lithely over a huge puddle in the middle of the walk. There was no question as to his identity. The darkness of that face, that commanding carriage, the sharpness of that voice — all were the same, the embodiment of the man who had monopolized her nighttime thoughts for weeks on end. That he was here, in Rockport, shocked her, rendering her limbs practically useless. In a defensive move she swung away from him, back toward the door.

"Arielle! Wait!" His voice was closer now, its firm demand a stark reminder of the anger he'd shown on more than one occasion. "Arielle?" He was behind her, tall and close, the aura of his presence affecting her deeply. The thunderous beat of her heart shook her entire body; defeated, she rested her forehead against the door.

He was not supposed to reenter her life — not after she'd finally acclimated herself to his departure! "What do you want, Chris?" she asked shakily.

"We have to talk. You have some explaining to do!"

It was the indignation in his voice that brought her head around, the intensity of his black-eyed gaze that mesmerized her instantly. "W-what?" As incomprehensible to her as his abrupt abandonment of her on that last night had been, this demand that she explain herself held her frozen in even greater puzzlement.

His dark head, its charcoal hair neatly trimmed and glistening with a smattering of raindrops, angled so he could eye the continuing precipitation, then he looked down at her hooded head once more. "Inside," he ordered, turning the doorknob for her and all but pushing her into the dry interior. His audacity was enough to revive her spirit, and to remind her of her wish that she had screamed and yelled at him when she'd been able.

With a fast-burgeoning indignation of her own she ripped off her rain gear, kicked her boots into a corner, then turned to face him, hands on hips, eyes royal blue and imperious, dark hair clinging to the deepened hollows of her cheeks.

"What are you doing here, Chris?" she boomed loudly, drawing a surprised expression to his face. "This is my home and you were not invited. The tables are turned; now *you* explain your presence or, so help me, *I* will call the cops!"

To her chagrin he smiled, recovering from his own shock long enough to drape his khaki trenchcoat over a hook to dry. He wore a natty three-piece suit of light gray flannel; it took great effort for Arielle to refrain from staring at him. When he turned to face her she took an automatic step back.

"I'm here to see you." He spoke more quietly. "There are several things I have to ask you." With the softening of his expression she saw that his leanness was more pronounced now; there were new lines by his mouth as though it had been a difficult month for him as well.

"Well . . . ?" she prodded, wishing to say as little herself as possible.

"May I sit down?" He looked over his shoulder at the comfortably worn armchair, the one she had curled in before the fireplace so many evenings during the past month. At her nod he moved smoothly and eased himself down, absently tugging at the leg of his pants as he crossed one over the other.

"Well?" She hadn't moved, wasn't sure if she could. Her knees felt rubbery, her stomach jumpy.

The dark eyes impaled her. "Won't *you* sit?"

"No."

For long and awkward moments Arielle fought the urge to squirm beneath his stare. In the end she did sit down, but only because her physical stability was seriously in doubt.

"You look tired, Arielle."

"I'm fine."

"Has everything been all right?"

"Yes."

She felt stiff and uncomfortable, much as she had felt that warm afternoon in St. Maarten when Chris had invited himself to join her for a drink. The last time she had seen him . . . She felt a crimson flush creep upward from her neck and was helpless to stop it. The last time she'd seen him had been in bed. Her eyes filled with tears and she looked down.

"Why did you come?" she whispered unsteadily. "I was doing so well . . . finally. . . ." In that moment it all flooded back. The pain, the anguish, the loneliness, the emptiness — all that might have been but would never be. Her shoulders shook as she cried softly, burying her face in her hands.

"I stayed away as long as I could." His voice came from directly before her. Without lifting her eyes she knew that he had left his chair and was kneeling in front of her. "Damn it, I didn't want to come! I wanted to forget all about you!" There was anger in his voice, and something else that bordered on desperation. Her tears slowed as she struggled to regain her composure.

"I thought you had," she whispered softly, her voice half-muffled in the moistness of her palms.

"I sure as hell tried," he growled, "but it didn't work. I've spent the past month thinking of nothing *but* you, Arielle. Please, please look at me."

At the pleading in his voice she raised her eyes. In that instant every ounce of her love reawakened and responded to the face before her. It was the same face she had looked at in profile for so many nights running — the face in the azure cameo. His hands rested on the arms of her chair, though he was careful not to touch her. His eyes were on a level with hers as his gaze delved into her.

"Tell me why you came to St. Maarten. . . . Tell me again."

"But I —" she started to protest, only to be interrupted.

"I know, but bear with me. After we've had all this out, I will leave very calmly and quietly, if that's what you want. But first, please answer me."

As he spoke she longed to reach out and touch his lips. Instead, she clutched her hands into fists in her lap. "I went to St. Maarten on vacation. That's all. I had some work to do there, some prints to organize into a book — which I never did get to until after I returned here." She added that last with a note of mild accusation, bringing a quirk to the corner of his mouth.

He kept his voice low and even as he continued the inquisition, the point of which continued to escape her. "Had you known beforehand that I lived in the villa, that I owned both cottages?"

"No."

"Were you at all . . . pleased . . . to discover my identity?"

"No!" The blue of her eyes flared wildly. "I didn't want *any* part of you. You may be a brilliant photographer, but I thought you were an absolute animal. . . ." Her outburst took even herself off guard. Quickly, she stifled the other words she might have added.

She watched his tall form as he straightened to its full height and crossed the room, head bent in thought. She simply could not imagine why he was here; after all, she had, in his words, been "bedded in the line of duty," then sent away dispassionately. What more could he want of her? He had taken his photographs and seized his sexual gratification. Or had the latter merely whetted his appetite? Apprehension surged through her, only to be aggravated by the ensuing line of his questioning.

"Who is Sean?"

"A friend."

"Damn it, Arielle!" he boomed suddenly. "You evade that issue every time I raise it. Exactly what is the nature of your relationship with him?" The rigidity of his body was so totally uncharacteristic that her own tension grew.

"He's a friend. What more can I say?"

"Do you sleep with him?"

"No!"

His eyes narrowed in accusation. "You've never denied that before."

"You've never asked as bluntly," she rallied, chin up, refusing to take the blame for his misconception. "I didn't feel, at the time you asked, that I had to go into deep explanation. He was — is — a friend. I don't know how I might have made it through these past . . ." As the gist of the confession she'd nearly made came to her she gritted her teeth together. Chris's gaze sharpened for an instant, then shifted to scan the room, taking in for the first time the homey atmosphere in which she lived. Arielle's gaze followed his, seeing as if for the first time the long white drapes at the front window, the Scandinavian-style rug on the floor, the numerous pieces of art, each done by one friend or another, that graced the plain white walls. When he looked back at her she glanced away, knowing instinctively that the worst was yet to come. Throughout her anguish two things had hovered at the back of her mind, both of which she had staunchly ignored. Now she could do so no longer. His eyes pierced her soul as he spoke in a low, tightly controlled growl.

"You weren't a virgin, Arielle. Despite everything you had led me to believe, you weren't a virgin. The fear, that little lost animal look, the hesitancy early on about lovemaking, your modesty . . . What was that all about?" His voice had gradually risen in pitch. So that *was* what had bothered him so terribly, the fact that he hadn't been the first. It was hurtful, though not surprising. But her attention was quickly snared as he went on.

"I worked with you so slowly and watched you bloom. From a frightened rabbit to a self-assured woman — you were really something!" He shook his head, amazed anew at the metamorphosis he had seen. "Then I felt so guilty at pushing you as far as I had. When I thought you were running out on me, I couldn't bear it! I *needed* you with me, regardless of your motives. I needed more time to make you love me. So," his voice slowed, "I forced you to stay."

He spent several moments pacing to the window, then back. Arielle could only watch and wait, unable to imagine what would come next. When he turned to her, there was pain in his gaze. "I *used* my camera —

I *used* it — to do what I didn't dare do myself. I was disgusted with myself for the lust I felt — and I was afraid to recognize all those deeper feelings which were turning me inside out — and I could do nothing to change it. I held off and held off, storming away from you time and again when I felt myself on the verge of losing control. Damn it," he seethed loudly, "all *that,* and you weren't even a virgin!"

For weeks she had refused to admit that this fact might have deeply affected him; now Arielle reacted with a violence she hadn't known she possessed. Jumping up from her chair, she stormed toward him, furious and hurt all over again. "No, I *wasn't* a virgin!" she screamed, her breath coming in short gasps, her chest rising and falling rapidly. "And would you like to know why? *Would you?*" In her turmoil, there was no longer any reason for the secret. "Because when I was a senior in college a group of fraternity brothers — there were four of them in all — decided to put the finishing touches to their season of merriment by deflowering the most improbable victim around. Me! The wallflower! The plump little girl everyone liked but no one dated!" Her eyes clouded with remembered anguish. "Oh, *he* dated me, all right! His name was

Peter Stoddard." She sneered venomously at the sound, then stiffened, took several deep breaths, and continued more quietly, all the while fighting the tears which had gathered behind her lids and now began to trickle slowly down her cheeks.

"His name was Peter Stoddard and he was a Very Big Man on Campus." She drawled the phrase out derisively. "When he first asked me out, I was too excited to question his motives. It was enough that someone saw me as a female." She paused, looked down, and turned away from Chris. As though it had been yesterday, the humiliation burned into her hotly. "He took me out three, maybe four times, each time coaxing me a little further. I wanted to be with him, to do what all the other girls talked so much about. I wanted them to respect me, too. When he asked me up to his room to study, I had an idea what would happen. A rough idea." The gaze she turned on Chris was hard and cutting. Wrapped up as she was in her tale, she was ignorant of the stunned look on his face, of the clenching of his own fists as he recalled his own college acquaintances and guessed the end of the story.

"Nothing could have prepared me for what he did. It was as though" — she stared blankly at Chris, seeing Peter — "once he had me in his room he didn't have to pretend anymore. He didn't even kiss me . . . just . . . just . . ." Choking on the words, she reached behind her for the chair and fell into it, hugging her knees to her chest in the only pose of comfort she knew.

"He raped you." It was a statement, loud and clear. But Arielle shook her head.

"No, Chris. It wasn't rape. That was the worst of it — almost. I didn't fight him. Maybe I thought that was how it was supposed to be. Maybe I was afraid to fight him for fear the pain would be even worse." Her voice lowered in shame. "Maybe I wanted him to make love to me, regardless, so that I'd be like the others."

"And what *was* the worst of it, as you put it?" If she had expected sympathy he offered none at the moment, his sole intent to hear the gruesome story out.

It took her much longer to speak this time. Suddenly purged of her anger, she was likewise totally drained of strength. Her breath came in loud gasps as her eyes filled again. "When he was . . . done . . . he was . . . diplomatic. He left the room . . . without saying a word . . . and saved his cheers for the hall. I . . . had to . . . lie there and listen as he . . . collected the congratulations of his friends . . . and the money they had . . . bet against his success."

Silence filled the room, broken only by her lingering sobs. But there was more to say; now that she had begun, she intended to finish. Slowly, and with conviction, she lifted her flooded gaze to Chris's sober face. "I would have liked to have been a virgin for you, Chris," she said softly and simply, filled with heartfelt regret. "You taught me so much. When I was in St. Maarten, with you, I felt like a whole person, a woman, a being of such value. You made me feel warm and enchanting, intelligent and beautiful. I had never felt that way before in my entire life. You did something to me, for me, that no man had ever been able to do."

Her voice died in her throat as she watched Chris move to where she sat. Once again he squatted before her, his expression almost beseeching. He lifted a strong hand to touch her cheek, then dropped it slowly and spoke deeply. "Didn't you know that I loved you?"

Arielle's heart skipped a beat. Her eyes widened in disbelief as she stared at him. Was this another aspect of his joke? Certain that she had heard him wrong, she started to shake her head, then stopped when she saw the torment on his face. He was no brooder now; nor was he arrogant, self-centered, egotistical, stubborn, or crass. Rather, he was open and as vulnerable as she was. A spark of hope flared deep within her heart. Struggling to keep it there, she sat dead still, waiting for the confirmation of what he had so simply expressed.

"God, Arielle, I love you. I've tried to escape it for the past month. But I can't." He paused to reach into the inside pocket of his jacket, not taking his eyes from hers for an instant. When his fingers unfolded the torn piece of red paper, she knew that that last-minute thought — that impulsive expression of the truth — would prove to be her salvation. "I might have been able to get over you if I hadn't found this. But if there was hope . . ." His eyes asked the question his voice could not.

Very slowly, happiness bubbled from deep within, bringing a smile to Arielle's lips. She whispered softly, "I wrote it, and I meant it, Chris. I do love you." There was a sparkle in her eyes that had been absent since that last afternoon on the island.

The movement was a slow one, neither was quite sure how much of the miracle to believe. Arielle raised her hands to touch him, to caress his face, then circle his neck as his hands slid behind her back to draw her against him. From there the embrace grew deeper until she cried out at the beauty of its force. "I love you so much, Chris. Don't ever leave me again!"

His lips stilled hers with a gentleness that belied the hunger raging within him. But the hunger was hers as well, and was not to be sated with a kiss alone. Both knew that; both fought it. There was still so much more to be said.

"I'm sorry, Arielle. If only I'd stayed and confronted you then, this past month of misery might never have been. I was hurt. You see" — he shifted onto the chair, deftly lifting her slender form and drawing her onto his lap, then soundly enfolding her in his arms — "I was sure that you were like the rest. I thought you had tricked me. The fact that you weren't a virgin merely convinced me that I had been betrayed again. God," he bit out in self-disgust, "I was so wrong!"

He buried his face in her hair as he pressed her cheek to his heart. She clung to him as vehemently as he did to her, breathing in his manly scent, feeling herself finally at home and content. "I love you," she whispered, then launched her own confession. "If only I'd trusted you enough to tell you the truth. But I kept remembering the pain and humiliation of my only other experience with a man. I was convinced that you had used me, that you wanted nothing more than some pictures and a night in bed."

"I want a hell of a lot more than that," he growled, playful for the first time as he tugged at her hair to tip her face back to his. "I want you *and* that body of yours — every day and every night for the rest of our lives. I want you to marry me, to be with me, to work with me and play with me, to have our children and grow old with me. Does that sound terribly selfish?"

In response, she lifted her hands to frame his face, her fingertips reveling in the roughness of his jaw. "It sounds like heaven to me," she murmured, mere seconds before she drew his lips to hers and repeated the sentiment in a different form. When finally she let him go, they were both breathless.

"Is that a working fireplace?" he asked huskily against her ear, puzzling her with the seeming irrelevancy of the question.

"Uh-huh. Why?"

"I'd like to make love to you before a fire." His tongue traced the outline of her ear, sending a tremor through her. "I want to see a warm glow on every inch of your body." His eyes caressed her; his grin sent shivers of excitement from limb to limb even before his hands began to reacquaint themselves with her curves.

Her blush of pleasure was hidden against the broad column of his throat. "The fireplace works," she told him coyly, "but I don't need its help to give me that warm glow. You can do that all by yourself." His lips silenced her momentarily, then she added with mischief, "I'd hate to see you get that beautiful suit dirty building a fire. . . ."

The look he cast her was filled with the devil and she drank it in greedily. Her eyes followed him as he slid out from beneath her, removed his jacket, vest, shirt, tie, shoes, and socks, then knelt before the hearth to build a fire. Helpless to resist the heady temptation, she moved after him to caress the rippling muscles of his corded shoulders.

"If you keep that up," he kidded thickly, "we may *all* burn down." His sure fingers struck the match and held it to the kindling. Then, with the confidence that was an intrinsic part of him, he gave the logs no further thought, but turned to Arielle, pulling her down to the thick rug as he began to undress her. She shifted eagerly to help him, then went quickly to work on the fastening of his pants. Slow and leisurely lovemaking would be for later that night. Now there was a flaming need in them both, a love-kindled desire which could only be assuaged by the fury of a wild and passionate coupling.

Later, as they lay, their bodies restfully entwined before the fire and Arielle stroked the damp flesh that had given, and continued to give her, such pleasure, they talked some more. "I think I scribbled that note in a last-ditch effort to plead my case," she breathed against his chest, inhaling his earthiness and the primitive aura surrounding them.

"Just as I left you the portrait —"

"The azure cameo," she said softly, her breath teasing the soft hair on his chest.

Chris tightened his hold, pulling her more firmly against him, begrudging her even the slightest distance. "The azure cameo. That it is. Soft and exquisite, as you are."

"Bold and magnificent, as you are."

For he was bold and magnificent — dressed, undressed, in every conceivable state — in Arielle's love-hazed view. That bold magnificence was never more pronounced than when he suddenly flipped her onto her back and rolled gently atop her, pinning her to the thick rug, weaving his fingers between hers, anchoring her hands not far from her soft flushed cheeks, which his thumbs then lightly caressed.

"Be mine, Arielle!" he groaned hoarsely. "Give me my freedom. I can only be free, totally free, when I'm with you!"

Her lips were a feather-touch from his, warmly echoing his need. "I've been yours for weeks, Chris. It's what I feel for you, *am* for you, that makes me whole. Without you, I've only half a heart. Oh, I *do* love you. . . ."

The fire crackled its warm applause as they kissed, deeply and passionately, their bodies fusing in the promise of things to come. Time lost all meaning in this one-ness. They declared their love in endlessly spiraling sweeps of delight, surging higher long after the flame in the hearth had settled to a golden ember. Only later, as they lay together, their passion spent and satisfied, did Arielle think again of the azure cameo and know that, in its precious vision, lay the picture of her future.

The employees of Thorndike Press hope you have enjoyed this Large Print book. All our Thorndike, Wheeler, and Kennebec Large Print titles are designed for easy reading, and all our books are made to last. Other Thorndike Press Large Print books are available at your library, through selected bookstores, or directly from us.

For information about titles, please call:
  (800) 223-1244

or visit our Web site at:
  http://gale.cengage.com/thorndike

To share your comments, please write:
  Publisher
  Thorndike Press
  10 Water St., Suite 310
  Waterville, ME 04901